*New Beginnings at
the Little House in the Sun*

New Beginnings at
the Little House in the Sun

Chris Penhall

Portuguese Paradise – Book 2

Stories that inspire emotions!
www.rubyfiction.com

Copyright © 2021 Chris Penhall

Published 2021 by Ruby Fiction
Penrose House, Crawley Drive, Camberley, Surrey GU15 2AB, UK
www.rubyfiction.com

A CIP catalogue record for this book is available from the British Library

ISBN: 978-1-91255-039-5

Prin... ...S.p.A.

*This book is dedicated to Sarah and Hannah and
my incredibly supportive family and friends.*

To Gareth, Ann, Kevin, Jean, Barrie and Sam

*To my late mum and dad – Jean and Eddie
– who were always reading and made books
a huge and important part of my life*

And to Mark, who bought me my first writing desk.

You're all fabulous and I couldn't have done it without you!

Acknowledgements

I would like to thank the Choc Lit and Ruby
team for the opportunity to release this story.

I'm incredibly grateful to everyone that has helped
me along the way, and to their continued interest and
support as I've written my second book. Thanks to the
Choc Lit team for giving my story that extra polish, to
my very wonderful Uni Chicks and their chaps who I've
known forever and who have been there for me through
everything – Jill, Sandra, Sue, Loui, Mark and Mike – my
Essex friends, work buddies, Portugal lovers, Hay Ladies,
salsa pals and all the good people I've met through the
years – here's to more of our dreams coming true!

Thank you to the Tasting Panel readers who passed
the original manuscript, especially to: Erin Thorn,
Yvonne Greene, Donna Morgan, Ruth Nägele, Hilary
Brown, Michele Rollins, Alma Hough, Fran Stevens,
Sharon Walsh, Cordy Swinton and Gill Leivers.

Chapter One

Alice pulled the door closed and turned the lock, allowing her forehead to rest on the blue-painted wood. She ran her hand along its grooves and grains, hoping to absorb all its memories and take them with her – the smiles, the tears, the joys, the laughter. How many times had she walked into the calm, protective sanctuary of this house, or stepped out through the wrought iron gate in the tiny front garden and met the challenge of a new day? It was the house she had loved and scrubbed and brought back to life. The house that Alice had built.

She stood back and looked at it for the very last time and tried not to cry.

This is a good thing, she told herself. *Everyone has to move on. I have to. I am.*

The waiting taxi revved its engine from the road. 'Goodbye, house,' she said, then blew it a kiss, turned away and jumped into the back seat. As the taxi began to move, she watched the ivy-clad walls slowly disappear, the cherry trees either side of the gate gradually obscuring the house from view as they drove away.

The cab paused at the end of the road just as the removal van delivering the new family's belongings arrived. She turned to watch it draw slowly towards her old home and as it stopped and her taxi turned away into the traffic, she felt suddenly adrift, floating, panicked. She was heading into a new life without the thing that had protected her and grounded her for more than fifteen years. It was like the cords were cut, and she'd been swept up into an empty space, blown away from the thing she had loved so very much. There was nothing to catch her now, nowhere safe to run to, nowhere to hide.

A hand took hers.

'I'm here,' said Luis, pulling her towards him. 'It's fine. It'll be okay.'

She sank into him and began to weep.

'I know, I know,' he whispered. 'But it had to happen. In the end, it's a good thing. You're free of him now.'

But in the process of getting Adam out of your life, you had to let go of your house, said the voice in her head. *Although he only got thirty per cent in the end! Ha!*

Thirty per cent too much, thought Alice.

'Your house gave you the gift of moving on,' whispered Luis.

Alice looked up at him. 'I've got mascara on your shirt again,' she said.

'I was expecting that. There's a reason it's dark blue and not white.'

She sank into him again. 'But you're right. My house did give me the gift of moving on, of money, and another kind of life.'

'With me in it,' he said. 'Don't forget that.'

'I couldn't do any of this without you.' She smiled at him.

He looked down at her. 'You look terrible. Your eyeliner has smudged all over your face and your nose is running.'

'Just as well you love me then,' she said.

'Just as well I do.'

The taxi made its way through the London traffic as Alice closed her eyes. She hadn't wanted to sell her beloved house, hoping to somehow keep it and rent it whilst she made her new life in Portugal with Luis. But she couldn't afford to buy her ex, Adam, out, and he had insisted on trying to get half of the value, even though Alice had repeatedly made the point that he had only contributed enough to own the downstairs toilet.

It turned out downstairs toilets were worth quite a lot of money these days, if the eventual allocation of thirty per cent of the house value to him was a guide price. But, as the voice in her head kept reminding her, *seventy per cent of London-house money was a lot of money.*

But Alice still couldn't get over the unfairness, try as she might. He didn't deserve it. And the house was now sold. It was someone else's.

She felt Luis stroke her hair, and fell into a listless sleep, her mind crowded with images of Adam's constant e-mails and messages digging at her, pushing her to let him have what he wanted. But not what he deserved.

It's for the business. For me and Veronique. Come on Ali, do the right thing.

That text had rung around in her head for weeks. *Do the right thing, do the right thing. It's only the right thing for him and his new girlfriend but certainly not for me.* She had repeated it to herself like a mantra to keep her fighting for what she deserved.

It had dragged on for almost a year, despite the apparent urgent need for investment in his business, because he would not negotiate.

Until finally, the letter from the solicitor had arrived and she knew she had to say yes. Just to be able to move on.

Dear Ms Matthews
Mr Kennedy has offered to accept thirty per cent of the sale price of the property. His partner is pregnant, and she is keen to bring this matter to a close as soon as possible …

'Alice, Alice,' Luis was whispering. 'We're here. Time to wake up.'

Her eyes flickered open, and she raised her head, her arms still wrapped around him. People were milling about the outside concourse, striding along and dragging their suitcases with them towards the departure hall. She sat up and stretched, shaking the dream away.

'Oh, your mum's here,' said Luis.

'Really? We said goodbye yesterday,' muttered Alice, surprised. She quickly began rummaging in her bag for a tissue to wipe the eyeliner off her cheeks. 'Nice of her to come, though.'

'Well, yes and no.'

'Is Joseph with her?'

'Um ... oh, yes. I can see him stood by the terminal building.'

Alice sat up straight and spotted her mother on the walkway holding a placard.

'Oh ...'

'"Good luck in your new life, Alice" is what it says,' said Luis, squinting to make out the words.

'Well, given it's Mum, that's quite low key.' Alice sighed and picked up her bag.

'And I think under that, in smaller letters, it says "A is a b ..." that word's been crossed out. "He didn't deserve thirty per cent. But at least you're rich anyway".'

Alice laughed and turned away. 'I can't look!'

Luis smiled. 'I love your mother, but I think she needs to do a course in snappy one-liners or something.'

Alice pushed the door open and stepped out, whilst Luis got the bags and spoke to the taxi driver.

'Hi, Mum,' she said, walking towards her.

'Alice!' shouted her mother. 'At last. I've been here for half an hour already. I was waiting inside, but they threw me out. Said political demonstrations weren't allowed. I said, have you read this placard?' She started to point it at Alice like it was an arrow. 'It's not political at all. It's about my daughter. What have you done to your face by the way? It's covered in black stuff.'

'Eyeliner, Mum.'

'Well, clean it off dear. You look like you're in that horror film – what's it called again – *Night of the Living Dead*?'

Alice gave her a hug. 'I'll wipe it off in a second. And thank you for the placard. It shows great ... great support.'

'That wellbeing course I've done has just made me, you know, open up, show that empathetic, caring side of my personality that I'd hidden for years.'

Alice's stepfather, Joseph, walked over to them and gently took the placard from her mother. 'Shall we join them in departures then? Can't stand out here forever.' He placed it gently against a wall. 'We'll collect it on the way back.' He smiled.

'Do you mind if we say our goodbyes here?' Her mum became tearful. 'I'm so excited for your new life, but so sad my baby is moving away.'

'It's Portugal, Mum, and you've already been out three times to see me.'

'Yes, but this is so final. And your house. I'm sad about your house.'

Alice could feel the tears begin to prick at the back of her eyes. 'Oh, Mum,' she said, hugging her again. 'It's fine. It's a new adventure. A new exciting adventure.' *But scary as hell*, muttered the voice in her head.

She saw Luis glance at his watch. 'We'd better get going,' he said.

Joseph grabbed Alice and put his arms around her. 'You're amazing. I'm very proud of you.'

'Thank you,' she whispered into his neck. Then, 'I'm scared.'

He squeezed her tight. 'I know,' he said quietly. 'But that's part of the fun of it. Fly, Alice, fly.'

She stepped back then kissed her mother, 'It'll be fun, Mum. Honestly. I'll be fine. More than fine.'

Her mother nodded. 'You will. Now, on you go, and let me know when you arrive in Cascais.'

Alice picked up her bag and grabbed her case as Luis said his goodbyes. Her heart began to beat hard, and that familiar sick feeling began to creep over her. As she turned towards the sliding doors at the entrance to the terminal she remembered that day almost two years ago when she'd virtually run through them – she thought she was running away from her problems, but it turned out she was running towards a new, brighter life.

Although today she didn't feel like that at all.

Luis took her hand again.

'Ready?' He smiled.

'Ready,' she said quietly, walking through the doors into the terminal.

Alice's stomach fluttered nervously as she and Luis passed through to the arrival hall at Lisbon airport. She'd flown back and forth many times in the past year or so, trying to sort out the mess that Adam was making of her life. But here she was: stronger, happier and officially starting a new life in the place that had helped her find the strength to fight her ex.

Their friend Ignacio was waiting for them as usual, this time holding up a card which said, 'Welcome home, Alice. It's all for the best.' She walked towards him, put down her case and hugged him tight.

'Oh Ignacio, it's so good to see you.'

He put his arms around her and patted her on the back like he was burping a baby.

'I had to be here. I was your airport chauffeur when you first arrived, wasn't I? And now it's your home I wanted to be the one to collect you again.'

'Like the banner, mate.' Luis laughed.

'I spoke to Alice's mother last night. We both agreed to make a statement to the world, to show Alice our support.' He lowered his voice. 'Although your mother thought I should put something in about Adam being a bastard, but I thought we should forget about him. Ignore him. Don't give Adam any thought.'

'Still going on those wellbeing and meditation workshops then?' said Luis, picking up Alice's bag and walking towards the exit.

'Yes. Since Alice's mother told me about them, it's changed my world. I'm taking it further and have made the decision to give up the chauffeuring altogether and become a coach and counsellor.'

Alice and Ignacio hurried after Luis. 'That's wonderful,' said Alice. 'But isn't that going to be difficult with you and Carlos taking over the café?'

'No, not at all. No.'

'Have you told Carlos?'

'Yes. There is a room in the café attic I could use, and it wouldn't affect the time I work with him at all. It's very exciting times. Brothers in arms! Is that what they say?' He paused for a moment and scratched his head. 'Because we are brothers. Or does it mean something else?'

'I was worried when the owner put it up for sale,' Luis moved the suitcase to his other hand. 'Carlos has been part of that place for so long, I couldn't imagine him not being there. So, from head waiter to joint owner within the space of six months. It's a relief and impressive at the same time.'

'He is very, very, very, very motivated. Nervous. Excited. Everything.' Ignacio nodded. 'Big changes, but good changes.'

As they all emerged outside, the warm, bright light greeted Alice like a welcoming hug. She sighed and breathed it in. *Home*, she thought. *This is home now*.

Ignacio strode ahead. 'I have a surprise,' he shouted. 'Look.'

Alice almost squealed 'Your yellow Rolls-Royce!' The sunlight seemed to illuminate the sleek, beautiful old car, loved and cherished by Ignacio for over twenty years.

'Out of retirement. For today only. And just for you.'

She virtually skipped over to it. 'Luis. This was what Ignacio was driving when I ran away from London.'

'And this is what he's driving now you aren't running away from anything,' Luis responded.

She stood on her tiptoes and kissed him, the heaviness she had felt earlier that day slipping away.

'And there's more.' Ignacio opened the door with a flourish.

A blue balloon bobbed out, got caught by the breeze and floated slowly into the distance. They all watched as it drifted high into the sky.

'Now that's an elegant balloon,' said Luis.

'There's more inside,' said Ignacio, virtually pushing Alice into the car. 'If you keep the door open they'll all fly out … oh, dear, they weren't like that when I left.'

Alice squeezed herself in and found herself surrounded by blue and white balloons. Luis climbed in after her and started to laugh.

'I think this was Mary's idea,' he said, knocking them back and forth.

Alice laughed too, remembering her landlady's love of all things pink, balloons included. 'Well, at least she's not chosen the usual colour.'

Ignacio clambered in the front and tried to speak to her through the gaps in the balloons that had drifted over the seats. 'They were in some bags. I emptied them in the car when I parked it and just walked away. I didn't look back, and I didn't know there were so many. Mary gave them to me last night before she and Frank left for Australia.'

Alice looked at Luis, his face beaming, and Ignacio, his head back, his shoulders shaking with laughter, and she found herself laughing too, unable to speak. As she laughed, she silently thanked whatever had accidentally brought them both into her life.

Serendipity, sighed the voice in her head.

Ignacio picked up a cool box from the passenger seat and held it up for them to see. He pointed at it. 'Champagne,' he managed to say through the laughter. He took out three glasses and a bottle. Alice watched him, mesmerised, as the cork exploded onto a white balloon, careered off the window, then landed on the seat.

Ignacio handed them both glasses silently, pursing his lips to try to silence the laugh. Luis snorted as a white balloon hovered over the top of his drink, whilst Ignacio shakily poured them a glass of champagne and a quarter for himself.

They clinked them together between the balloons but were still laughing too much to say anything.

Alice sipped the champagne, allowing the bubbles to tickle her throat. 'Home, home, home,' she said eventually. 'I'm home.'

Then she opened her window and started to guide the balloons out, so as Ignacio began to drive, a trail of translucent blue and white balls spilled languorously from the car, leaving a slow, graceful trail of bubbles as they went.

Chapter Two

The car drove up along the familiar drive to the apartment block – Alice's on-off home since she'd arrived the first time, when she'd been so lost, stressed and scared for the future. It seemed like a lifetime ago that she'd decided to stay with her friend Kathy in Cascais rather than facing Adam and his demands to sell their house. And then somehow ended up apartment-sitting for Mary and Frank and looking after their cat, Aphrodite.

She smiled to herself, looking forward to finally putting down roots in the place that had seduced and comforted her from her very first day in Portugal. Luis sat next to her, his eyes closed as he rested, a curl of hair falling onto his forehead. He scratched his neck absent-mindedly, and she took his hand. Opening his eyes, he smiled back and kissed her lightly on the cheek.

'Thank you,' she said.

'For what?'

'Just ... for it all.'

He kissed her again. 'And thank you. For it all.'

The car stopped, and Ignacio jumped out. 'Here we are.' He opened the boot and took out the cases.

As Alice climbed out, she was overwhelmed by the scent of jasmine hanging lightly in the air, and a peacock called from the nearby park. Above her purple blossom decorated the jacaranda trees and, beyond the bushes of luscious pink bougainvillea, the blue of the pool shone in the afternoon sun. In the distance she could hear the constant comforting roar of the sea.

She kicked off her sandals and wiggled her toes, the heat of the path warming her feet.

It's fine. It's all fine. It will be fine, she thought. *It's an adventure, that's what it is. You are in the middle of an adventure.*

'Are you sure you don't mind me heading straight off?' said Luis, softly. 'I can't leave Elvis with Carlos for much longer.'

'Of course not.' Alice picked up her suitcase. 'Kathy's popping over later with the baby, and Elvis needs a long walk along the beach, I expect. Carlos isn't much of a dog person to be honest, so I doubt he's had much of a run over the past couple of weeks.'

'You're an angel.' Luis kissed her once more and jumped in the back of Ignacio's car.

'Alice. See you tomorrow in the square at ten o'clock sharp,' reminded Ignacio, turning on the engine.

'Thanks for collecting me,' shouted Alice as he began to drive away.

Slipping on her sandals again, she hurried towards the foyer and called the lift. As she travelled to the top floor, she pulled a sheet of paper from her handbag and stared at it, reading through it for at least the hundredth time.

Vende-se. For sale.
Attractive, historic, three-bedroomed property
in the old town.

One bathroom, kitchen, two reception rooms,
courtyard garden. Off street parking

In need of some renovation.

In need of some love, said the voice in her head.

She opened the apartment door and walked in. Everything was exactly the same as it had been when Mary and Frank had come back from their travels and she'd moved out to stay with Luis. The silver, white and scattered pink everywhere was a bit of a shock compared to the cluttered, almost-building site feel of Luis' place, though.

'Ah Mary, I just love the fact that you love pink so much,' she said out loud, hoping Aphrodite would hear her voice and patter in to say hello. But the cat was nowhere to be seen.

Alice pulled the terrace doors open and stepped onto the balcony, enjoying the burst of heat on her face. She could just see the ocean glistening between the trees as soft, white clouds floated gracefully across the bay.

Resting on a chair she put her head back and stretched, enjoying the feeling of space and seclusion. She just needed time to herself and was grateful that Luis understood. At least she hoped he understood. *He says he understands*, she scolded herself. *Stop overthinking it!*

Her eyes fluttered shut as she lost herself in the warmth of the sun, her mind slowly emptying of all of the challenges she'd had in the past couple of years. She breathed slowly, repeating to herself, 'All is good, all is well. All is good, all is well. All is …' she felt something scuttle around her lap '… Ahhhh!'

Whatever it was dropped onto her hand. Too frightened to open her eyes, she whispered. 'Aphrodite … that is you, isn't it?'

A loud purring confirmed that it was indeed the cat. Whatever it was on her hand moved again. She opened her eyes slowly – Aphrodite jumped onto her lap and began to toy with a tiny gecko which suddenly raced up Alice's arm.

'Ahhh!' she screamed, waving both arms around and jumping up, shaking her body to try to get rid of the gecko in the unlikely event it was still there.

'Oh, Alice. I have missed you. I just love the way you dance.'

Alice jumped again and turned around. Her friend Kathy stood in the living room as Aphrodite stalked past her towards the stairs. 'I think she's offended.' Kathy laughed and took her son out of his pushchair. 'The door was open for some reason.'

Alice giggled, then felt something on her neck. She jumped again and shook it off. 'Oh, for goodness sake,' she shouted.

The baby chuckled as the gecko fell to the floor, then scurried along the balcony and down the wall.

'Oh, James. How are you? You've grown so much.' Alice kissed his head softly.

'More to the point, how are you?' Kathy sat down and balanced him on her lap.

'Well, mixed to be honest. Fancy a cup of tea?'

'Yes, go on. I could do with a gin and tonic. Sleepless night again thanks to this one and his cold. But a tea it is.'

Alice walked into the kitchen to an array of new pink items, obviously bought by landlady Mary. 'I didn't know you could get kettles this shade of very bright pink,' she said, filling it with water and switching it on.

'Have you checked in the cupboards?' shouted Kathy from the living room. 'Mary's left you a few treats.'

Alice opened one of the doors. Inside were several containers with little labels on them. 'Drink Me' they said. Laughing, she took them all out to see if there was a description of what was in them. 'There's no list of ingredients,' she said, walking to the doorway and waving one of them at Kathy.

'And the problem with that is what?' asked Kathy, deadpan.

A series of images appeared in Alice's mind of the various effects of Mary's tea in the past, from simply accidentally falling asleep on the sofa to cleaning frantically and speedily, talking gibberish, and that terrible incident with the olive oil, flip flops and washing-up liquid when Kathy and Alice had tried to make their own version.

She shivered with a combination of embarrassment and delight. 'Common or garden tea today, I feel.' Alice put in a couple of tea bags and added the water and milk. 'I'm sure I'll dive in and take the risk of her latest concoctions when I'm feeling reckless and brave.'

Carrying the mugs through to the living room, she put them down and sat on the chair opposite her friend.

'It's lovely to have you back.' Kathy set the baby down on the mat and gave him a plastic book to look at.

'He's sitting up really well now. He was all wobbly when I left.'

'Yep, and he's almost crawling,' said Kathy, 'which is both a good and a bad thing.' They both paused and took a sip of their tea. 'So, did you cry?'

'Yes, for almost the three months I was there sorting everything out. But it's done now.' Alice sighed. 'No going back.'

'All that love in that house,' said Kathy softly.

'Yes. But I suppose if I had managed to buy Adam out—'

'—which he didn't allow because he is a controlling and bullying pig,' interrupted Kathy.

'Quite. Well, if he had let me buy him out, I'd have still had that tie to the past, I suppose. So, hard though it is, I have to commit to my future completely.'

'Talking of commitment …?' Kathy smiled hopefully.

'Luis and I are happy as we are at the moment,' said Alice. 'But talking of commitment. What about you, Kathy. Isn't it about time you took the plunge?'

'Oh yes, well. I have a bit of a surprise.' She beamed. 'Stephano and I are getting married … again.'

'Fantastic. I'm so pleased for you.' Alice jumped up and hugged her 'When?'

'No date yet.'

'Oh.'

'Well, we've already been married once. Then that horrible divorce. And then him running away to Brazil.' Kathy gazed into the distance for a moment. 'And him turning up again, and then all that on-off sleeping together. And then the unexpected pregnancy. It's exciting and unsettling at the same time.' She almost laughed, then shook her head. 'Honestly!'

'Well, its lovely news. When are you thinking – this year, next year?'

James began to grizzle, so Kathy picked him up.

'No idea to be honest. The fact that we've agreed to marry each other again after the last time is impressive in itself I think, so we're letting that sink in.'

'Small steps,' said Alice.

'Tiny steps,' said Kathy. 'Tiny, tiny, tiny steps.'

James quickly graduated to a full-blown cry.

'Oh, he needs some milk,' said Kathy. 'Here, take him while I dig it out.'

'Come here, gorgeous.' Alice walked around the room, bouncing him up and down, as he combined tears with giggles. 'Are you tired? Are you hungry? Mum's getting you your lovely milk now.'

As James erupted into tears again, Alice handed him back. 'Time for your mother then, I think.'

Kathy put the bottle in his mouth, and he began to slurp it contentedly.

'So, big day tomorrow?'

'Yes,' said Alice. 'I'm meeting Carlos and Ignacio in the square to talk about interior design at ten.'

'I'm so excited for them. Carlos is very nervous about taking over the café, though. Mostly excited, though.'

'Understandable, I suppose. Then at one, I'm going to see the house.' Alice beamed.

'The little yellow house?' asked Kathy. 'Is Luis going with you?'

'Yes. He can put his renovation eye over it. I'm all emotional at the moment. Desperate to put my money into a little holiday let venture.'

'So, these living arrangements?' asked Kathy.

'Well, the farmhouse is taking so long to finish, that we thought it was best if I stayed here whilst all the big building work is going on. Luis, on the other hand, loves living on a building site!' Alice took another slurp of tea. 'Don't look at me like that! He's going to be staying here too. Mary said bringing Elvis over is fine. Aphrodite sorts of likes him.'

Kathy didn't say anything.

'I can't move in with him until I've bought my own place. It's going to be my holiday let business. He understands. I don't know why you don't. I want the security for myself after this fight with Adam over my house.'

'Well, a bit of it was his.' Kathy smiled. 'I'm trying to be the voice of reason here!'

Alice put the tea down. 'I'm a very complicated person. So no arguments please.'

As Kathy opened her mouth to say something, James stopped drinking and burped loudly.

'For a moment there I thought we were going to have a very deep and meaningful discussion,' sighed Kathy.

'Oh, I love you James!' Alice laughed. 'Another cup of tea, Kathy?' She walked into the kitchen and switched the kettle on. *Tomorrow is another day*, she said to herself. *And it will be good.*

As Alice walked out into the morning sun the following day, she rummaged in her bag and made sure she still had the house details. The trees dappled patterns on the grass and swayed gently in the spring breeze. Everything smelt fresh and floral and alive. Her mind fizzed with excitement as she hurried through the back streets of the old town to the square. The birds sang happily, and the white, purple and pink of the spring flowers burst from verges and window boxes.

She heard the clink of china from a kitchen window as cups and plates were moved, a family chattering noisily over breakfast, and then she skirted around a workman painting a wall a bright, luscious yellow. As she walked closer to town, the cobbled streets widened slightly and she could see more people moving around, beginning their day. She loved Cascais first thing in the morning, when the cafés were just setting up and the shops were about to open.

She sat down at a table in the square, waiting for Carlos

and Ignacio to arrive for their meeting. Taking her phone out of her bag, she messaged Luis. Slept well last night. How about you? Missed you though xx

Carlos walked towards her carrying a tray with three coffees on it. She stood up, and he greeted her with a kiss.

'Alice, Alice. Welcome home,' he said, placing the cups on the table and sitting down. 'It's all very busy, so busy. Stress, stress, stress.' His usually smiling face was serious.

'Where's Ignacio?' asked Alice, taking out her notebook, pen and laptop.

'He'll be here in a second,' huffed Carlos. 'I wish he'd never done that mindfulness course. He is being very irritating. I do not want to breathe in and out for ten minutes before work. I have too much to do!'

'It's because he thinks it'll help.' Alice smiled.

Ignacio stepped out of the café and walked towards them.

'Here he comes,' sniffed Carlos not looking behind him. 'I can sense his serene presence.'

Alice was surprised.

'Not really.' He laughed. 'He's got a squeaky shoe. That also is irritating.'

Ignacio bent down and kissed Alice 'Ola, ola! Did you have a good rest after your difficult day yesterday?'

'I did. It's lovely to be back to be honest. Even though it was hard to walk away from my house ... the house.' Her phone buzzed. Missed you too. Me and the pooch will be over this evening. Can we stay over? Or will Aphrodite get in a mood? Xx

Aphrodite will deal with it. She loves Elvis. See you later xx, she quickly texted. She put the phone down and looked up. 'Well, exciting times,' she said. 'Let's get down to some planning.'

Ignacio shifted uncomfortably in his seat. 'We have no idea what we're doing,' he admitted.

'Well, that's why you've got me in to help with the design and décor.' Alice laughed.

'He means he doesn't think we know what we're doing at all.' Carlos sighed. 'I know exactly what we're doing. I've been in the restaurant trade since I was fourteen.'

Alice smiled. 'Yesterday you said it was very exciting … has anything happened?'

'The past. He reminded me of the past. Last night.' Ignacio took a deep breath and stared into the distance.

'Yes, you go ahead and meditate,' muttered Carlos.

'The past?' Alice looked at Ignacio and then Carlos, but neither of them answered. 'So,' she said, trying to sound brisk and efficient enough to stop them arguing. 'Do you have any ideas of the kind of style you want inside?'

Ignacio leaned forward. 'I'd like it to feel like you are in a garden but inside.'

'And outside,' said Carlos, leaning forward too. 'We are opening up the patio as well. I'm very excited about that.'

'Me also.' Ignacio beamed at his brother, and Carlos beamed back.

Alice was relieved their disagreement lasted less than a minute. 'Do you have specific ideas of what you want – colours and such?'

Carlos looked thoughtful for a moment. 'Green, I think.'

'And brown – tree trunks, you know,' Ignacio chipped in.

Alice wrote it down on her notepad. 'Anything else?'

The brothers looked at each other and then at her.

'No,' said Carlos. 'We'll leave it to you. We saw the photographs of your house, remember? We know you will create something beautiful.'

Alice paused, surprised. 'My house? I just decorated that for me … well for Adam too, but he couldn't have cared less.' She smiled sadly. 'Something good has come out of all that then, apart from money.'

Ignacio put his hand on hers. 'We trust you.'

'That's lovely, and I'm very honoured, but I need a bit more guidance.'

Carlos looked at his watch. 'I have to go and get the kitchen organised.'

'And I have an airport pick-up,' said Ignacio.

'Oh,' said Alice, slightly irritated and a little bit disappointed. She'd been looking forward to talking to them about ideas so she could go and research them. They all stood up. 'I do need a budget,' she said.

'Of course.' Carlos became suddenly efficient. 'I've got the details on my computer at home. I'll e-mail it to you later. Come in and have a look at the space now if you like.'

Ignacio began to walk away but paused. 'Don't worry. Like I said, we trust you. You'll make it beautiful. We have enough time before we take over, and some space after that to renovate. And we thought it would be good for you, whilst you are … between houses. We know you love a project.'

Alice nodded, put her notepad away and grabbed her bag, following Carlos inside. It was dark and old-fashioned with little natural light, which is why she usually sat outside.

'Here.' Carlos opened a wide glass door at the back of the room. 'Here it is.' They stepped into an overgrown patio with some old tables and chairs stacked in a corner, a few empty discarded pots sat next to them. Wisteria crawled half-heartedly up the dingy white walls, tangling with lilac bougainvillea, and orange hibiscus listlessly hugged the corner.

Her heart fluttered. 'Wonderful,' she said to Carlos. 'I'm going to the park to get some ideas. I'll see you soon.'

He laughed. 'And *adieus* to you, my friend. We are very, very glad you are back.'

Alice walked across the road towards Fisherman's Beach. 'Hello. I've missed you,' she whispered as seagulls swooped and soared in the sky, the riggings of the fishing boats moored in the bay tinkling as they bobbed and swished on the swell of the sea.

The daily fish auction close to the jetty was nearing its end, and Alice paused for a moment, enjoying the spectacle, then turned towards the hill and ambled happily to the park near the stone bridge, her mind full of ideas for the café and plans for the little yellow house she hadn't even viewed yet. As she moved through the shade of the eucalyptus and pine trees, the calming aroma of sage and rosemary washed over her. She retrieved her camera so she could take some photographs.

'Are you ready?' Luis squeezed Alice's hand as they stood outside the house.

'I've virtually moved in already in my head,' she said. 'I hope it's how I imagined it would be inside.'

'You could have viewed it before.' He laughed. 'It's been on sale for quite a while.'

Alice looked up at him. 'I know, but I didn't want to jinx it. You know me – it's been such a long road with my London house that I didn't want to step forward until it was all finished.' She pretended to rub her eyes in order to cover some unexpected tears for her old home.

'*Ola, bom dia*!' A smartly dressed man opened the door. 'Miss Matthews? I am Steven, the estate agent looking after this property. Do come in.'

She tentatively stepped into the hallway. It was dusty and smelt old and neglected, cobwebs drooping from the ceiling, and old leaves on the floor. The doors to either side were open, allowing shafts of light to illuminate the dark floor at the base of the staircase. She shivered. This was it. This was going to be hers.

'Come,' said Steven holding the kitchen door ajar, and they walked into a bright, light room opening onto a tiny garden. Three of the walls were decorated with patterned tiles.

Alice looked up at Luis who was beaming down at her. 'Everything you expected?' he asked softly.

'Yes, everything!' She laughed. 'How I imagined it would be. What do you think? Do you think we could make it beautiful again?'

Luis walked around the room, knocking the walls, examining the cracks, his face serious. 'Yes,' he said eventually. 'We'll see what the survey says, but I've seen worse!'

They followed Steven up the narrow staircase to the first floor, where there were two bedrooms and a room that was probably the bathroom but had nothing in it, then to the top floor, where a vast light bedroom opened onto a run-down rooftop terrace. Steven struggled with the patio doors, eventually pushing them open so they could see the rooftops of Cascais tumbling down towards the blue of the bay.

Luis stood behind and put her arms around her. 'Now, I know you love it, but we have to be sensible.'

'I know,' she said softly. 'I am eminently sensible, as you are only too aware. Although currently a bit emotional.'

'You are.' He laughed. 'But I've a feeling that the money from your London house may be burning a hole in your pocket. Just because you've got the deposit ready and can buy it all in one go, doesn't mean you should.'

'Absolutely ... but I do love this house. It's just as I thought it was going to be. I can picture it decorated and furnished. It'll be perfect for holiday lets.' *Once I have my house, I'll feel better*, she thought. *More grounded, more settled.*

'*You haven't got it yet*,' muttered the voice in her head. '*Anything could happen.*'

In an attempt to shove the thought away, she turned to Luis and held his hands. 'Once you've finished the old farmhouse, will you help me with this?'

'I was going to whether you asked me or not,' he said, squeezing her hands. 'But, like I said, let's sit down, you can work out what to offer, then you can get a survey done. It's been on the market for a while, so we need to make sure nothing's wrong structurally.'

A mobile phone ringtone interrupted the tranquillity, and they heard the agent talking. 'It's what?' they could hear him asking. 'When were you told? ... okay ... well ... you should have mentioned it before I left the office.'

He walked towards them, looking embarrassed. 'Miss Matthews, I'm so sorry to have wasted your time. My colleague has just called me to say that an offer of the asking price was made first thing this morning by a cash buyer and the property is now off the market.'

Alice felt her stomach sink as a cloud drifted over the sun. *Two houses in one week*, she thought, the sense of being cut adrift suddenly overwhelming her again.

'Oh, baby.' Luis pulled her towards him.

Chapter Three

'It's okay. It just wasn't meant to be.' Luis had said, leading Alice back to the café where they were now sitting drinking coffee. 'We'll look at some others together.' He smiled at her. 'It'll be fun.'

'There'll be plenty more out there,' she said.

'There are. Now say it like you mean it!'

She laughed. 'I know. I will. I just had my heart set on it, that's all.'

Carlos walked past, a tray in his hand. 'It will mean you have more time to spare to design the café,' he said. 'You will be less rushed. Every cloud has a silver lining.'

Alice looked around at the square with all its different coloured parasols and chairs, full of life and warmth. 'I need to start making jewellery again,' she said. 'I suppose …'

'One thing at a time.' Luis stood up. 'I've got to rush – I'm pricing up a renovation job in ten minutes.' He kissed her and threw some coins on the table.

'What time are you coming over later?' she asked.

'About six. I'm bringing Elvis. Is that still okay? They've turned the water off at the farmhouse again so we can't stay there. And I'm playing with the band at the bar on the beach tomorrow lunchtime, so we could go down together and have lunch after?'

'Lovely.' Alice stood up too. 'I'd better get going as well. I haven't really had time to unpack and buy food.'

'*Ciao* for now.' Luis waved and walked towards the sea.

'*Adieus*,' said Alice, turning towards the town. But as soon as he'd disappeared from view, she felt cut adrift again. *Told you*, said the voice in her head. *Nothing runs smoothly. Why you thought it would be all plain sailing beats me. It never is with you.*

She took a deep breath. 'I'm going to browse some estate agents' windows,' she said aloud, as that was the only way to silence the voice. 'So, screw you.' Inwardly smiling at her own bravado of telling herself off, she walked purposefully towards the railway station and found an estate agent's window to gaze at. The display was full of possibilities, but none as enticing as the little yellow house.

She gave up, her mind flitting from one thought to another – *house, no house, little yellow house, nearly, now gone, all in the space of two days*. Forcing herself to focus on something, she wrote an imaginary shopping list in her head instead ... *orange juice, bread, ham, olives ... no house ... Vinho Verde, cheese, water ... must sort out my stuff to make bracelets ... cat food*. She continued to add things as she walked around the supermarket.

Broken tiles, beads, ribbon ... sad about the little yellow house. She got into a taxi, and it continued as she travelled back to the apartment. *Cotton, scissors ... need to go to the stalls to see if they need any more bracelets before I make them ... I'll find another house. I'll find another house ... oh, bloody hell*.

Jumping out of the cab, she rushed upstairs and threw the shopping into the kitchen. Then she changed into her swimming costume, before hurrying downstairs to the garden and stared at the cool, blue tranquil pool for a moment. 'Calm down,' she muttered. Then she dived in. The chatter in her mind died down as she became suspended in the water, the sound of birdsong and waves muted as she glided up towards the air, and when she surfaced, she felt peaceful again. Climbing out, she lay on a sunbed, allowing the sun to dry her skin, and closed her eyes.

She woke up to the sound of splashing and children laughing. A tiny gecko skittered along the wall, and a dragonfly hovered over the grass. Alice glanced at her watch and jumped up, surprised. *Two hours*, she thought. *I've been asleep for two hours. Luis will be arriving soon!* She picked up her towel and ran over the lawn to the path, enjoying the sensation of the warm, dry grass on her feet. She pulled on her flip-flops, then hurried into the apartment block.

'I thought Aphrodite was okay with Elvis,' said Alice as the cat dug her claws into her hand and hissed at the dog.

'They were last time they met,' said Luis, holding the lead whilst Elvis barked loudly and repeatedly. 'It's just been a month or so. They'll calm down in a minute.'

'I hope so. I'm not letting Aphrodite out in case she wanders off in a huff and never comes back.'

'Maybe put her in the bedroom while they settle? If I put Elvis in there he'll wreck it as he's so big.'

Aphrodite began to crawl up to Alice's neck, her claws now gripping her shoulder.

'I don't suppose Mary's left any of her medicinal tea?' said Luis, pulling Elvis onto the balcony. 'Only joking ...'

Aphrodite yowled and hissed. 'She used to sip it when I had some, but I don't think it's a good idea.' Alice walked to the kitchen, the cat still hanging onto her neck. 'Well they can't have any, but I think I will. What about you?'

'Given the current tension in the situation,' shouted Luis from the balcony. 'I'll give it a go. A nice bit of camomile tea, isn't it?'

Not quite, thought Alice, remembering the effect it used to have on her. 'It's a bit stronger than that.'

'I'll have some anyway. At least we'll be relaxed. The house is more of a building site than when you left to be honest, so ...'

Alice turned the kettle on, took out some cat treats from the cupboard, opened the bedroom door and put Aphrodite and the food in there. Pulling it shut, she said, 'My mind was so full of everything earlier that only diving in the pool would get rid of the chatter, so a bit of tea would do me good to keep me grounded.'

Luis settled Elvis under a table on the balcony and joined

Alice in the kitchen. Pulling her towards him, he kissed her long and languorously, stroking her hair, then running his hand slowly down her spine. 'Oh, I've missed this. I've missed this with you here.' He sighed.

'Me too,' she whispered.

The kettle switched itself off, and the dog barked.

He laughed. 'Moment ended!'

Alice poured the boiling water into the cups and passed one to Luis. 'Those last three months in London were so intense,' she said. 'Once everything was sorted out with Adam, I thought it would be okay. But the house sold so fast ... and then putting my life into boxes.'

'I know. But we're here now. Together.'

They both sipped their tea.

'That's quite nice,' said Luis.

'Mmmm.' Alice savoured the familiar taste and a sense of serenity slowly creeping up from her toes.

'You know you can move in with me as soon as the house is finally finished. We could decorate it together.'

'I will.' She smiled. 'I've got loads of ideas already.'

'But...?' Luis took her hand.

Alice stood up and walked to the window, 'No but. That's what I want. More than anything. But I have to have something that's my own. I can't go back to half owning somewhere like I did with Adam.'

'I'd never do that to you.' He pulled her to him.

'I know you won't. I know. But it's your house. I need my house. I mean I know I'm going to let it out, but I need to do it.

He kissed her again. 'I get it. I get you.'

The silver moon gazed down at them. 'I've missed the big moons.' She laughed. 'There's something about the moon over the sea in Cascais.'

Elvis grunted from under the table.

'He agrees with you.' Luis laughed. 'Now, whilst the

animals seem almost settled, I have something to tell you ... they've asked me to sing one song tomorrow at the gig.'

'Have they?!'

'Yes, but I can't sing. I told them, but they insisted. So, I need to practise. I apologise in advance.'

As he began to search his phone for the song, Alice decided to let Aphrodite out of the bedroom. She opened the door a crack and the cat skipped out and ran into the kitchen.

Luis plugged his phone into the speaker and turned it on.

'*Volare*,' he sang, then looked in the air as if the words were hanging somewhere above him. He laughed as the music played on. 'I'm not sure I can do this.'

'Yes, you can. That first word sounded absolutely fantastic.'

'I did a bit of busking in Melbourne years ago,' he said. 'But I was actually rubbish.'

'Come on ... you can do it.'

He picked up the melody again and grabbed her hand. She giggled as he pulled her to him, leading her into a slow, close dance to the music, him singing at her and trying not to laugh too much. As the song ended he dipped her so she nearly touched the floor.

'Don't hurt your back,' she squeaked, and they collapsed into each other's arms, laughing.

'That was wonderful,' she whispered.

'No, it wasn't. You're biased. It's just because you're sleeping with the singer.'

'Speaking of which,' said Alice quietly, gazing up at him.

Elvis grunted again.

'How domesticated.' Luis turned Alice to see Elvis laying down, with Aphrodite curled around his paws.

'That didn't take long,' Alice said.

'Perfect timing.' Luis took her hand and led her to the bedroom, closing the door behind him.

Alice stretched and ran her foot along Luis' leg as he slept.

She looked at the tiny flecks of grey speckling his dark hair and unshaven face, and her stomach did the familiar loop the loop – the same loop the loop as when she'd first met him. The same loop the loop she felt every time she saw him. He grunted sleepily and turned over, snoring quietly again. She called it the 'I Love Luis Loop the Loop'. The morning sun peeped through the blinds, dotting the floor with tiny specks of light, and as Alice slid out of bed, she stepped on them one by one, inelegantly balancing on one foot then another. 'Follow the yellow brick road,' she muttered under her breath.

Dramatically opening the doors onto the balcony, she stepped outside and stretched her arms wide. *And you are doing what exactly?* There was that voice again. 'I am welcoming the day,' she said out loud. 'I am welcoming my new life.'

The trees rustled gently in the breeze, and a stork hovered in the distance over the bay; its long, elegant frame stretched like a ballerina. She breathed in slowly and smiled. This was home now. *Yes, but you haven't actually got a house. The little yellow house is gone. Your home in London is gone.*

'It's an adventure,' she said out loud. *And I can't turn back the clock*, she thought.

A cat yowling brought her back to reality, followed by a dog barking angrily.

'Whoops! Forgot we had pets,' she said, walking to the door whilst Luis jumped out of bed, suddenly awake.

'I slept in,' he said, peering at his phone. 'I've usually got Elvis out and walked by now. Mary's relaxing tea is amazing.'

They opened the door to see the large Alsatian and the tiny black-and-white cat sitting next to each other and gazing up at them. Aphrodite turned and walked to the kitchen, whilst Elvis trotted to the door.

'Now,' said Luis. 'I'm quite instinctive about these things. I'm getting the vibe that—'

Elvis barked.

Luis laughed. 'Yep, I think he wants a walk.'

Aphrodite put her head around the kitchen door and stared at Alice.

'Yes, Miss Aphrodite,' said Alice. 'I will get your food immediately. Sorry for the delay.'

Luis pulled on his clothes and opened the door. 'I'll get some fresh bread and coffee for breakfast when I'm out.' He kissed her as Elvis ran to the lift. 'See you in half an hour or so.' Then he popped his head round the door. 'I forgot to say – I've done some photos for Duarte de Silva's new flash boutique hotel south of the river, and he wants to talk to you about your bracelets.' The lift door pinged open and then he was gone.

'Well, Aphrodite,' said Alice, pouring her food into a pink cat bowl, 'Duarte de Silva wants some more of my bracelets. Exciting or what!'

As she turned the tap on to fill the other bowl with water, an image of Adam throwing her bracelets into a drawer and slamming it shut stabbed into her head like a dagger. *Really, Alice, making bracelets at your age. Isn't that for children?*

She turned the tap on full force, so the water splashed the walls and her face. 'Hotel owner, Duarte de Silva doesn't think so,' she said. Turning the tap off, she walked to the balcony and sat down. 'And he owns a record label. And some restaurants.'

Stop thinking of Adam and his rubbish every time something good happens, Alice Dorothy Matthews, the voice in her head muttered.

'I'm going to go down to the stalls in town tomorrow to see if they want any more of my jewellery,' she shouted to Aphrodite, who was purring over her food in the kitchen. 'My jewellery that apparently is very popular.'

Alice sighed and stood up. Adam had tried to steal half the house when it wasn't his. Now it was someone else's. She pulled the sheet of paper with the details of the little yellow house out of her bag – now it was someone else's too. She scrunched it up so she could throw it in the bin. 'The dream of owning you has kept me going over the last few months. I hope your owners are good to you.'

It's a house not a person, reminded the voice.

'Yes, I know, but it is a bit like a person to me.' She stood over the bin, then unscrunched the paper and put it back in the bag.

Chapter Four

Luis took Alice's hand as they walked to their seats, as Elvis followed, weaving around the clusters of people and tables at the café by the beach. 'The guys have already set up,' he said, 'but I've got to go and make sure the guitar's in tune, then I'll be back. Can you order me a beer?'

He rubbed Elvis behind the ears. 'Go and stay with Alice, okay?' he said, patting him on the head, then he went over to join the rest of the band.

Kathy and Stephano arrived as Alice sat down, and Elvis lay under the table whilst little James chattered to himself happily in his pushchair.

'Alice.' Stephano gave her a hug. 'Lovely to see you back.' Kathy pulled out a chair and collapsed into it.

'Wine. I need wine,' she said wearily.

'As bad as that?'

'No sleep last night.'

Alice laughed. 'Oh dear.'

'Wait till it happens to you.' Kathy's eyes twinkled wickedly.

'What, having a baby?' Alice spluttered. 'I'm in no position to have a baby at the moment.'

Her friend raised her eyebrows then looked down at the menu.

Alice watched Stephano fussing over James as he talked to the waiter, and her heart lurched. Her situation was hardly perfect, and she was fighting with her sensible, rational self about it. But ... she glanced at Kathy who she knew was deliberately not saying anything. 'I know you're deliberately not saying anything to get me to say something I don't want to,' muttered Alice.

Kathy continued to study the menu.

Alice sighed. 'Okay, you're right. We're not trying. But we are not *not* trying.'

Kathy looked up and bit her lip.

'Stop laughing. I know you're suppressing a laugh.' The drinks arrived and Alice poured herself some water, whilst Kathy took a long gulp of wine.

'I've got a day off,' she said. 'Stephano's taking James out later, and I intend to drink wine and go to sleep in about two hours. Happy days.' She touched Alice's arm. 'Continue.' She smiled.

'Well, we've decided that we will not try to prevent me getting pregnant. Although it would be better if it was when Luis' house is finished. And when I've bought one of my own.'

'That's very "go with the flow" for you,' said Kathy. 'But as you will be forty next year, it's quite sensible.'

'It doesn't feel it,' said Alice. 'I mean it is, because we can't wait forever. But that sensible part of me – that very, very sensible part of me – thinks I'm reckless.'

'You've never been reckless.'

'No. Anyway, nothing's happened yet. Thankfully.' Alice sipped her water. 'Not thankfully ... shall we say I'm conflicted?'

Stephano sat down and bounced James on his knee. Alice smiled at the scene.

'It'll happen,' said Kathy. 'Now where's your man?'

Alice pointed at the stage, where the band was about to start playing. 'He's ready to rock and roll.'

Luis took the mic in his hand. 'Welcome to Don Sebastiao and our occasional Sunday lunchtime gigs. You know what we do – if you want to dance, feel free, but don't bump into the restaurant staff or your food may end up on the floor!'

The diners laughed and clapped, and Alice beamed. Luis always looked so happy when he was making music, so lost in the moment, that it was a joy to watch.

'Apologies in advance, but for some reason they've

suggested I sing the first song, even though I'm a guitar player. So, here we go.' He put the mic on the stand, picked up his guitar, tapped his foot to get the time, and began to play, the band joining in as he went.

'*Volare* …' he sang.

Kathy leaped up and held out her hand. 'Dance, madam?'

'If you insist.' Alice laughed, standing and straightening her dress. They moved to the edge of the café, merging with the other dancers on the cobbled pavement. A group of small children giggled, jumping up and down, and chasing each other around.

'Good way to spend a Sunday lunchtime,' shouted Kathy over the noise.

'Indeed, it is.' Alice spun slowly around and wiggled her hips. As she moved and sang, the warm sun on her back, surrounded by happy people, she felt the shift inside her again. Like every time she relaxed a bit more, she subconsciously shed another protective skin from the past and freed something that was holding her back.

They sat down when the song finished, and Luis walked over to collect his beer. 'How does it feel to be with the singer, gorgeous?' he asked.

'I was going to get a T-shirt printed with "I'm with the singer" on it,' said Alice. 'But I decided it would make me look like a groupie.'

Luis pulled her to him, gave her a long kiss and then walked back to the band, beer in hand.

'Oh, I really fancy him.' She laughed with Kathy. Baby James giggled, and she waved at him.

Alice picked up her glass and sat back, watching the other diners enjoy themselves, but felt suddenly and inexplicably uncomfortable, as if she was being watched. Turning around, she caught the eye of a woman sitting at a table on the other side of the café. The woman smiled at her then looked away, the boy sitting next to her engrossed in his mobile phone. She shivered for a moment, then brushed the feeling away. *It was nothing*, she told herself. Just an echo from the past come to trip her up.

Kathy leaned forward and touched her arm. 'Bracelet lady,' she said. 'I love them all, but I love the green one the most.'

Alice took it off her wrist and gave it to her. 'I've got another one at home – have it.'

'You're awash with bracelets today – two on each wrist.' Kathy smiled.

Alice waved her hands and the bracelets made a jingling noise. 'I decided to advertise my own goods by wearing them. And I'm going into town tomorrow to see if any of the stalls want any more. And ...' She tailed off, knowing what her friend would say if she told her who else wanted her jewellery.

'And ...?' prompted Kathy.

'Nothing.'

'And ...?'

Alice poured herself some wine. 'Duarte de Silva wants me to design a special line for the boutique shop in his new hotel.'

'Be careful of him.'

Alice took a gulp. 'I knew you'd say that.'

'Honestly, I just don't trust him.'

'Well, Luis seems to think he's okay. And Carlos and Ignacio – he's given them a lot of advice about the café.'

Kathy put her drink down. 'Well, there's just something about him. And his daughter lied and tried to split you and Luis up.'

'Yes, Marcella is a nasty piece of work but she's off abroad somewhere now, because Duarte found out about her behaviour. I don't think we were the first people she'd tried to do that to, so he finally did something about it."

'That's all very well, but his sister-in-law tried to split you and Luis up, too. So it's not a good track record for that family at all. Be careful.' James started crying. 'Oh, baby, come on, are you hungry?' Kathy tried to distract her son whilst Stephano was getting a bottle of milk out of the bag.

'How much do you have in that?' Alice laughed.

'Oh, the usual: milk, nappies, wipes, water, emergency dummies, books, toys, kitchen table ...' The baby grabbed hold of Kathy's wrist and began playing with the bracelet. 'Well, that's calmed him down,' she said.

The song finished, and Alice turned to look at the stage but, as Luis waved at her, James began to scream and cry. She looked back to see beads and ribbons scattered on the floor, whilst Stephano was frantically searching through the bag once again. 'Oh dear ... he seems to have redesigned the bracelet,' said Alice.

'There's that lime-green submarine in there somewhere,' said Kathy wearily. 'Just keep looking. It's the only thing that will quieten him down.'

Noticing that a meltdown from Stephano and Kathy as well as their son was imminent, Alice knelt down and picked him from his father's knee. 'I'll distract him for a moment whilst you empty the huge contents of your bag on the table. Come to Auntie Alice,' she cooed, smiling at his tear-stained face and picking him up. 'Come with me, and we'll have a look at everything.' She walked around the tables, chatting as to him she went, and his tears slowly began to subside. Luis was standing next to the stage, and James giggled as he kissed him on the cheek.

Alice and Luis' eyes locked. *Maybe this will be us soon*, she thought. As she turned to take the baby back to the table, she caught the eye of the woman again, who immediately averted her gaze. By the time she handed James back to Kathy, Alice noticed that the woman was now staring at Luis.

Stop it, she told herself. *He's in the band. People will stare at him. Honestly.*

Ah, yes, but remember he had a reputation. When you first met him, people told you he had a reputation.

That was a long time ago.

We all have a past, the voice in her head whispered again. *You haven't! Well, only a boring and mundane one, darling.*

She spluttered with laughter.

'What are you smiling at?' asked Kathy, who seemed more at ease now James was being happily fed by Stephano.

Alice looked around her. 'Just everything,' she said. 'Shall we order some food? Luis will be finished soon, and I'm very, very hungry all of a sudden.'

After lunch the waiter began to clear the plates from the table, and Luis took his phone from his pocket. 'I've been looking at some possible houses for you, Al,' he said.

'Ooh, what have you found? I was going to get onto it later.'

They both looked down at the small screen, their foreheads touching. Luis put his arm around her and pulled her closer. Kathy and Stephano began to pack the baby's bag as James slept soundly in his pushchair. Close to where they'd been sitting some sparrows pecked at the crumbs on the floor, and a robin flew up and perched on a chair next to them whilst Elvis eyed them sleepily from under the table.

'That one looks nice,' said Alice. 'I like where it is.'

'The white one?' said Luis, looking more closely. 'That's not far from the little yellow house.'

'That's probably why I like it.'

'What about this one?' he said. 'It needs more doing to it than that one, but I can help out.'

Alice thought for a moment. 'The word "Project" jumps out at me, to be honest. I mean the little yellow house was a project, but this looks like a Project with a capital P.'

'Shows promise though,' said Luis. 'Why don't we have a

look at the outsides later when I take Elvis for his evening constitutional?'

'Good idea.' Alice squeezed his hand. 'Thank you,' she whispered.

'Can't have my girl feeling in limbo,' he said softly. 'The sooner you get your own house, the sooner you can move into mine!'

Alice put her arms around him and pulled him closer.

'Oi, lovebirds! there are other people here,' said Kathy. 'Get a room!'

They laughed and stood up.

'I'm just jealous,' said Kathy, smiling down at James. 'Having the time or energy to even peck Stephano on the cheek seems but a distant dream!'

'He is the perfect contraception,' chipped in Stephano, who was finally hanging the newly re-packed bag on the back of the pushchair.

'I'll get the guitar, back in a minute,' said Luis, Elvis trotting behind him.

'You two will be great parents,' whispered Kathy.

'Well, we've been letting it happen for nearly six months, and nothing ...'

'You've had a lot of stress, just be calm.'

'Nearly forty ...'

'Calm ...'

'Can't have a baby till I've got the house anyway ...'

'Calm ...'

'Need to get a house quickly—'

'—calm down, Alice,' cut in Kathy. 'You're going with the flow, remember?'

'Yes,' she said, sharply, then glanced at Luis, chatting to one of his band mates, guitar in hand, and felt the familiar loop the loop. 'Yes, I am going with the flow ... it's the new me. Just sometimes the old me peeps her head above the parapet.' As he walked back towards her, she saw the woman standing by her table and talking to her son, apparently preparing to go. But as Luis passed, the woman glanced at him again and caught his eye.

Alice caught the flicker of something in Luis' expression as she did so. He nodded politely and hurried back to the table.

'All okay?' she asked.

'Yes, yes ...' He smiled. 'Let's go home. Well, to the apartment. My home has no water or electricity.'

He took her hand, and they followed Kathy and Stephano towards the road, Elvis padding happily ahead.

Chapter Five

Alice dodged around the tourists as she walked down the sea road into town, her bag of bracelet samples hung over her shoulder. An early morning call from Ignacio asking for her to meet him and Carlos in the square meant she was rushing to talk to the two stall-holders she knew, rather than arriving cool, calm, collected and the very embodiment of a talented, creative, yet well-organised businesswoman.

The call had come when she was mashing up an avocado with chilli and lemon. She had managed to drop some on her arm whilst trying to talk to Ignacio, then rubbed her eyes so the chilli made them sting. She'd quickly eaten her breakfast and hurried out of the door, looking as smart as she could under the circumstances. Pausing next to an ice cream van, she took a few slow breaths and attempted to walk serenely to the first stall. '*Ola*, Bernice,' she said to a woman moving boxes from her van.

'Alice,' she said warmly, putting the boxes on the table and grabbing her hands. 'I'm so pleased to see you. Visitor numbers are picking up, and I need more bracelets from you – can you let me have thirty by Friday?'

'Of course.' Alice tried to work out in her head how many she had ready back at the apartment.

'That is very good. It's getting busier because it's getting warmer, and I need to stock up.' Bernice examined the bracelets Alice was wearing. 'I love this turquoise one – what about another five of those to see how they go?'

'Yes, no problem.'

'Excellent.' Bernice hugged her and started to move the boxes again. 'Marianne isn't on her stall by the station today, if you wanted to talk to her, too. Just text her.'

'Okay. I'll see you on Friday.'

As she turned to go, Bernice said, 'We've missed you. Welcome home.'

Alice smiled. *Home*, she thought, *home* ... just need to find an actual house.

The square was quiet, with a few customers scattered around the tables in the different restaurants. Carlos and Ignacio were sitting just outside the café, deep in conversation, paperwork spread out in front of them.

Alice pulled out a chair and sat down. '*Ola*,' she said. They both looked up, surprised. 'Why are you both so serious? Is anything wrong?'

'No, no Alice.' They both kissed her in greeting, and Carlos waved to another waiter to get her a *galao*.

'We have had an idea,' said Carlos, appearing quite excited.

'Carlos has had an idea,' said Ignacio firmly.

'Excellent.' Alice looked at them both expectantly as Carlos smiled back, and Ignacio pursed his lips.

'Wait a minute, though,' said Ignacio, picking up a napkin and wiping something from Alice's shoulder.

'Avocado for breakfast?' asked Carlos.

'Oh, no, it's not on my dress?'

Ignacio laughed. 'Just a spot.'

'I wondered why Bernice looked at me like that ...'

'Anyway.' Ignacio leaned back and folded his arms.

'Tiles,' said Carlos.

'Lovely. What about them?' asked Alice

'We want a wall of specially designed tiles, individually painted.'

'I like the green and brown idea,' Ignacio sighed, 'but ...'

'But it won't be individual to us,' explained Carlos.

Alice stirred the coffee the waiter had brought over for her, realising she was in the middle of one of their disagreements again. She said nothing. Carlos shifted in his seat and moved closer to her, brimming with excitement.

'We want you to design the tiles and paint them,' he said.

40

'I've never painted tiles. Are you sure?' Alice took a sip of her drink, realising she was not allowed to say no.

'I told you, it's too much. We should just paint the walls and hang pictures,' huffed Ignacio, leaning back in his seat.

'I know a lady—'

'—Another of his ladies.'

'She is an artist, like you,' Carlos continued. 'She teaches people tile painting, and she has a kiln in the back of an old camper van in her garden.'

Ignacio rolled his eyes.

'I was talking to her the other day, and she said … it would be individual and distinctive to have our own tiles.'

'I'm not sure I'll be able to do them well enough.'

'It's a small wall, Alice. I have every faith. She said you can join her class. It's on Tuesdays.'

Ignacio shrugged his shoulders, obviously resigned.

Alice's heart began to race. *I need to get the bracelets done, speak to Duarte de Silva, find a house, do a training plan for my friend's company*, she thought. *I can't … no, I can … calm down.* She took a deep breath. *Being busy is my default setting. It'll do me good, stop me feeling in freefall.*

She put her hand on Carlos's. 'Of course I'll do it. Text me her details, and I'll arrange to go to the class.'

'I'll text her now and tell her.' Carlos almost bounced up and walked into the café.

Ignacio sighed. 'He likes to compose flirtatious messages without anyone looking at him.'

'Maybe this could be the one to capture his heart?' Alice smiled.

'Like the last one to capture his heart for three weeks … and the one before that who captured his heart for a magnificent two months. My brother needs to concentrate on the business at the moment.'

'How's the mindfulness and meditation going?' asked Alice, trying to take the conversation in a different direction.

'Oh, excellent. I was talking to your mother yesterday about using the room above the café for my soon-to-be counselling practice. She thinks its excellent. I'm frankly very excited.'

Carlos reappeared at the door, beaming. 'You're booked in for tomorrow at ten a.m. That is okay, isn't it? It's two hours.'

'That's absolutely fine, of course.'

Carlos began to clear the cups from the table.

'Any ideas about the design?'

They both looked at her, faces blank.

'No, we trust you,' said Ignacio.

'Yes, it's up to you.'

A good thing or a bad thing or both, she thought. 'Okay, well. I'll get some ideas for you in the next two weeks and we can decide. We haven't got much time if I've got to paint them all too.'

The alarm on Ignacio's phone buzzed. 'Time to go for my next airport pick-up.'

'Okay, well, I'll pop down later in the week to keep you up to date.' Alice texted Marianne, the stall-holder, before she stood up. *I'd better get myself properly organised if I'm making bracelets and making tiles*, she thought, strangely excited about being busy again. The three of them said their goodbyes and set off in separate directions.

Alice messaged Luis. He was waiting for her in his truck at the bottom of the hill, Elvis barking at her from the back seat.

'How did it go?' He kissed her and turned the engine on as she sat down.

'They're having brotherly disputes,' she said. 'And they're sending me to tile painting classes so I can paint bespoke tiles for the wall at the back of the restaurant.'

'Another string to your bow.' He laughed.

'I'm not sure I can get it done in time, but still, I'll give it a go.'

The car pulled out of the town onto the Guincho Road.

The sea was rough and wild, white foam ridges tumbling into the deep, dark blue of the fierce waves. Alice sat back, the car window open, enjoying the wind flying through her hair.

'I need to warn you about what you're about to see,' said Luis.

'I know it's a bit of a building site at the moment.' Alice smiled.

'I want you to promise me you'll see through it. It's been more than three months since you've visited it, remember?'

They turned in from the sea road, up the hill along a winding track to the old farmhouse that Luis had bought two years ago and had begun renovating as quickly as his time and money would allow. He stopped the car and jumped out, with Elvis following.

Alice didn't move. Mounds of earth surrounded the house, which was covered almost completely in plastic sheeting. Luis solemnly took her hand and she stepped out, following him to the top of one of the mounds. She could make out the silhouette of the building and heard the shouts of the workmen from inside.

'We can't go in – I haven't got any hard hats spare – but half the floors are down,' he said. 'And I've got the bathrooms in the store shed ready to install. They're making good the terraces at the back and from the top bedroom at the front at the moment. They've been painting them, hence the sheeting – it's got a bit windy over the last couple of days, and they're protecting the paintwork.'

In the distance Alice could make out the tangle of rose bushes in the garden and the contours of the lemon trees.

Luis squeezed her hand. 'In a few months, we can live here, together,' he said. 'We'll be a family. I can just see the kids running around the grounds, in and out of the kitchen. There'll be a swing over there—' he pointed animatedly to a plot next to the house '—and I'll build a tree house in that old oak over there.'

Alice looked up at him, his face open and happy, and felt still and calm.

'I love you, Luis Simal,' she said.

He smiled at her. 'I love you too, Alice Dorothy Matthews.' They stood next to each other, with Elvis sitting patiently at Luis' feet. *This is what happiness feels like then*, thought Alice. *This is it.*

Chapter Six

Alice had placed all her bracelets in piles on the floor. She gathered her beads and ribbons, as well as the shattered and smoothed shards of old tiles that gave her jewellery its unique look, to sort into boxes. Aphrodite jumped on a piece of green material that Alice was folding up and tried to bite it, pulling it into the mountain of jewellery, which collapsed and slid over the tiled floor.

Alice laughed. 'You're not helping.'

Luis walked back into the living room carrying two glasses of wine. He put them down and turned on his laptop. 'Need to check out what I have to do at this renovation job I'm starting tomorrow,' he said, pausing to hand a drink to Alice. He sighed. 'We need a bit of gentle music and to dim the lights to get the mood right, I'm afraid. But there's no dimmer switch so we have to use our imaginations!'

'That's All' by Frank Sinatra filled the room as Elvis yawned loudly. Luis' phone buzzed and Alice saw him looking at it out of the corner of her eye. Something changed. Something wasn't right. Alice knew it.

She looked up. He was reading a message on the screen as if he couldn't believe it.

'Are you okay?' she asked.

He didn't meet her eye. 'Yes, yes. Someone's contacted me about the band. It's okay. Fine.'

Putting the phone down, he smiled. 'Drink up. I'll get you another one. I'm getting another one.' He gulped down the rest of his drink and walked to the kitchen. 'Only one more. I've got to be at the job at eight, so I'm leaving early.'

'Are you sure everything is all right?' Alice knew it wasn't, and her heart began to pound.

Luis came back from the kitchen, his face now composed, bottle in hand. 'Yes, of course. Shall we get an early night?'

Alice got off the bus just outside the house where her tile painting class was starting, then rang the doorbell at the gate that led to the garden. It opened slowly and she followed the path towards the chatter and laughter echoing from the wooden outbuilding shaded by eucalyptus trees, as classical music floated towards her. Pausing uncertainly at the door, she took a deep breath and walked in. The six women inside were oblivious to her presence.

'Hello?' she said quietly. Then 'Hello ... I'm looking for Gina?' Her voice rose uncertainly.

A woman with black hair pinned up loosely around her face and a bright, kind smile walked over to her.

'Alice? How lovely to meet you.' She hugged her tightly, then shouted. 'Everyone – this is Alice. A friend of Carlos.'

The room rang with friendly greetings as Gina pulled her up a chair. Alice almost shivered with pleasure – she hadn't been in a room full of people making things and laughing since she was at university, and had only realised in that moment how much she had missed it. The table was covered in palettes of paint and brushes sticking out of jars, sponges scattered haphazardly next to mugs of water, and white tiles waiting to be decorated.

Gina sat down next to her and took her hand. 'Carlos has asked me to look after you,' she said. 'He told me you are a talented artist, but you are new to painting Portuguese tiles.'

'I am,' said Alice. 'But I'm excited to learn.'

'Why don't we get you to do some basic tiles today as practice? Then we can think about the design next week, once you know how it works.' Gina placed a square cream tile in front of her, next to glasses of blue and yellow paint and a fine brush. Then she pulled out some tracing paper and a pencil from a drawer in the table and put them next to a book of traditional Portuguese patterns.

Alice felt her fingers tingle with anticipation and wiggled them without realising she was doing it.

Gina laughed. 'You are going to create some beautiful tiles, I can feel it. Now, choose a pattern, trace it onto here, then we transfer it onto the tile, paint it over, and then I put it in the kiln.'

'You make it sound easy, but I don't think it is,' said Alice.

'You'll learn how to do it beautifully. And next week, once you see the results, you will get your confidence.' She stood up, then sat down again, leaning close to Alice. 'Carlos is a lovely man isn't he?' she said quietly.

'He is lovely and very kind.'

'Gina,' one of the other pupils called her over. 'Can you help me with this?'

She stood up. 'Call me if you need anything.'

Alice began to turn the pages of the book, studying the patterns and examining the colours, unable to decide which one to choose to start with. The woman sitting to her right smiled at her and pointed to a design of a small boat and some lines for waves in blue. 'This one is easy to begin with,' she said.

'Thank you.' Alice felt at home and sensed a glow wrap itself around her. Picking up the pencil, she began to lose herself in her drawing, listening to the chatter in the background and being carried along with the music. Eventually a bell rang, and Alice looked up with a start, the spell broken.

'It's the only way I remember when the two hours are up.' Gina laughed. 'Otherwise we'll be here all day.'

Alice cleared her space and handed her the four tiles she had finished

Gina examined them closely. 'These look very good,' she said. 'I'm impressed.'

'I'm so pleased,' said Alice. 'I want everything to be perfect for Carlos and Ignacio, and I was worried I wouldn't be good enough.'

'You are good enough,' reassured Gina. 'I can see you are very talented just from what you've produced today.'

'Thank you. I'll see you next week.' As Alice turned to go, Gina touched her arm.

'Send Carlos my regards,' she said.

'I will,' said Alice.

That went well, she texted Luis as she left. It turns out I love tile painting! xx

Then she messaged Kathy. Still on for a coffee in the square at two?

Yes! The phone buzzed back immediately. I need to speak to an adult person. Although I may not make any sense about anything.

Alice laughed at the message. And your point is? she texted back.

'Just parking the pushchair,' Kathy sang at a giggling James. 'When did I start singing everything to you?' she sang again. 'I've got baby brain. I have, I have!'

Carlos knelt down and pretended to tickle him. 'You are my best customer,' he said. 'You are, you are ...'

James giggled again.

'*Galaos* ladies?' he asked, looking up. 'And a gin and tonic for you, James?'

'That will happen soon enough,' sighed Kathy. 'The years will fly by, but time seems to be going in slow motion at the moment.' She flopped down into her seat.

'So, two *galaos* for you then, and one for Alice?' Carlos laughed, picked up a tray and walked inside the café.

'Give me caffeine intravenously,' muttered Kathy.

James erupted with laughter as Carlos reappeared at the door, waved at the baby and disappeared again.

'Ahh, there he is,' said Kathy. 'Carlos the ladies' man. Do you think he'll ever settle down?' She rummaged around in the baby bag. 'I mean, I never see him with the same woman ... ahh, there you go.' She pulled out a plastic book and handed it to James. 'I was thinking the other day ...' Her face went blank, then she looked at Alice for a moment. 'I can't remember what I was thinking the other day.' Kathy put her head in her hands and groaned. 'What's happened to me? I used to read books. Now I'm excited about what happens at the end of *Thomas the Tank Engine*.'

'I'm rather fond of the Teletubbies myself,' said Alice. 'You were talking about Carlos and I was about to say ...' she lowered her voice and leaned over the table. 'He seems rather taken with Gina, the tile painting tutor. I was at her class today. She was asking after him, too.'

James shrieked with laughter again. They both turned to see Carlos pulling faces at him from the doorway, then looked at each other and began to laugh themselves.

'Here are your drinks,' said Carlos, walking towards them. 'I gave you extra caffeine Kathy. On the house!'

'You know me so well,' she said. 'Thank you.'

Alice felt her phone buzz. You can paint some tiles for the house on the hill! It was Luis. And I have a surprise for you. Two viewings tonight for your perfect home. Don't say I never treat you! x

Alice smiled. *Whatever I saw on his face last night was another echo of the past*, she thought. *I just need to calm down.*

Ummmm ... whispered the voice in her head. But it was almost too quiet for her to notice.

'What do you think?' Luis knocked the kitchen wall.

'I think it has potential,' Alice said slowly. 'But it's a bit dark to be honest.'

Luis smiled at her. 'I knew you'd say that. You love light and bright.'

'I suppose because the windows are so big, I assumed they would let in a lot of light.'

Luis glanced outside. 'At the back here, there are too many other buildings. They block everything.'

Alice felt a greyness press down on her. 'I'm getting a bit

worried. Do you think I'll find anything I want as much as the yellow house?'

He stroked her hair. 'To quote your mother – Alice Matthews …' He paused.

'Yes …?' Alice said encouragingly.

'That's all I've got to quote your mother.' He laughed. 'This is from me – we've looked at the outside of two houses and the inside of two others.'

'Yes, I didn't like that last one we saw tonight at all … '

'… and you have been back in Cascais less than a week …'

'I'm homeless …'

'You've got Mary and Frank's place to stay in and, when the water and electricity is back on in the farmhouse, you've got that too, so not homeless.'

'Houseless, then.'

He laughed again. 'It will happen, Alice, it will. It has to be the right house, though.'

She grabbed his waist and hugged him, her head on his chest. 'Yes. I know. Sensible Alice disappeared for a few seconds there.'

'You've got a lot on anyway – your bracelet empire, being a design consultant for Carlos and Ignacio's restaurant …'

'Excellent job title.'

'Just thought of it.'

'Creating a new and exciting tile pattern for a wall and then painting all the tiles …'

'That'll keep you occupied. Also that online training consultancy freelance job you took on months ago before you sold your house.'

'An eminently sensible job which basically saved my financial bacon when I was sorting that out. I'm not giving that up. Not for a while anyway.'

'And Duarte de Silva. Have you messaged him yet?'

'God, no. I forgot.' Alice stood back and began to look for her phone in her bag.

'I think he wants us both to go and look at his new hotel. The setting is gorgeous – I went down last month to get some ideas and I've already submitted the photos. It'd be great to go down together. I want to be the first to show it to you. It's magical,' said Luis.

Alice messaged Duarte to tell him she was interested in the job and put her phone back in her bag.

Luis grabbed her hand and walked to the door. 'Shall we say bye to the house and get something to eat? Elvis needs a run as well.'

'Bye, house,' said Alice, and they stepped into the street.

'Did you like it?' The estate agent was standing by her car, with Elvis sitting patiently next to her.

'Not for me, unfortunately,' said Alice.

'Okay. Well, I'll keep in touch. I may have something very interesting coming up in the next couple of weeks.' She got in the car and started the engine as Alice and Luis began to meander along the street. The night air was warm and still, light with jasmine and peony, as Elvis walked softly next to them.

'These windows,' sighed Alice, gazing up at the bright blue shutters. 'They are so beautiful. I wonder who's living behind them.'

'I often think that,' said Luis. 'People like us, maybe? Or there is a famous writer living in that tiny blue house with the white windows. If you listen you can hear the tap, tap, tap of the keyboard.'

Alice stopped walking and listened. 'Can't hear a thing,' she said.

'I was using my imagination!' Luis laughed. 'We could populate the whole town with our imaginations, couldn't we?'

Alice squeezed his hand.

Luis checked a message on his phone, and Alice caught that flicker again.

'Is everything okay?' she asked.

'Yes, of course. Why do you ask?'

'Just a feeling,' she said softly.

'Everything is fine,' he said, but his voice had a faint trace of irritability. 'Let's go to the square, shall we?'

The sound of laughter and chatter began to fill the narrow streets as they got closer to the square, faint sounds of a piano in the background and the distant barking of a dog from inside one of the cafés. The parasols seemed to glow white, green and red, as they walked towards a table, the clinking of knives and forks and the hum of conversation sounding like music to Alice.

Luis' phone buzzed as they sat, his face once again held a trace of something he wouldn't say.

Ignacio walked over to them and pulled up a chair, putting a large book down and sighing. 'I am working on all of the different ways that people across the world cultivate forgiveness.'

'That's a big book,' said Alice.

'It encompasses many things. Your mother recommended it to me. It's to give me an overview of some of the many ways people have of looking at the world. Forgiveness is very important, it appears,' he said. 'I tried explaining it to Carlos earlier when I was late for a business meeting as my meditation class ran over. I was very stressed when I got here and snapped at him, I'm afraid.'

'He'll understand,' said Alice, trying not to laugh. 'Where is he?'

Ignacio raised one eyebrow and smiled. 'He is on a date. With another of his ladies.'

'Do you know who with?'

'No. I don't ask about his love life and he doesn't tell me.'

Luis stood up. 'I've got to make a call,' he said. 'They want me to play in the band on Sunday, but I thought we could just chill together.' He kissed her on the cheek, but Alice felt it again – a faint uneasiness.

Ignacio leaned forward. 'Alice, have you noticed that there is a woman that has been staring at you since you sat down? She's with a boy over there by the statue.'

Alice looked over and saw the woman who had been at the gig at the weekend. She was watching Luis as he headed towards Fisherman's Beach whilst talking animatedly on the phone.

'Oh, yes. I saw her on Sunday.' *Here we go again*, the voice in her head whispered. *Another woman from his unfortunate past.*

The woman said something to her son, then stood up and followed Luis.

Alice felt sick. *Nope, nope, not again*, she thought. *Not this again.*

Ignacio looked at her. 'I'm sure it's nothing,' he said kindly.

'I'm sure it is,' she said firmly, taking the menu and attempting to study it. *It's nothing*, she thought. *Nothing.*

Follow them, said the voice in her head.

It's nothing. I don't want to interrupt Luis. He'll think I'm mad.

Doesn't matter what he thinks. What about you?

She tried to focus on the menu, but the words were just shapes on a page.

Ignacio gently took it off her.

'The old Alice would have sat and done nothing,' he said quietly. 'She would have just sat there and worried.'

She looked at him. 'I know.'

'She would have put everyone else first. That's what the old Alice would do.'

'Yes.'

'Just sat there ...'

'I'm going to check he's all right. She's probably just nipped into a shop or something.'

She stood up and hurried towards the sea road, glancing at the boy who was sitting on his own, engrossed in a game on his phone.

This is the new me, she thought. *Facing things, not running away. And it's nothing. I know it's nothing. Just the past waving at me. The new Alice. The new me.*

She tripped over a cobble and fell into a table.

For God's sake, muttered the voice in her head.

'Sorry, sorry,' she said to the three surprised diners as she steadied herself. 'Loose cobble there. Enjoy your meal.'

You wouldn't know the new Alice if she tapped you on the shoulder and said 'hello Alice, I'm the new Alice.' The voice in her head sounded despondent.

She straightened her dress and looked around, trying to see where the woman had gone. And there, in the street leading from the square to the bay, she saw them in intense conversation. Luis was shaking his head. Then, suddenly, he moved back and stood against a wall, looking beyond the woman, his face unreadable.

Alice's heart began to beat fast, pumping as she rushed over. *No, no*, she thought. *Walk calmly, don't show you're worried.* Her pace slowed as she moved until she was finally standing next to Luis, who hadn't noticed her.

'Are you okay?' She touched his arm.

He looked down, his face stricken. 'Oh Alice. Alice. What will you think of me ...?'

'What's going on?' She looked at him and the woman. 'You're worrying me. Is everything all right?'

The woman glanced back towards the square. 'I'm just checking my son is okay. Sorry. I didn't want to leave him, but I needed to speak to Luis.' Then she stroked her stomach absent-mindedly. She was pregnant.

Alice froze, unable to speak. *No*, she thought ... *no*.

The woman stepped forward. 'I'm really sorry,' she said quietly. 'This is not the way I wanted it to go ... but Luis wouldn't answer my messages, and he needed to know.'

Alice stared at her, her head a cacophony of questions. *She was pregnant? Luis' child? Who was she?*

She felt a hand take hers. Luis had stepped towards her and was gazing at her. 'I'll tell her.' Alice saw he was shaking. 'I have a son,' he said. 'I didn't know about him. I've just found out. Fran just told me ...this is Fran ...'

'It was from a long time ago,' the woman said quickly. 'An insignificant fling. I didn't tell Luis then. I didn't know till I got back to London.'

Alice stared at him, and then at the woman. She didn't understand. She had heard the words, but they didn't make sense. They did make sense, but they couldn't be true, because if they were, everything had changed. Everything had changed in just one second. People continued to meander past, talking happily, and a group of drummers began to play in the square as if nothing had happened. But it had. Everything had happened. All at once. In an instant.

'I tracked Luis down on Facebook. I knew he'd be playing in a band somewhere ... but I still wasn't sure whether I wanted him in Mario's life.'

Luis squeezed Alice's hand. 'What will you think of me?' he said again.

'I went to the gig at the restaurant on Sunday to see. I still wasn't sure.' She looked at Alice. 'We were both irresponsible and ...' She glanced at the floor. 'Luis wasn't the kind of man I wanted in my son's life.'

Alice glanced at his stricken, guilty face. He stared at the wall opposite, seemingly unable to focus on anything.

'But when I saw you two and how you were together, with your friend's baby.' She stopped suddenly and looked towards the square again. 'I trust you to be in my son's life. Our son's life.'

Luis looked up. 'Does he know it's me?' he asked.

'No.'

His voice began to rise. 'If you had told me I would have been part of his life.' He looked at Alice. 'Believe me, Alice. I would.'

Alice looked at him. She took a deep breath, fighting away the tears.

'I'm not the man your father was,' he said quietly. 'I want you to know that.'

She looked up at him. 'I know.'

'I would never have walked out on my child like he walked out on you. Or not taken care of them. If I had known I would have—'

The woman cut in. 'We were young and we were irresponsible and we were arrogant. I made the decision. Please don't feel bad about that. It was my decision. It was mine … and we have been okay. He's a good boy.'

Alice felt a switch flick her onto autopilot. She was suddenly sensible again, feeling nothing. 'And now he wants to meet his father?' she said, pulling Luis towards her.

'I messaged Luis a couple of times, but he didn't respond.'

'I saw you at the restaurant the other day, but you looked different.' Luis spoke in a rush, his voice quiet, but Alice could hear the emotion he was trying to hide. 'I wasn't sure it was you. And when you messaged me you didn't say what it was about, so I thought I'd let the past be the past. And not reply.'

Fran touched his arm gently. 'So this was the only way I could speak. I'm sorry. It's a shock.'

'Can I meet him?' asked Luis. 'I'd like to meet him.'

'We're here for a couple of days more,' she said. 'Shall we arrange to do it properly? I'll tell him he is meeting his father, so he's prepared. He asked me to find you.'

'Okay.' Alice could feel Luis begin to gather his strength again. 'Could I say hello now, though? Not introduce myself as his father. Not till tomorrow.'

Fran smiled. 'Of course. Can you make it as casual as you can? I need to prepare him.'

Alice stepped forward and held out her hand. 'I'm Alice,' she said. She felt almost an onlooker to something so intimate between them. But it was her life too.

'Good to meet you.' Fran pulled her into a hug, holding her tight as Alice once again felt herself begin to float from her safe anchor. Fran stood back and looked at Luis. 'Ready?' she asked.

He nodded and they walked to the square so he could meet his son. Alice stood back, watching them make their way around the tables to where the boy was sitting. She tried to read Luis' face, but it was too far away, and as the boy looked up it was as if she was pulled back to the past. To when she and her sister, Tara, met their stepfather, Joseph, for the first time.

They had no real idea what a father was either, as theirs had abandoned them when they were little, leaving their mother in debt. And then they were evicted and lost their home so had to move to a tatty bedsit, before their mother gave in and moved in with her parents. They didn't know what they were looking for until Joseph came into their lives.

This is the right thing, she thought. *The right thing*. But it was as if she was standing next to herself, watching someone else reacting to what was happening.

Then Luis was standing next to her. He couldn't meet her gaze. 'Alice ...' was all he could say. 'I ... don't understand what has just happened. Is this real? Am I dreaming this?' She took his hand.

'You're shaking,' she said. 'Please don't. It will be all right. It will.'

They stood for a few moments, unable to speak, life going on around them as if nothing had changed. 'Big day tomorrow,' said Luis eventually. 'I'm going to meet him after work. After she's spoken to him.' He hesitated. 'You will come, won't you?'

'I'll meet him afterwards,' she said softly. 'You need to meet him without me first.'

He kissed her cheek. 'You've been there, done that, bought the T-shirt in your own life,' he said. 'Whatever you think is best.' He cupped her face gently in his hands. 'This isn't going to be a problem for us, is it?'

'No, no ...'

He put his arm round her waist, and they walked towards his car. 'His name is Mario,' he said. 'I have a son and he is called Mario.'

Chapter Seven

They barely spoke when they got to the apartment. There was so much to say, but Alice felt she didn't have the words and Luis seemed unable to concentrate on anything. When they eventually climbed into bed, he put his arms around her, pulling her to him. 'I love you,' he whispered. 'Please forgive me.'

'There's nothing to forgive,' she said softly. 'And I love you too.'

Then they had rolled away from each other, Alice wide awake, her mind jumping, her body tense, listening to Luis' listless breathing until he eventually sank into a restless sleep, and then she did too.

She awoke to Aphrodite biting her toe.

'Owww!' She sat bolt upright, squealing, the cat following her foot's every movement, waiting to pounce again. Covering her legs with the sheet, she sat up. The sound of rain pitter-pattered on the window, and she heard the shaking of leaves on the trees in the gardens. The only sign of Luis was the indents in his pillow and a stray black hair.

Alice suddenly felt sick. He wouldn't be coming home to her after work. He would be meeting his son properly.

Her mind began to fly – there were too many thoughts for her to settle on any one thing. All she could hear was *It's the right thing. He's doing the right thing. You're doing the right thing. These things happen. It will be fine.*

But the sick feeling didn't go. She stood on the cool, hard tiles and checked her phone. There was a message from Luis. I love you, it said. Wish me luck xx

Then there was one from Duarte de Silva sent very early that morning. Let's have a meeting to start this off. Can you meet me at my restaurant in Lisbon at 11.30? It's Casa de Andre in Baixa.

Relieved to have something to take her mind off the

earthquake that had just happened in her life, she messaged him back. Yes of course. See you there.

There's nothing I can do about this, she thought. *So I have to throw myself into any opportunity to occupy my mind. Thank you, Duarte de Silva.* Opening the wardrobe, she scanned the hangers for something suitable to wear. 'Aphrodite, what does a bohemian and creative businesswoman wear?' The cat went for her feet again.

'Shoes, obviously,' she said picking her up and stroking her neck. Her favourite orange floral trousers caught her attention. 'What do you think?' she said, putting Aphrodite on the bed. The cat padded off and wandered into the kitchen.

'Okay, maybe too much.' *You can't go for those trousers every time you feel threatened* said the voice in her head. *You bought three pairs when Adam was trying to intimidate you into selling the house.*

She put her hand out and found the yellow and green pairs. 'When I put them on I feel brave and visible and empowered, actually. But for once I agree with you voice in head,' she muttered. 'Plain, yet classy, green sundress and lots of my own jewellery. Plus I'll put my hair up in some kind of … thing.'

Aphrodite began to yowl hungrily, then Elvis barked from the balcony.

'Why aren't you with Luis?' she asked the dog, who looked up at her then walked to join Aphrodite in the kitchen. 'Oh yes, I forgot. He can't take you to work today … oh dear, you're going to have to come with me to Lisbon. Are you up for that?'

He barked and stood by one of the vibrant pink plastic food bowls that landlady Mary had left for them.

'I'll take that as a yes,' she said, spooning out some food.

The rain had stopped by the time Alice stepped out, her bag of bracelet samples in one hand, Elvis's lead in the other and an umbrella stuffed into the handbag draped over her shoulder.

'Be careful of the cobbles,' said the porter as she left. 'They can get very slippery when it's raining.'

'Will do,' she said, slowing down to avoid falling over.

Elvis virtually pulled her down the hill and up again towards the station. The strong breeze blew her carefully pinned up hair, which she had covered with enough hair spray to keep it in place for a couple of months. She had thrown herself into creating the right look as a way of distracting her thoughts from Luis and what was to come.

The train moved away from Cascais, the sea grey and angry to her right, whipping up the waves far into the distance. Rain began to splatter the windows as it halted in Estoril, and droplets fell in through a gap above her.

Oh dear, she thought, touching her hair. *Please stop raining before we get there, rain.* She sat back in her seat and tried to ignore the churning in her stomach. Was it because of the meeting with Duarte de Silva? Was it because of Luis and the feeling that the rug had been pulled from under her again, or was it because someone else had bought the little yellow house?

All of them, she thought. *All of them.* Her finger traced a line on the window, and she grabbed the sill, the feeling of being suddenly adrift punching at her, then receding again.

You've never been adrift before. There's always been an anchor. Be careful.

I am careful, she thought.

Of yourself, I meant said the voice in her head, as the carriage slowed just before Belem, pausing in front of a building called Champalimaud Centre for the Unknown. She snorted with laugher and continued to giggle quietly for five minutes, knowing in her heart that it was due to a kind of mild hysteria.

The train pulled into Cais do Sodre station in Lisbon, and Alice took a deep breath. *I am a businesswoman*, she thought. *I am going to create an empire of bracelets. And other things.*

Picking up Elvis' lead, she swung her bag of samples and they made a satisfying jingling sound as she walked along the platform to the exit, shaking her arms to make her jewellery sing, too.

Walking along the river, with her large dog and her colourful bag, Alice thought about the sepia postcard of the girl on a Lisbon street that Kathy had sent her on the day she had decided to run away to Portugal. In the picture the pavement had been wet from a downpour, but the girl didn't care. Sunshine was coming. Let it rain. 'Today, that's me,' muttered Alice to herself. Rushing over Praca do Comercio, she crossed the road to Rua Augusta, enjoying the comforting hum of the trams criss-crossing the streets.

As it began to drizzle again she took out her umbrella and tried to open it. Half of it fell limply, useless.

'Oh dear,' she said to Elvis. 'I'm going to get soaked.' Looking up at the sky, she sighed. 'It's not going to stop. Half an umbrella is better than none.'

Her phone buzzed, and she rifled through her bag for it, trying not to fall over in the process. Change of plan. Meet us at the entrance of the food hall next to Cais do Sodre. Duarte DS.

Alice sighed. 'Back we go,' she muttered, beginning to retrace her steps and hoisting the broken umbrella above her head, one side drooped to ninety degrees. It looked like two different umbrellas stuck together, but she pretended not to notice and hurried through the narrow streets rather than following the river, Elvis trotting along beside her. Turning a corner too quickly, she slid on the wet cobbles through a large puddle, which spattered her legs with warm, grey, dirty water, then she almost skidded to a halt outside the food market.

Unfortunately, Duarte was standing outside talking to a tall, casually dressed man and just as Alice caught sight of herself in a window, holding half an umbrella above her head, hair damp and messy from the rain, muddy marks splattered up her legs, a bag of samples in one hand, a handbag over her shoulder and holding the lead of a large, wet Alsatian in the other hand, it was too late to hide

You're a businesswoman who's building an empire of bracelets and other things, are you? asked the voice in her head.

The other half of the umbrella broke and fell over her, showering her face with rain. She looked like she was wearing an umbrella hat.

Both men looked at her, and Duarte smiled widely.

'Alice,' he said, kissing her on both cheeks. 'Welcome back to Portugal. I hope everything has been sorted out with your house.' He stood back. 'It's a pity about the weather,' he said.

'Hi,' said Alice. 'Yep, my umbrella decided to die today.'

'We had a change of plan,' said Duarte. 'This is Saul Pires.' The man next to him smiled and nodded. 'He's my consultant chef for the new hotel. Just flew in from New York.'

'Hello,' said Alice, accidentally shaking the umbrella and so loosening some stray droplets onto her nose.

'Nice to meet you,' he said. 'I'd shake hands, but you don't have any available.'

Alice laughed. 'Wasn't expecting to bring Elvis,' she said. 'The dog.' Alice held up the lead. 'Not the singer. Obviously.'

He smiled. 'That would be quite something. If it was the singer and not the dog.'

She glanced at him. He looked familiar. *Saul reminds me of someone*, she thought. *Someone from a while ago. Who?*

'Saul's got a meeting here later, so we thought we'd kill two birds with one stone. My driver will look after Elvis.'

A man in a suit darted forward and took the dog's lead, and the three of them walked into the market.

'Lunchtime and it's already busy,' exclaimed Duarte, as he skirted the tables packed with people eating and drinking, the queues to the food outlets snaking around the walkways, full of hungry customers chattering happily. 'Come,' he said, walking left to a quieter part with stools next to the counters of cafés. He indicated where they should sit. 'We can hear ourselves speak here, at least.'

'And the food's great,' said Saul. 'They are very creative with *bacalhau* ... I mean the salted cod ...' he clarified to Alice.

'Yes, I do like *bacalhau*,' she said, longing to sit down and dry out.

As they sat, Alice saw her reflection in the steel of one of the ovens and decided to abandon her carefully arranged hair, which now looked like a straw wig on a scarecrow. She began to pull the pins out, shaking it free, and stroking her hands through the damp curls to try to make it look less untidy.

A menu was put in front of her on the table and she looked up. Saul and Duarte were both staring at her, but then quickly looked away and studied their menus. Alice checked her buttons were done up and there was no avocado on her dress.

'Let's all have the fish platter,' said Saul, waving at the waiter.

'So, Alice,' began Duarte. 'Has Luis explained about the hotel and your jewellery?'

'He just said you wanted me to design a line of bracelets for you. I've bought some examples of my more recent designs. In fact, I'm wearing three of them.'

She held her arms up to show the tangle of beads, ribbons and recycled ceramic tile.

'They are beautiful. But I need something slightly different. A different line to the ones you sell here or on your website.'

'The online selling got put on the back burner whilst I was dealing with selling my house in London,' she said. 'But I'm about to get it up and running again.'

'They are very nice bracelets,' said Saul

Alice smiled. 'Thank you.' She put her bag of samples on the table. 'Do you want to see some more?'

Duarte waved his arm and shook his head. 'No, no. That's fine. What I want is for you to visit the hotel and be inspired by it and the surroundings and come up with exclusive designs based on what you see.'

'I'd love that,' she said a bit too quickly, excited by the prospect of creating designs for Duarte, as well as working for Carlos and Ignacio. *I'm an artist*, she thought. *An actual artist.*

The food arrived and they began to eat.

'Saul here is going to visit the hotel too to source local produce and fine-tune a menu based on that,' said Duarte, pulling a *langoustine* apart, 'Luis has already done the photographs I'm hanging in the rooms, but he can come too.'

'Luis?' asked Saul.

'My partner … boyfriend …' explained Alice, wondering if partner sounded like it was just business and boyfriend like they were both sixteen.

'Ah,' said Saul

'This food is delicious,' said Alice, using her bread to wipe up the oil and juice.

'Saul is off to Paris then London and the hotel isn't quite ready for anyone to visit yet, let alone paying guests. I'll get you both down there in a few weeks and you can stay for a night to get the feel for the area.'

'Sounds good,' said Saul. 'My personal assistant will sort out the dates.'

Duarte looked at Alice. 'Does that sound like a plan?'

'Yes. I'm sure I can fit a night away into the diary,' said Alice. 'For work. I'll ask Luis, too.'

'I should have got you to design some of the rooms.' Duarte picked up a jug of water and poured himself a glass. 'Alice has a great eye, Saul. She designed the interior of the beautiful house she has just sold in London, all by herself.'

'A woman of many talents.' Saul smiled.

'Go on, show him Alice. She has photographs on her phone she carries everywhere.'

Alice's heart lurched – she didn't want to look at pictures

of the house that someone else was now living in. It was all too raw. 'Oh, I'm sure Saul doesn't want to—'

'—I'd love to,' he interrupted. 'I'm working on a new project, and I'm always interested in other people's ideas.'

'Alice, you need to be proud of what you do.' Duarte waved his glass around expressively. 'Jump at every chance.'

Alice took her phone out of her bag, pausing for a moment before putting it on the counter so Saul could see. *I will not cry*, she thought. *I will not. I am a bohemian businesswoman, etc, etc.*

Opening up the photograph folder, she began to guide him around the rooms, and as she did so, experienced a mixture of pride and anger. She felt her heart was going to break.

'This is the kitchen. The floor was my own design ... I sourced this great tile place and they helped ... the bedroom curtains were from material I bought in Petticoat Lane ... there's a great place in Primrose Hill where you can buy all sorts of knick-knacks, so I haunted there for a while until I got the hallway right.'

'That is a gorgeous house,' said Saul. 'Very classy, very different. I'm impressed.'

'Oh, thank you. I've never thought ... I just show people the photos because I miss it. I was just making it nice for me to live in.'

Duarte's phone rang. 'Excuse me,' he said. 'I have to take this.'

Saul smiled, then his phone rang too. 'Excuse me,' he said apologetically.

Alice decided to check hers for messages. There was one from Luis.

I'm nervous about tonight. L x

I know. But it will be fine. Don't try too hard, she replied.

He responded immediately. I love you, Alice xx

I love you too xx

Are you sure you don't want to come tonight too? x

I won't come tonight. But I'm there if you want me x

Her stomach did a loop the loop. But not the good one. She couldn't shake the feeling that something she was supposed to share with Luis for the very first time had been taken away from her. *But*, she thought, *that little boy deserves to know his father. Stop being so selfish …*

You're allowed to have feelings, even if you don't think they are the right ones. The voice in her head almost sounded kind for once.

Looking at her phone, she scrolled down to her sister's number. Then scrolled up to her mother's. They would understand.

'Do you want a lift back to Cascais?' Duarte shouted across the room.

Alice looked up, surprised.

'Cascais,' he repeated. 'It's still raining.'

Alice put her phone back in her bag. 'Thanks,' she said. Saul was still on his phone, so she waved goodbye to him and followed Duarte out into the street.

Chapter Eight

'Can you look after James tomorrow afternoon?' Kathy's voice sounded weary. 'I've got to go into the salon and Stephano's mum is ill. I wouldn't ask but ...'

'Of course I'll look after him. I'd love to.'

'What's the matter?'

Alice paused. 'Nothing. Why do you think something's the matter?'

'Your voice. It's too jolly.'

'I'm just happy.'

'I know you're happy. But something's not right.'

Elvis began to nuzzle Alice's neck.

'What's that noise?'

'Are you training to be a police interrogator or something?' joked Alice.

'Now that's a thought.' Kathy laughed.

'It's Elvis. Luis couldn't take him to work today.'

James began to wail in the background.

'Peace over,' said Kathy. 'Can I drop him off around two?'

'Yes, see you tomorrow.' Alice put the phone down, walked to the balcony and rubbed her head. Clouds were scudding across the darkening sky, lit up by the red of the setting sun. She glanced at her watch. Luis would be meeting his son right now. She tried to picture him walking into their hotel lobby nervously, scratching his neck and smiling too hard, and realised she wanted to be with him more than anything. But he needed to meet Mario alone. That was the right thing to do.

Aphrodite stretched lazily along the tiled floor and rolled onto her back.

'Waiting for a cuddle, are you?' Alice smiled, kneeling down and stroking the cat softly. 'I should be looking at designs for tiles on the computer,' she said. 'And making more bracelets ... thinking about the café interior design ... and that plan for the online training. Oh, and looking for a house'

Alice waited for the anxiety to overwhelm her, but she couldn't feel anything. She knew it would happen, though.

'Come on Elvis,' she said. 'Let's go for a walk. I'll take my laptop and do a bit of work at the café.'

The square was quiet, the rain having kept people inside, but there was still a welcoming murmur of conversation and laughter. Alice peered into the café and waved at Carlos, then sat down at a table under the awning and switched on her laptop. Elvis lay down next to her and yawned

'No Luis tonight?' asked Carlos when he came over.

'Not tonight. Something came up.'

'A *galao* or some wine?' He smiled.

'*Laranja fresca*.'

'Ahh, more Portuguese. You are doing well. Fresh orange juice it is.' He waved inside to get someone to bring the drink and then sat opposite Alice.

'Something's wrong,' he said.

'Oh no. Are you okay?'

'Not with me. With you.'

Alice paused for a moment. 'There's nothing wrong with me.' She looked intently at the laptop screen.

'Yes, there is.'

'Why do you think there's something wrong with me?' said Alice, typing in the wi-fi code and deliberately not looking up.

'Because I know you.'

They sat in silence for a few minutes. Sometimes Alice wanted to be a closed book, not an open one.

'And I saw Luis ten minutes ago with a woman and a boy who looked around ten or eleven, or twelve. Difficult to tell these days.'

'Oh. Yes. Well. He had something on.'

'They walked over there and didn't come to see me.' Carlos seemed a little put out.

Alice finally looked at him. 'He just had some business.' She smiled in what she hoped was a reassuring way.

An orange juice was placed on the table. Carlos grunted. 'I'd better get back to work. Any ideas on the tile pattern?'

'That's what I'm working on now.' Alice clicked onto a page of Portuguese tiles and showed it to him. 'And I saw some fantastic tiles at that foodie place in Lisbon today. I'll get some ideas together before next Tuesday when I'm back at Gina's.'

Carlos smiled. 'Ahh, Gina. What a lovely woman. Pity about all the new age stuff, though.' He walked into the café, humming happily and tunelessly.

Alice put on some headphones to listen to music, browsing through tile designs as she made notes and drew some ideas, losing herself in the blues and the yellows and in the interiors of houses, churches and public buildings, so when Elvis began to bark excitedly, she had almost forgotten where she was.

A hand gently stroked her shoulder, and she glanced up to see Luis smiling down at her. Alice stood up, relieved that his evening had obviously gone well. 'I was engrossed in my work,' she said.

'She gets lost in it,' said Luis. 'Totally absorbed.'

Fran stepped forward and hugged her. 'He's been telling us all about your bracelets and artistic endeavours,' she said. 'It sounds like you've found your happy place.'

'I suppose I have.' Alice switched off the laptop.

'This is Mario.' Fran moved to one side to reveal Luis' son standing awkwardly, looking at the floor.

'I'm Alice, hello.' She put her hand out to shake his. He looked up and took it uncertainly, studying her closely.

'Are you the lady who was dancing at the café last week when the band was playing?' he asked.

'Yes, I was. That's me.'

He laughed. 'Were you the lady who tripped over and fell into a table over there last night?'

'I'm afraid so.' She laughed too.

His face lit up. 'I like you. You're funny.'

'Not deliberately, I can assure you.' Alice began to put the laptop into her case.

'Mario is very much into computers and games and technical things,' said Luis.

'My mum is always telling me to stop playing computer games,' he said. 'But I'm nearly eleven. What else am I supposed to do?'

Fran stroked his hair. 'Plenty of things,' she said softly. 'But let's not get into that now.'

Luis took Alice's hand. 'Fran has said it would be nice for me and you to spend some time with Mario tomorrow together,' he said. 'They are only here for a long weekend, so it's their last day.'

'I would love to,' said Alice. 'I'm looking after baby James in the afternoon. Can we do after that? Around six?'

'Six would be great for me,' said Luis. 'I'll finish work by five. What about you two?'

Fran smiled. 'That would be fine for us.'

'Can we go to the ice cream place again?' asked Mario.

'We've just been there,' said Fran. 'Why don't we wait and see tomorrow?'

'Okay.'

'So, then, tomorrow it is. Say bye, Mario.'

'Bye, Dad,' said Mario who was now focused on his phone again. He didn't notice the smile spread across Luis' whole face.

'See you tomorrow. We'll meet at your hotel.' Luis put his hand out to shake Mario's hand, thought better of it, ruffled his hair awkwardly instead, then stepped back, embarrassed.

Alice took his hand and squeezed it as they sat down. 'I need a beer,' he said to Carlos, who had been standing watching and now nodded silently.

'How was it?' she said.

Luis sighed. 'I don't know. He's nice and talkative … but two days ago I didn't have a son. And now I do. So, I don't know how any of it is supposed to be.' He leaned forward. 'This is not going to be bad for us, is it?'

Alice leaned over the table and kissed him. 'No. No, it's not. I promise. You asked me that last night, remember? We'll just take it in our strides.'

Carlos brought out the beer as Alice picked up her ringing phone. 'Hi Kathy. Everything okay?'

'I'm okay. Are you okay?'

Alice paused. 'Ye-es,' she said slowly.

'I knew there was something up.'

'What do you mean?'

'Luis has a son. I mean … how are you feeling? How is Luis?'

'How did you know? Are you psychic …?' she glanced up as Carlos cleared some plates from a nearby table.

'I'm fine,' said Alice. 'I'll see you tomorrow.' She rang off and looked up. 'Carlos?' She waved at him, but he ignored her and looked studiously ahead.

'Are you both okay?' Ignacio hurried around the corner towards them and sat down.

'What do you mean?' asked Luis, puzzled.

'The news. Your son … what a shock. What a blessing …'

'How did you know?' Luis asked as Carlos walked over to another group to take an order.

Alice's phone rang again. She felt a knot in her stomach as she saw the name. Mum.

'Hi, Mum,' she answered.

'Oh, darling. Are you okay? Do you want me to fly over? We can come over, can't we Joseph?'

'I'm fine, Mum. What are you talking about?'

'Luis has a son. I mean, you must be all over the place?'

'I'm fine, Mum,' reassured Alice. 'I'll call you tomorrow.'

'Carlos ...' Luis was waving at him to try to get his attention.

Alice looked at the sky, then at Ignacio's concerned expression, then at Luis' bewilderment and Carlos's deliberate avoidance and began to laugh. 'If we timed that, from Carlos hearing it to my mother calling, it would be less than five minutes.'

Luis sipped his beer and began to laugh too.

'It's because we care,' said Ignacio softly.

'Thank you,' said Alice. 'It's okay Carlos, we forgive you,' she said as he weaved his way back to the restaurant via some distant tables.

Luis put his beer down. 'I need to tell my parents,' he said.

'Yes, you do,' said Alice.

He sighed. 'I can't face it now.'

'When you're ready,' she said.

Spots of rain began to pitter-patter slowly on the cobbles.

'I'll give you a lift back to the apartment,' said Ignacio. 'I've done my last airport pick-up of the day.'

As Alice stood up, the expected rush of anxiety finally overwhelmed her. *I've got forty bracelets to make*, she thought. *Design those tiles, come up with a concept for the restaurant and outside space, design bracelets for Duarte de Silva and book in time to do the online training plan. And find a house. Find a house. Add – support Luis through this.*

'That would be great,' she said. 'I've got to catch up with some work when I get home.'

'You look tired,' said Luis. 'Are you sure?'

'Yes. I don't want it to slip. I've wasted too much time this evening. I couldn't concentrate, what with everything ...'

Luis stood up and took her hand. 'You're here going with the flow,' he said gently. 'Remember, no need to get stressed about work. You're too organised.'

It's not the work you're really anxious about though, is it?

muttered the voice in her head, as they followed Ignacio out of the square.

The following morning Luis left for work early so he could be back in time to see Mario, and Alice threw herself into bracelet making so she could get ahead before Kathy dropped the baby off. She sat at the table surrounded by boxes of beads, smoothed shards of tiles and ribbon, with Etta James playing in the background. Aphrodite lay next to her, purring happily, and the sun shone warmly into the room. Losing herself in bending and shaping the wires and assembling the jewellery so the colours and textures coordinated perfectly, she laughed when the playlist suddenly shifted to Ronan Keating singing 'Life is a Rollercoaster'.

'It sure is,' she said to the cat, who lazily opened her eyes, stretched and went back to sleep.

Ticking 'making twenty bracelets' off her to-do list for the day, she stood up and walked to the balcony, stretching her arms above her head. Two toddlers were in the children's pool playing, whilst their father watched. *What is my father doing now?* she suddenly found herself wondering. *Does he care about where I am or what I'm doing? How would he react if I arrived in his life like Mario has in Luis'?* She felt a sudden knot in her stomach and a brief surge of anger which surprised her.

Irritated with herself for even thinking about the man who had abandoned her all those years ago and left the family homeless, she picked up her laptop, walked down to the garden, sat under a tree and began to browse for houses for sale in Cascais. The heat on her back soothed her as she clicked from estate agent to estate agent, trying to find something that captivated her like the little yellow house had. Every one of them had tiles, either on the doorstep, in the rooms inside or as a feature on the outside walls, and she began to save them into her 'tiles for Carlos and Ignacio' file in the hope that some of them would inspire an original pattern for their wall.

'Shouldn't you be wearing a sunhat?' Kathy shouted from the path.

Alice looked up in surprise, lost, as usual, in her work. 'Are you talking to me or your baby?' she asked.

'I keep forgetting I'm not everyone's mother.' Kathy laughed, guiding the pushchair over the grass.

'I'm sitting in the shade, so worry not.'

'I am worried though. About Luis and the sudden appearance of a son. I mean, how are you coping?'

'We're fine,' said Alice sharply.

'Of course, you are,' said Kathy. 'Not.'

Alice closed her laptop. 'It's all new. I mean we didn't know he existed last week. We haven't processed it … we haven't talked about it much.'

'Does he live here or …?'

'In London, so they won't see each other loads, I suppose.'

'How are you feeling?'

Alice sighed and stood up. 'He has a son. It's important he's in his life.'

'Yes, but how are *you* feeling?' Kathy repeated.

'Fine,' said Alice, taking the pushchair and walking towards the apartment block.

'Oh, I appear to have been dismissed,' called Kathy after her.

'Yes, you have. What time's Stephano picking him up?' Alice shouted over her shoulder.

'Four-thirty.'

'Okay, see you soon.'

'I'll go now then, shall I?'

'Bye!' Alice laughed and walked through the doors. 'Shall we have some fun?' she whispered. 'How about a bit of Disney whilst I finish up my work for today, and then we can go to the park to see the peacocks.'

James burbled happily as they caught the lift and fell asleep as soon as Alice put on the television. The background chatter from the cartoons combined with birdsong and children's laughter, whilst the trees rustled gently in the breeze relaxed her and she worked into the afternoon, calm and focused. Standing up to get a glass of water, she checked her phone. There were two messages.

I'm going to be late. So sorry. Problems at work. It could be a couple of hours. Is that okay? Stephano.

I can't leave work till after five and I can't get hold of Fran. Can you go and meet them and apologise for me? I'll be there asap. I'm meeting them at their hotel – The Navigador. L xx

Alice glanced at her watch and began to hurriedly close the shutters and gather her things. It was four-thirty already, and she didn't want to keep Fran and Mario waiting. They needed to know that she and Luis were reliable.

James stirred and Alice paused. 'Please stay asleep,' she said softly, but with a slight panic to her voice. 'You're going to have to come with me, and I haven't got time to feed or change you.'

After a few moments, whilst Alice stood completely still and tried not to breathe, he slipped back into his sleep. She opened the door, ran to the lift and called it, then pushed the front door, hoping James wouldn't hear it ping, but he seemed to be sleeping deeply. As the door opened, she waved at the doorman behind the reception desk and put her finger in front of her mouth, pointing at the baby with the other hand.

The doorman nodded in acknowledgment, and Alice sped out of the automatic doors into the sunshine and a cacophony of noise.

Ha, ha, ha, laughed the voice in her head.

She almost ran down the path, across the road, and through the quiet back streets to the hotel. Mario and Fran were waiting in the lobby as James slowly began to stir.

'Hi,' she said. 'Luis has been slightly delayed because of

work. He'll only be half an hour, but he couldn't get hold of you. Are you happy for me to look after Mario on my own?'

Fran frowned slightly, then put on a bright smile.

'No, of course. But I hoped Luis would be a bit more reliable ...'

Alice paused for a moment, not sure what to say and decided not to be rude. 'He is reliable,' she said, brightly. 'This has all happened rather out of the blue, though, and he has work commitments. He is on his way.'

Fran nodded but she still looked tense. 'Of course,' she said. 'Yes, I just want everything to be easy and straightforward and we're going home first thing tomorrow ...'

'Luis will be coming,' reassured Alice.

Fran looked at James. 'That is your friend's baby, isn't it?'

'I'm looking after him and his father is delayed at work, unfortunately, so I'll take Mario back to the apartment and wait for Luis.'

'Oh, he's a cutie,' said Fran, friendly again. 'I'm sorry ... this is just so big.'

'Yes, it is.' said Alice. 'I understand.' But something stopped her from telling Fran that she knew exactly what it was like to grow up without a father, that her mother had had to find her own way of coping too, and that she didn't want Mario to feel the way she had. Not that she cared any more. No. Not at all. All she said was, 'It's important.'

Fran nodded. 'I'm glad you feel that, too. I was terrified Luis would have met him and they wouldn't ...' she trailed off, realising Mario could hear, then looked at the clock on the wall. 'I've taken the opportunity to book a facial and my appointment is in five minutes, so I'll see you all later. Mario has my number on his phone.'

'Bye, Mum,' he said, looking up from his phone for the first time.

Fran turned and rushed off, glancing back as she turned the corner, waving to her oblivious son.

'Is my dad not here?' he asked.

'No, he's very sorry, but he will meet us at the apartment. Work problems, I think.'

'Who is this?' he asked, nodding at James, who was beginning to grizzle.

'This is James. I'm taking care of him for a friend.' Alice looked at the baby and realised he was on the edge of a full-blown hearty cry. 'It's okay. We'll get you home soon. Daddy will be back soon.' Digging around in the bag Kathy had left her, she picked out a noisy toy and waved it around in front of him. His face broke into a smile, and she put it in his hands. Then she took Mario by the hand, and they walked quickly out onto the pavement. 'Follow me,' she said. 'If we keep moving, he may not notice he's hungry and needs his nappy changed.'

'Nappies? Yeuch!'

'I agree completely,' said Alice. 'But I think I'm going to have to confront it when I get home.'

They turned towards the sea and began to walk. 'What's that noise?' asked Mario.

Alice could hear something but couldn't make out what it was; a happy, discordant musical sound, with what sounded like several trumpets playing almost in harmony.

'Ah, it's the student Mariachi band,' she said. 'They try their best, but they need a lot of practice.'

As they walked past the entrance to the square, the band piled out onto the road, almost surrounding them with music.

James' face began to crumple, as Alice hurried on, Mario scurrying alongside her, with what felt like the Mariachi band following on behind.

'They'll go in a minute,' she muttered. 'They'll go …'

'I don't think he likes the music,' said Mario.

'I'm just going to get to Fisherman's Beach and give him a drink,' said Alice, as she made a concerted effort to pull away from the band and move in a different direction.

Pausing on the promenade, she rummaged around in the bag again and found the bottle of milk.

'There you are,' she said softly to the baby who was now crying. 'There we are ...'

He took the bottle and began to drink as they headed up the hill as fast as they could walk.

'Are we nearly there yet?' Mario mumbled.

'Ten more minutes if we walk quickly,' she said, and they hurried on.

As they turned into the entrance to the apartment gardens, James finally threw his bottle onto the floor and began to cry big, tired tears. Mario picked it up as Alice almost ran to the block, through the doors, into the empty lift and up to the apartment. Pushing the door open, she took him out of his pushchair and rocked him in her arms as she walked around the room.

Mario sat on the sofa and began to play with his phone again as Aphrodite pounced on his unsuspecting leg.

'I'll get you a drink in a minute,' she said.

'Okay,' said Mario. 'Your cat is funny.' He looked up. 'Is this what it will be like when my mum has her new baby? I've never had a brother or sister before. Will they cry a lot?'

James grabbed one of her earrings and began to tug on it. Mario laughed. 'I'm not sure what it will be like,' said Alice. 'But I'm sure it will be lovely.'

James lost interest in the earring and began to grizzle again. '*Que sera, sera*,' sang Alice softly, walking out onto the balcony as he slowly began to calm down. She heard the door click open and turned to see Luis standing there smiling at her.

'Look at you,' he said. 'Earth Mother.'

'*Of course you are!*' sniggered the voice in her head.

'Well you know.' Alice tried her best not to laugh out loud.

'Hello, Dad,' said Mario standing up. 'Where are you taking me?'

'You go on,' said Alice. 'Stephano's been delayed so I'll stay here. It's fine.'

She could see Luis hesitate. 'Go on,' she said. 'Why not show him your new house? I loved a building site when I was young. When Joseph used to take me up to his projects, I had such a lot of fun.

Luis walked over to her and kissed her gently on her check. 'Okay. Come on, Mario,' he said, turning to the boy.

They closed the door behind them, and Alice stayed on the balcony watching them walk towards the car. But as it moved away along the drive, she sensed the shadow of a protective wall involuntarily creeping up inside her, for the first time in two years.

Chapter Nine

'*Ola*, Alice,' said Gina as she walked through the gate to her workroom for another tile painting lesson. 'What a beautiful day. So much inspiration everywhere.'

'It is gorgeous here. You are very lucky.' Alice began to walk up the path, the bushes next to her bursting with blue and yellow flowers. Gina fell into step beside her. 'I've still not got a clue about the tile pattern. Ignacio and Carlos have left it all to me and I don't want to get it wrong.'

'You have reminded me – there is something I need to find for Carlos.'

'If you aren't busy after the class I've got to pop in to see them about some business.'

Gina smiled. 'Oh, actually, I do have a free hour before I have to meet my mother later. Maybe I can join you once I have tidied up?'

Alice smiled at her. 'Of course you can. That would be very nice.'

'How lovely. I'm looking forward to it. Now, then,' Gina was business-like again. 'So inspiration is coming slowly?'

'Yes, but I'm a bit overwhelmed. I have found a lot, but I'm not getting any original ideas.'

They stood at the door of the workshop where the other ladies were already hard at work, chattering and relaxed, with music playing in the background. Alice could feel her heart skip faster as the smell of paint oozed from the pots. She closed her eyes and breathed it in.

'*Ola*,' the women said in greeting. '*Como voce esta*?' said one. '*Tudo bem*?' said another.

Alice waved. '*Ola, bom dia*,' she said and sat down next to a small pile of tiles Gina had already laid out for her. The ones she'd fired the previous week were also set out waiting for her to check them. She examined them closely and nodded. 'Not too bad. I need to work harder on the lines though.'

Gina picked up one of the tiles and held it up to the window so the light made the shapes easier to see. 'I think you should practice some more, and maybe next week you will have that incredible lightbulb moment.'

'Lisbon is a wonderful place for tiled houses,' said one of the women. 'You can get lots of ideas.'

'There are beautiful houses in Alfama. I go and take photographs of them to inspire me,' said the lady sitting next to her.

'I'll do that. Good idea.' Alice picked up a book of designs and turned the pages. Finding two to practice on, she took a page of tracing paper and began to work. And, for a while, the ever-increasing to-do list in her head disappeared.

Two hours later they began to pack up and the list slowly returned.

'Are you still sure I can meet you for coffee?' asked Gina quietly.

'It'll be lovely.' Alice smiled. 'I'll be there at around one.'

A busker sat at the base of the statue of Luis De Camoes in the square singing 'Hey Jude', accompanied by the happy chatter of the people dotted around the tables of the different restaurants clustered on the cobbles. Alice was taking photographs of the inside of Carlos and Ignacio's soon-to-be café whilst Carlos bustled around, taking orders to the kitchen, then plates and glasses outside.

'Carlos, you still haven't told me the budget,' she said as he rushed past her.

'I'll send it to you on the e-mail,' he shouted over his shoulder.

'You said that last week,' she said.

'Yes, yes, yes, busy, busy, busy,' he muttered. 'I will … Gina!'

Alice turned to see Gina standing in the doorway, a red hairband framing her face, the light shining behind her as if she was backlit in a movie. Carlos had temporarily paused, three plates balanced in his hands, as if time had stood still. Then someone shouted his name from outside and he began to move again.

'Lovely to see you Carlos,' she said, stepping aside.

'Hi,' said Alice, wishing she could dress her hair the way Gina could. 'Shall we grab a table outside?'

The midday sun scorched the ground as they stepped into the daylight, and they sat in the shade of a large parasol, hiding from the heat.

'I knew I'd find you here.' Kathy waved from the steps at the other end of the square. Almost running towards them, she threw herself down on a chair. 'Stephano's mum is making up for yesterday and has told me to have the day off. I don't need to go to the salon, so I'm mooching.'

'You look too overexcited to mooch,' said Alice.

'A nice beer will calm me down.' Kathy pulled her sunhat off and smiled at Gina. 'Oh, hello. I haven't seen you in ages.' She stood up and kissed her on both cheeks, then flung herself down again.

'Kathy ... when are you coming back to tile painting classes? I miss you. And the tea.'

Alice raised an eyebrow. 'What tea?'

'Just usual tea,' said Kathy innocently.

'The herbal tea that Mary gave her the recipe for.' Gina laughed. 'It's very relaxing. You need to give *me* the recipe.'

'Anyway,' said Kathy, changing the subject. 'I can come next Tuesday. Orders from mother-in-law to take more time for myself, so she can have more time with her grandson, which I'm happy about.'

'The usual herbal tea, is it?' muttered Alice quietly. 'Be careful. You know it can have unfortunate effects.'

'It's fine. It's just her normal recipe. Not the extra strong one we accidentally made that time.' Kathy suppressed a snort and covered her mouth.

'Is everything all right?' asked Gina, looking confused.

'Just something silly.' Alice smiled. 'Carlos!' She waved at him as he rushed past.

'I know, *galao*, Sagres,' he said, still moving. Then he paused. 'And you Gina, what would you like?' he asked softly.

She looked up at him. '*Galao para mi.*'

'*Dois galois* it is.' And he disappeared.

Alice and Kathy exchanged smiles.

'I used to come to the square a lot when I was a girl, not so much when I was married. Not at all since I was widowed,' said Gina. 'It was a long time ago. I miss it.'

'It's one of my favourite places,' said Alice. 'And I love sitting here in this spot. It's like a canopy of parasols in the summer, and I can watch everyone come and go.'

'It's like her office.' Kathy leaned back in her chair, rolled her shoulders, stretched her arms and sighed. 'And relax. I'm trying to relax.'

'I'm going to Alfama tomorrow afternoon to take some photos, and hopefully I'll be inspired for the tiles for the interior of the ...' Alice trailed off as Gina's attention switched to a figure walking towards them.

Alice and Kathy followed her gaze. Ignacio was striding across the square, then stood stock-still. Alice and Kathy looked at each other and then looked back at them. Gina began to fiddle with her hair, as Ignacio seemed to realise where he was and began to move.

'Ladies,' he said. 'Lovely to see you. And this is ...?' He looked at Gina.

She looked up at him. 'Gina,' she said

He took her hand and kissed it. 'Of course! How could I not know!'

Alice and Kathy looked at each other again and smiled. 'Gina is the lady who is teaching me how to paint tiles,' said Alice.

'Ah, Gina. I remember now! You planted the seed in his mind for the tiled wall. What an excellent idea.'

That's not how I remember it, thought Alice. 'Before you go,' she said, 'I was supposed to meet you both here half an hour ago about the designs and costings.'

'One of those days,' he said. 'Can we reschedule for tomorrow morning?'

Again, thought Alice. 'Of course. Eleven? Is that okay?'

'Excellent,' he said. 'Lovely to see you Gina.' Then he walked inside the café.

'That's Ignacio, Carlos's brother,' said Kathy.

'Oh …' Gina fiddled with her hair again. 'Of course. Now I remember.'

The busker standing nearby stopped playing and began talking to some people on a table next to them. One of them ordered him a beer and he started to strum his guitar.

'What a lovely song,' sighed Gina. 'My father loved to listen to Simon and Garfunkel. "Homeward Bound" was his favourite. He used to travel for work, and he'd sing it as he walked up the steps to our apartment.'

Alice sat back in her chair. *Thanks for reminding me*, she thought. *Home. Home. I haven't got one … I have got one … no house of my own …*

'Talking of which,' said Kathy as Carlos placed their drinks on the table, moving on to the next group to take their order. 'Any of those houses you saw with Luis any good?'

Alice put her hands around the glass and enjoyed the heat from the hot coffee. 'No. None suitable. Nothing gave me the feeling I got from the little yellow house.'

Kathy took a sip of her beer. 'You could just buy a modern apartment, you know? You're going to be moving in with Luis permanently when his house is finished. You don't have to buy a house that you fall in love with. You won't be living in it … you'll be renting it out.'

'I know. You're right. It's just … I want to have somewhere I can put my stamp on. I can't explain it …'

'But practically speaking—'

'—You are absolutely correct,' interrupted Alice. 'I just … I'll work it out.'

Kathy stood up suddenly, panicked. 'I've forgotten something. What have I forgotten?' She looked under her chair and checked in her bag, looked at Alice, confused, then laughed. 'I haven't got a pushchair and that great big baby bag because James is with his gran.' She sat down. 'Baby brain,' she said and took a long gulp of her drink.

Ignacio reappeared with a sports bag. 'I left this here by mistake earlier. I've got a Hot Yoga session later in between airport pick-ups.'

'I was thinking of trying that,' said Gina. 'I have been doing Ashtanga for a few years, before that Kundalini, and I want to try it slightly differently.'

Ignacio smiled. 'I will feed back my experience next time I see you. You will be at the café again?'

'Of course I will.'

Ignacio waved as Carlos walked towards them. 'My brother and his yoga! He needs to concentrate on the café at the moment rather than all that bending and breathing.' A customer beckoned from a nearby table, and he went to deal with them.

'I'm rather a fan of yoga and such things,' whispered Gina to Alice. She glanced at her watch. 'I'd better go. I'm meeting my mother in half an hour, so I have to get to Estoril. I will see you next week at the class Alice, and don't forget to come too Kathy, if you can.' She kissed them both, waved at Carlos and almost glided out of the square.

'She reminds me of one of those beautiful Italian film stars from the sixties,' mused Kathy.

'She is lovely, isn't she?' said Alice. 'Carlos obviously thinks so too … as does Ignacio.'

'There could be trouble ahead,' whispered Kathy. Alice kicked her under the table, and she stopped. Instead, she finished her drink and looked directly at Alice, who knew exactly what was coming. 'How are you coping with the Luis situation then?'

'Just coping with it.' Alice clicked on a photograph on her phone and showed it to her friend. 'I've been taking screen shots of tile patterns to help me with ideas. What do you think?'

'Oh no you don't!'

Alice suddenly felt she wanted to cry but didn't know why. She breathed in and said steadily, 'It's very sudden. We aren't really talking about it. Luis is doing his best, and I'm letting him get on with it. Mario is lovely and ...'

'And ...?'

'He and Fran are going home today, so I'm sure it will all sink in then.'

Kathy leaned across the table and squeezed Alice's hand. 'This is big, Alice. Don't forget yourself in all this, as you usually do.'

'I'm not. I'm thinking of myself, and what it was like for my mum, and I'm acting accordingly ... and all I want to think about is what shade of pink that bougainvillea above the menu on the wall is over there ... and should I be taking more photos to sell to your friend's gallery? How do I decorate the terrace at the back of the restaurant? And has Aphrodite got a secret stash of geckos somewhere? I have had enough of the big stuff for a while, selling my house, moving countries ... you know.'

'Shall we get an ice cream and go for a paddle?' asked Kathy, suddenly standing up.

'Excellent idea,' said Alice. '*Ate amanha*, Carlos. Until tomorrow.' He waved from the table of women he was serving, smiling again.

Luis was sitting on the balcony when Alice got home, Elvis at his feet, with Aphrodite curled up on the sofa inside in the shade. She could feel his tension even from the doorway, and his foot tapped repeatedly.

'Luis?' she said. 'You're home early ... why are you out there? You must be roasting. It's so humid today.'

He turned around, surprised, then almost jumped up. 'Alice ... I'm sorry I didn't hear you come in. My mind was somewhere else.' He put his arms around her. 'You are suffering from humidity hair,' he said softly.

'Wet and frizzy ... yes I know. I was going to go for a swim to disguise it as fresh from exercise hair.'

'I'm so glad you're here.'

Her heart began to beat faster. Something wasn't right.

'Mario and Fran have gone back to London.'

'Have you arranged to see them again?'

'Fran has decided to rent a house during the summer holidays nearby so I can get to know him better before the baby is born. Her partner is going to be visiting too.'

Alice stepped back and looked at him. 'That's good, isn't it? You can get to know each other better.'

'Yes, but ... I phoned my parents.'

'Was it that bad?'

'They want my sister to meet Mario and Fran in London. Cassie lives there so they think it's a great idea. They can meet Mario by proxy. I don't want that. It's too soon, isn't it? I mean I've only just met them. A few days ago I didn't even know he existed.'

'I don't know what anything is, Luis. I really don't. I think you just have to go with it.'

'It means I have to go too, though ... my sister can be ... she can be ... not very diplomatic ... oh God. This time last week it was just you and me. I'm supposed to be helping you look for a house and getting my place ready for us to move into ... and looking forward to having a family ...'

Well, you're not pregnant yet. Better hurry up, whispered the voice in her head. She felt her stomach lurch nervously and put a hand on it. 'Mario is a nice boy. It's a good thing. It's just ... I feel a rug has been pulled from under us a bit and it's no-one's fault.'

Luis walked back out onto the balcony. 'My mother is very excited. My father very quiet. My mother kept asking if I was sure he was mine, and if Fran wanted money and … all the things I'm ashamed to say came into my mind as soon as she told me. That's bad, isn't it?'

She followed him out and put her arms around his waist. 'No. I think it may be a normal reaction. And …' Alice sighed. 'Does she want maintenance? I mean if she does that's absolutely right, but you have to think about that and take it into account.'

'You still love me, don't you, Alice?' he whispered, not seeming to hear her question. 'I'm just so ashamed of the way I used to be.'

'I still love you. And I love that you are doing this and not running from it.'

He gently stroked her face. 'It's all got very serious, hasn't it? It mustn't stop us being us, though.' He smiled. 'I'm going in a couple of weeks, so let's make sure we have some fun to make up for it before then.' He took her hand and led her towards the bedroom. 'Starting now.'

The following day they both tried to bring some normality back into their lives, so Luis popped out to the farmhouse to check on the work being done before he went to his renovation job, and Alice took the train to Lisbon to do some research, walking along the river and up into Alfama.

After a couple of hours of exploration, she wandered into a beautiful old church and enjoyed its cool shade for a while before venturing back out into the scorching hot sunlight. As she put her camera in her bag in the archway, she noticed a blue and white mural on the wall next to her and the germ of an idea began to form. *Maybe I don't just have to do decorated tiles?* she thought. *Perhaps I could do a mural.* She felt a sudden rush of excitement and decided to go home.

The Tagus was alive with river traffic as Alice walked

towards Cais de Sodre station from Alfama, ferries criss-crossing busily under the watchful eye of the statue of Christo Rei on the southern bank. The sense of movement and determination picked her up and almost carried her past the cars and lorries to her left, with the water lapping quietly to her right. As she arrived at Praca do Comercio, its plaza dotted with tourists taking photographs, the brightly coloured trams busily moving to and fro around it's edges, framed by the grand buildings on either side, she paused and smiled, trying to commit the scene to memory. She never tired of it and would stop and stare every time she passed.

Taking a sip of water, she took off her hat and waved it in front of her face in an attempt to cool herself down as a bead of sweat slowly made its way down her back. Turning to look at the river, the whisper of a breeze caught her hair for a second and she started to walk again.

Commuters began to fill the pavement, hurrying towards the station on their way home, so she decided to get a drink before joining them on one of the busy trains. Crossing the road towards the food court she had visited the week before, she breathed a sigh of relief at the shade it offered. Her dress was stuck to her body and, as she pulled it from her back, she visualised jumping into the pool at home, then floating around, cool and calm, until it got dark.

'Hello. It's Alice, isn't it? I'm sorry, I'm very bad with names.'

Alice looked around, startled. Saul Pires was standing in front of her smiling.

'Oh,' she said. 'Oh, I was miles away. Thinking of a cool swim actually. How are you?'

'Hiding from the heat. I have a meeting at six-thirty, but I don't want to go outside yet. So, I stayed and annoyed the guys at my café for a while. I was supposed to be in New York but that got pushed back, so I'm making myself useful here.'

'New York – how exciting.'

'Yes and no. Are you in a hurry or would you like a complimentary cold beverage?' he asked.

'I was just going to sit for five minutes and then head back to Cascais.'

He smiled. 'Should we prop up my bar for a little while together then, before we go our separate ways?' He pointed to the bar stools. 'My treat.'

Alice nodded, noticing that he looked more familiar than the Saul Pires she had met just a day or so ago. At the time there was so much going on it was just a shadow of a thought at the back of her mind. But now he was in front of her again, she realised what it was. He really did look like Harry, or 'Harry the Holiday Fling', as Kathy used to refer to him. Or 'The-Man-She-Used-To-Think-About-And-Wonder-Why-She-Didn't-Respond-To-His-Letter-After-She-Met-Adam-And-Of-Course-Regretted-It-When-Things-Got-Tough', which is how Alice described him to her sister over a boozy lunch years before. 'Catchy name,' Tara had said, and it had stuck.

'What would you like?'

'A large orange juice and soda,' said Alice, trying to climb onto the tall, slim bar stool without looking like she was clambering up a rock face. Finally managing to sit down, her legs dangled loosely and uncomfortably.

'So, Duarte is trying to get us to go to the hotel in a couple of weeks. I hope you can make it.'

'A couple of weeks? I haven't heard from him, but I'm sure I can.'

'He's an interesting character.' Saul passed her the drink and she took a long, refreshing gulp. 'Have you known him long?'

'About eighteen months or so,' said Alice. 'He bought some of my bracelets. I was just starting to make them, so it meant a lot to me. And he loves the photos that Luis takes. It's nice to feel appreciated.'

'Luis. That's your partner, yes?'

You even sound like Harry the Holiday Fling, thought Alice, *only with a Portuguese accent.*

But he isn't, whispered the voice in her head.

'Yes. He renovates houses, too. That's where he is today.'

'Well, I will look forward to meeting him when we are at Duarte's hotel. He's a lucky man.'

Alice took another sip. 'Is he?'

'To have someone like you in his life, yes.' He smiled at her, holding her gaze for a second. 'I travel for my work so much it's difficult to form any kind of meaningful relationship.'

'Oh, yes, that's not easy.' Alice looked away and felt herself blush but knew he wouldn't notice as her face was so flushed from the heat. She swung her legs, and one of her flip-flops dropped to the floor.

'Excuse me, Saul …' one of his chefs called over.

'I'm sorry, I have to go. Work beckons.'

'Of course. I'd better get back too. So much to do, so little time,' Alice began to slide off the stool.

'Allow me,' he said, helping her down.

'Kind,' said Alice, as her feet touched the floor. She bent over and grabbed her flip-flop, leaning against the stool to put it on. *Oh, I am so cool*, she thought. *A cool, elegant, stylish businesswoman.*

'Hopefully I will see you soon,' said Saul.

'Yes,' said Alice, glancing up into his intense brown eyes. They were so much like Harry the Holiday Fling's that for an instant she felt she was losing the power of speech.

He shook her hand and turned to go as Alice felt a bead of sweat ooze down her back. She inwardly sighed. 'Bye,' she said. 'Nice to have bumped into you.'

'Have a good journey home. And perhaps you and your partner can join me for lunch soon? We are all part of Duarte's hotel project after all.'

'That would be lovely.'

'What's your number? We can sort something out?'

'Oh. Okay ... actually.' Alice remembered she had some business cards in her bag. A remnant from when she was about to conquer the world with her bracelets just before she began to battle Adam for the house. 'Here we are,' she said, handing him one. 'The website is a bit basic. I'm going to be updating it, but the phone number and e-mail address are up to date.'

'Thanks. See you at Duarte's hotel.'

She turned and waved. 'See you.' As she walked towards the exit, she picked up her phone and messaged Luis. On my way home. Fancy a trip to the beach at Guincho for a refreshing walk? xx

He replied immediately. You read my mind. I'll pick you up outside the station. X

Then her phone pinged again. It was a message from Saul Pires. Here is my number. I look forward to meeting you and your partner. I'll be in touch. Regards. Saul Pires.

Surfers bobbed half-heartedly in the bay, as if the heat of the day had sucked the life out of the waves whilst Alice and Luis walked through the shallows, side by side, Elvis running ahead.

Luis brushed her hand softly. 'We haven't really talked, have we, about what's happened?'

'No, but it's happened so quickly.'

He sighed. 'I haven't told Fran yet, about my sister wanting to meet them. I mean I don't know her, do I, really? I don't want to overwhelm Mario.' He stopped and looked at her. 'I want to be here with you. I didn't want it to be like this. But I have a son ... suddenly ... and I know I ... oh I don't know.'

A biplane soared above them, carrying a banner behind it, its humming bringing them back to their surroundings.

'It is what it is,' said Alice quietly.

He squeezed her hand. 'So, I don't want to go to London the week after next. I have you, I have my work, the house to do. But I have to go.'

'I know.'

'But my mother has got so excited. Like she's exploded with it.'

'It's okay.'

'They haven't even met you yet, Alice. They need to meet you.'

'It will be okay. It will be fine,' she said firmly. 'I'll spend the time you're away looking at houses to buy, and it looks like I'll be going to Duarte's hotel then too to do research, so I'll be occupied.'

'Oh?'

'Yes, I bumped into a business friend of his – Saul Pires – and he told me.'

'Saul Pires? Saul Pires the chef?'

'Yes.'

'Oh … well, be careful. He has a reputation.'

'Do you know him?'

'No. But he was on TV recently – one of those cookery shows in the UK. It was shown here and there was all this stuff in the papers about his love life.' He smiled at her. 'When you were in London for three months I sat alone in my building site house watching television in my vest.'

Alice stopped walking 'Really, Luis. This is about my work. You actually think that a celebrity chef with a complicated love life would be interested in me? I'm flattered.' She laughed. 'But as you know, I only have eyes for you. And you've got a vest?'

'Too right I have. I totally rock the look too,' said Luis. 'I'll race you to the beach bar. Last one there buys the drinks.'

'Not fair! You're much, much taller than me.'

'Life isn't fair,' he said, letting go of her hand and running off.

'I'm only having a fruit juice anyway,' she shouted, as she tried to run after him. 'So there.'

Chapter Ten

For the next week, Alice and Luis got on with their daily lives, burying themselves in work, pushing the sudden change in their lives away, pretending everything was normal.

But it wasn't, and on the day Luis left the apartment to fly over to meet his son again, Alice dealt with it by putting on her swimming costume and heading towards the garden. Elvis had been dropped off to stay with Carlos, so it was just her, Aphrodite and her own thoughts in what felt like a very empty apartment.

She looked up from the pool as a plane flew high above, a tiny white stream of cloud behind it crossing the sky. She decided it was the plane Luis was taking to London and imagined him sitting, headphones in, blocking out his nerves with music. Submerging herself in the cool, clear water to stop the unpleasant, heavy feeling that had begun to push its way through her, she swam until it was washed away.

We just have to get through this bit, she thought. *In the meantime I have to find a house to buy … make more bracelets … sort out the design of the tiles … come up with an idea for the café patio… mark some online training … find a house to buy … GO WITH THE FLOW.*

A dog ran past a bush nearby, dislodging some bougainvillea and Alice watched as the petals fluttered to the ground like pink snow. Pulling herself out of the pool, she picked some up and carried them to the apartment, her mind filling with ideas of designs, her worries temporarily gone. Sitting down at the dining table, Alice began to sketch, the world empty of everything apart from the task at hand for a while.

Then her phone buzzed.

Absent-mindedly picking it up, she saw a message from Mary. It began with, Dearest Alice, I have some news. But don't panic …

Alice dropped her pen, her heart beginning to race.

You're panicking, said the voice in her head. She started to read on.

A few months ago someone offered to buy the apartment. We said no even though it was for a ridiculously high price. It's our apartment and we love it, and despite our travels Down Under to see our grandchild we fully intended to keep coming back to paradise – that is, Cascais. However, our son-in-law has this week been made redundant and, as you know, there is another baby on the way very soon. It's put everything into perspective, and we want to stay close to them to enjoy our grandchildren, have family time and maybe help them out a bit financially when they need it.

That's why we've made the very difficult decision to sell our beautiful home and resettle here in Sydney. The offer came at the right time, and I am certain it happened for a reason. I know you are going to buy a property and the apartment is yours if you want it, but I think that it may be too much of a stretch for you financially. If you can afford it and you do want it, it is yours. You just need to let us know in the next two days. No matter how much we love it, it is bricks and mortar at the end of the day, and love and family are more important.

I know that you and Luis will be moving into the farmhouse when it's ready, so if you decide not to buy our home, it's good for us to feel you will be secure anyway. The only thing I would ask is that wherever you go, you look after Aphrodite. She became your cat, after all, and was pining for you when you were away.

I've written the valuation at the bottom of the page for you to consider. Sensible Alice, this is a hard-headed business decision. There are other properties to invest your money in. Your home will be where your heart is, and that's with Luis.

And remember, whatever happens, you will be fine. I know it now and I knew it when I first set eyes on you.

Send my love to Kathy.

Mary xx (Mystic)

P.S. There is some very strong relaxing tea hidden at the back of the airing cupboard. I wouldn't let Frank anywhere near it after he drank some too quickly and, well, anyway … best not to know … but I know even though there is no need to panic, that you will panic. IT IS FOR MEDICINAL PURPOSES ONLY. DO NOT GO OUT EVEN IF YOU HAVE A SIP (IN THE MORNING YOU WILL FEEL FABULOUS.)

Alice scrolled down to the price of the apartment, took a sharp intake of breath, then jumped up and ran to the airing cupboard. *That's three homes in about six weeks*, she thought. *Three homes I've lost.*

Careless, muttered the voice in her head.

She knelt on the floor and began to rummage around the back of the tank.

Hurry up with that tea. The voice in her head sounded like it was shouting. *Even I need a bloody break!*

Alice pulled out a pink tin and sat back. A label was tied to the handle. 'Drink me in emergencies only,' it said on one side. 'Making phone calls after consumption is not advised. Operating machinery is forbidden. One tea bag per twenty-four-hour period only.'

On the other side was written 'Do not use phone for eight hours after use'.

She switched the kettle on and gazed out of the window over the gardens. 'This was never mine,' she said to Aphrodite who was brushing around her legs, purring. 'I was always going to move out. It's just now I have to move out. Soon.' Pouring the boiling water into the cup, she looked down at the cat. 'But you're coming with me. I hope you're happy about that.'

The steam brushed her face as she took the tea to the balcony and sat down. *It's fine*, she thought. *It's fine. It's really fine. Just pushed things forward a bit.* She took a sip and closed her eyes. *I'll be more proactive about looking for a house to buy now then. I'm not going to worry Luis about this … he'll only panic with the farmhouse in the state it's in at the moment … I'll see if Kathy can come with me to look. Or Stephano. Carlos or Ignacio might … This is delicious, this tea is.*

She took another sip and felt a relaxing warmth spread itself around her body. Aphrodite jumped onto the sofa and began to curl herself up, so Alice decided to join her. With every sip her muscles relaxed and a smooth calmness seeped over her. She lay down on the sofa opposite the cat and closed her eyes. 'In the morning I will feel fabulous,' she muttered.

The room was dark when she heard her phone ring, the moon illuminating the floor from the open windows onto the balcony. Music drifted in from one of the apartments below, and she could hear happy chatter from the garden. Alice wondered whether to even bother to get up. She was so comfortable. So relaxed. Why try? Why change? *This moment, this very moment*, she thought, *everything is perfect*.

Could be Luis, whispered the voice in her head, woozily. *Could be Luis, the love of your life.*

'Luis,' she said so loudly it woke up the cat.

She rolled onto the floor and tried to stand, but her legs felt like butter and she knew they would never support her weight, so she continued to the bedroom on all fours. By the time Alice arrived at the bedside table, the phone was silent. Leaning against the bed, she picked it up. 'It was Luis,' she shouted to Aphrodite who had followed her in and was watching from the doorway. 'But he didn't leave a voicemail. Oh dear. Oh dear ... oh dear ... am I slurring my words? I'd better not call him or he'll know I've been on the tea.' Alice laughed at her own joke, then sighed. 'I'll send him a message.'

Ola! How are you? I am well. I am here with the cat. The thing is this ... and I'm not in a panic about it AT ALL. But you know, once all is said and done, we will be fine. I'm so looking forward to getting together and sorting it all out. How are things where you are? How is? We will have an ADVENTURE! Can't wait to see you. Then she added a unicorn emoji by accident and as she tried to delete it, she accidentally added a sun, then a smiley face, a glass of wine and a potato. So she gave in, pressed kiss five times and sent the text, dropping the phone as she did so.

'Did I do it properly, Aphrodite?' she asked as the cat jumped on the bed. 'Better check.' She picked up the phone and scrolled down to see, but her eyes wouldn't focus, and the room was very dark. 'God, I'm sooooooo tired,' she whispered. 'But it's Luis, the love of my life. I must send it.' Stabbing at the phone with her thumbs she tried again, placed it on the floor and climbed onto the bed. She was asleep in seconds.

Alice almost bounded out of bed the following morning, full of energy and feeling upbeat about absolutely everything.

'Mary was right about that tea, Aph,', she almost sang. 'I feel fabulous. Even your horrible cat food smells okay today.' Alice spooned it into the pink cat bowl and switched the kettle on. 'Common or garden tea today, though.'

Aphrodite ignored her and began to eat noisily.

'I'd better switch my phone on. I remember turning it off in case I sent any messages. And the instructions were specifically *not* to use the phone.' She laughed. Alice took her cup back to the bedroom and removed her swimming costume from the drawer as she waited for the phone to come back to life.

Shall I have a swim before or after breakfast? she wondered, picking the phone up to check the messages that had come in overnight.

You've been drinking Mary's tea again! And don't panic about what? All going okay here (apart from my sister, obvs). Will call you this eve. Love you. L xx

Alice giggled. 'I must have sent him a message under the influence. Whoops!'

Then she read one from Kathy.

Meet me at the salon at 11. I have a break then. What the bloody hell was that all about? Don't panic about what? P.S. I haven't laughed like that in a while. Kathy xx

Another message, this time from Ignacio, appeared.

I showed this to Carlos and we feel you have found some of Mary's very, very strong tea, which Frank warned us all about. Panic about what? I and C :)

Alice put her head in her hands and sighed. 'Oh. Dear. I didn't follow the instructions and sent it to everyone.' Then she laughed again and pulled on her swimming costume. As she was walking out of the door, the phone pinged again.

An adventure would be most welcome. SP.

Who on earth is SP? she muttered, walking into the lift. As she arrived on the ground floor, she remembered.

Saul Pires. She'd sent a tea-fuelled text to Saul Pires that was meant for Luis.

Waving at the doorman Alice almost ran to the pool. 'Oh, bugger,' she muttered as she dived in.

Chapter Eleven

Alice pushed the door open of the salon and was greeted by the receptionist.

'Kathy is in number three,' she said, waving.

'Thanks.'

Kathy was organising the room and looked up as Alice pushed the door open. 'That text was very funny,' she said. 'Oh, I miss Mary's tea. I've been trying it all you know – camomile, peppermint, camomile AND peppermint, lemon-balm tea, rose tea, just tea … but nothing, nothing has that frisson of excitement you get just by taking a sip of Mary's concoctions.' Kathy carried on moving things around. 'I mean, despite what the labels say, you never really know what's going to happen next.'

Alice picked up a bottle of lavender oil and sniffed it. 'This is probably just as calming. And it doesn't have a warning on it.'

'It probably says "Do Not Drink",' said Kathy.

'Fair point. I do feel physically very good after last night. And despite everything, quite calm and upbeat.'

'God, that's amazing. Normally you would be throwing yourself in swimming pools, having weird internal arguments and getting in a tizz.'

'No …' said Alice. 'I've just gone for a swim, given myself a talking to and have arranged to go and see four houses this afternoon. Does that count as a tizz?'

'So, then. What are you not in a panic about?'

'I accidentally sent that text I sent you to Saul Pires.' Alice bit her lip.

Kathy's eyes widened. 'Saul Pires the chef?'

'Yes.'

'Tell me more.'

'Another time.' Alice looked at the floor. 'Mary and Frank are selling the apartment.'

Kathy sat down on the newly made treatment bed, obviously surprised. 'Oh. Well … she hasn't messaged me or anything.'

'I'm sure she will, it—'

'—I mean, we're really good friends. Why would she not tell me too?'

'I think it's all happened really quickly.'

'Maybe … but …'

'I think she wanted to tell me because I live in the apartment. I'm sure she'll be in touch soon.'

Kathy stood up and smoothed the bedding. 'I'm going to miss her,' she said briskly.

'Why don't you message her?' said Alice. 'I think a lot has been happening with family and everything.'

'I'm sorry. I'm just constantly tired and ready to take offence at everything.' She hugged Alice. 'So, two things – why did you send a message to Saul Pires even by mistake, and are you in a panic? Be honest. And how are things going with Luis? That's three things … I have a condition called baby brain!' She continued to move around the room, picking up bottles and filling tubs with balls of cotton wool.

Alice pressed herself to the wall to get out of the way. 'It was dark when I sent the messages. I think I just pressed loads of buttons and sent them to contacts beginning with I, J, K and L … and P … or S … judging by the response.'

'Why do you have Saul Pires' number?'

'He said he wanted to take me and Luis out for lunch as we were working on the projects at the hotel … oh dear … you don't think I've given him the wrong impression, do you?'

Kathy took Alice's hands, looked directly at her and said 'Time will tell, time will tell … only joking!'

'Kathy!'

'Your face! I think anyone would struggle to make anything of that message to be honest. Although …'

'Yes, "but he has a reputation". Everyone has a reputation here. Everyone.'

'But he has!' Kathy opened the door. 'Right, I've got ten minutes. Let's grab an ordinary cuppa from the café, and we can walk and talk.'

'Okay ... second question. I'm not in a panic, as I'm being proactive. I've got four places to see this afternoon.'

'Excellent. But you know you can move in with Luis? That's the plan.'

'Yes, but you know me ... and he's got a lot on his plate all of a sudden.'

'It's your plate, too.'

'I have to let him get to know Mario.'

'You do.'

'And give them space.'

'Yes, but ...'

'... but?'

'Mario is a part of your life too now. You and Luis are a couple.'

'Yes. He is, but I just think I need to stand back a bit so it's easier for them both.'

'Have you spoken to your mum?'

'Not really.'

'Well, don't you think she would have an interesting perspective on that particular issue?'

Alice sighed. 'Maybe.'

'Not maybe. Definitely.'

They stood at the counter and looked at the menu board. 'I'm still feeling the lack of Mary's tea,' said Kathy. 'I'm having a coffee to give the opposite effect entirely.'

'Luis does seem to be wound up about his sister being involved all of a sudden.'

Kathy laughed. 'Yes, from what Stephano said I'm not surprised.'

'She can't be that bad?'

'No, he says she is a very nice person but rather full of her own importance. An uber solicitor, and all-round superwoman.'

'We'll get on then,' said Alice. 'Not.'

Kathy's phone rang. 'It's mum-in-law,' she said. 'I'd better take this. Baby update!'

'It's okay. I'll grab my coffee and head into town. I'll call you tomorrow. I'm off to Duarte's hotel the day after.'

'Ciao for now,' said Kathy, distractedly. 'Mwah!'

Alice looked at her phone to check the address of her first viewing and set off through the back streets towards town. *Today is the day*, she thought, *that I will find my dream house.*

But what about Luis and his new son? Everyone seems to have children apart from you, Alice, said the voice in her head.

She felt heavy all of a sudden and paused. *No, I won't allow you to do this to me*, she thought. *And by you, I mean me.*

Someone dropped some plates with a clatter in the distance, and she realised she was around the corner from the first house on the list.

'Big smile, Alice,' she muttered, straightening her dress and smoothing her hair. 'Today could be the day.'

But, after four disappointing viewings Alice had to accept that today wasn't the day, so visited some more agents and grabbed the details of ten more properties to browse then went to the square and ordered some food.

Carlos handed Alice Elvis's lead. 'Now you have recovered from all of that tea, perhaps you can take him for a walk.'

Alice looked up, a pile of house details in front of her on the table.

'Is he missing Luis?' she asked as the dog nuzzled her hand.

'Yes. And so are you.'

'He's only been gone a day.'

Carlos pulled up a chair. 'I know you're smiling Alice, but I don't think you are okay. You have had a shock with Luis and his son. It's a big thing. And now Mary selling the apartment.'

'How did *you* know that?'

'Kathy called. Explained the panic and the strange text, too.'

'A lot of change all at once,' she said quietly. 'And I can't even find a house to buy. I saw four earlier on and put my foot through the floorboards of the first one. And that was the best of the lot!'

Carlos pushed the leaflets away and moved the plate of salad she had ordered and ignored closer towards her.

'You need to eat,' he said kindly. 'Then get some air on the beach with Elvis.'

Alice kissed him on the cheek. 'Thank you,' she said. 'Oh, I've got an idea for the tiles by the way. Once I'm back from Duarte's hotel, it's full steam ahead on those.'

Carlos smiled and leaned closer. 'How is Gina?'

'She's fine. Helpful. Nice.'

'You know that Ignacio mentioned he may take up tile painting too. On top of his chauffeuring. And all of his counselling and meditation. And taking over the café.'

'Oh, well. Maybe he wants a hobby.'

Carlos snorted. 'He hasn't got time for a hobby. And …' He leaned even closer. 'I think he is having second thoughts about the café.'

'Oh,' Alice said. 'I don't know.'

'I think he is having a mid-life crisis. At exactly the wrong time. He should have it next year – that would be more convenient.' A customer waved at him from another table. 'I have to go,' he said. 'Now eat up and look after yourself. Maybe a trip over the river even if it is for work will do you good.'

Elvis grunted and settled next to her whilst she finished her food.

'I sense there could be trouble ahead,' she whispered to him. 'And not with me this time.'

Alice picked up her phone and tried to call Luis. There was no answer, so she left a message, and walked Elvis up through the town to the prom towards Estoril. She put her headphones on, hoping a blast of Ed Sheeran would block out the world now Mary's tea was wearing off.

After she dropped the dog back to the café for Carlos, she spent the evening sketching the design for the mural for the café, music still on in the background, the chattering in her head beginning to rise despite it.

I'm almost forty. I spent almost fifteen years waiting for Adam, believing his promises. Wasting that time. And when I meet a man who wants to be with me and have a family with me, he suddenly has a family ... and even bloody Adam has a baby now.

She stood up and moved to the balcony, listening to the cicadas singing their own song in the garden below.

'They all have fathers who want to be with them, don't they?' she said out loud. 'Mario, Adam's son ... James has Stephano ...' There it was. Tears pricked at her eyes. She didn't know where they had come from, or where or when that thought had begun. But now it was there.

'That was the past,' she said to the gulls who were swooping across the night sky. 'Mum married Joseph, and he is a better man than my biological father could ever be.'

She walked back into the living room and began to rifle through the house details. 'Once I get that house I'll feel a lot better,' she muttered to Aphrodite, who jumped on the table and sat on the papers as Alice picked up the phone to answer a call from Luis.

'Hey gorgeous. How's Cascais?'

His deep, warm voice comforted her and she began to smile.

'Lovely. How's London?'

'Wet!'

'How's today been?'

'Oh … well … I saw Mario and Fran briefly after school. It was fine till Cassie joined us. She is such a … a …'

'… a what?'

'Everything has to be done her way. She's annoyed Fran by saying she should have a test to make sure Mario is mine.'

'Subtle.'

'In front of Fran and Mario. And we should sort out money.' Luis' voice began to rise.

'Well, you did say …'

'Yes, but she'd been there for five minutes and Mario was there. And she keeps trying to wind me up about everything. What I do … how I live … the reason I left Australia in the first place. She just needs to leave it all alone. But she thinks it's funny.'

Alice wanted to put her arms through the phone and hug him.

'When are you seeing them next?'

'I'm spending tomorrow with them and Fran's partner. And Cassie is insisting on tagging along too. She's going to mess everything up. I mean I've only known Mario for about three weeks … well, actually, I've only met him about three times.'

'It's all new. You're bound to be stressed.'

'I miss you. Wish you were here.'

'Wish I was too, but you know, I think me being there would cause even more chaos.'

Luis sighed. 'What are you up to this weekend?'

'Tile painting tomorrow and on Sunday heading to Duarte's hotel for research.'

There was silence for a moment.

'Luis, are you still there?'

He sighed again. 'Saul Pires will be there?'

'Yes. And Duarte. You could have come too, as you know. He said he wants to meet you as we're all involved in designing something for the hotel.'

'Do you have to go? Could you wait for me and we'll go together another time?

This time Alice was silent. Her mind went blank. *What was going on?*

'What do you mean?

'I just … oh, never mind.'

'We've had this discussion. I mean, Luis, you aren't serious, are you?'

She could hear him breathing, but he didn't respond.

'This is part of my job … I didn't try to stop you going to London after all.'

'I just …'

'I have to go. Don't you trust me …?' Her voice trailed off. She could hear someone's voice in the background.

'Who's that? Is everything okay?

'Look, I've got to go,' he said irritably. 'I'll call you tomorrow.'

'Love you,' said Alice. But he had already ended the call.

She got ready for bed and then sat looking at her phone, trying to work out what to say to Luis. She wanted him to know she was there for him. It's all a bit stressful, isn't it? xxx She pressed send. Then I love you xx. She sent that and fell into a listless sleep.

When she left the apartment the following day, Luis had not responded to the messages, so she was grateful to be able to throw herself into working on the mural in Gina's workshop.

'Thanks for letting me come, Gina.' Alice had a piece of tracing paper in front of her and was busy transferring part of her design of the mural onto it.

'Oh, you would never have it done in time if you only came once a week.' Gina put some painted tiles into a box. 'It means I can catch up with some tidying, so it helps me. I'm behind with firing some of my pupils' creations too.'

'I'm mixing traditional with something a bit different so I

may need some advice when I finally start painting.' Alice put aside one finished tile and started to work on another.

'How big is it going to be?'

'It's a section at the back. They were going for a whole wall, but that's not practical.'

'They could do that in sections another time if they wanted.'

'Exactly.'

'Actually, I'm trying something new too. I've made some vases and I'm going to smoke fire them instead of putting them in the kiln.'

Alice looked up. 'Oh, yes, I've read about that. I've never done it myself.'

'Well a former pupil has left a leaflet with instructions. I was going to buy an incinerator but have decided to put together a brick one, like a barbecue. Then I can use it as a barbecue as well. And it's safer. Do you want to try it too? Not today. The handyman hasn't finished it yet.'

Alice briefly felt an idea hover somewhere at the back of her mind. 'I'd love to, but probably after I've done the tiles,' she said.

'You could try one or two tiles to see what they look like.'

'Yes, that's a good idea.'

'You can set it all up – set fire to the wood shavings and monitor it. It'll be another skill for you to master.'

'Thanks – I appreciate that.' Alice started to work again as Gina walked out of the room towards the kiln.

Alice smiled. *Gina doesn't walk. I'm sure she's on wheels*, she thought. *No wonder Carlos and Ignacio look at her the way they do.*

'*Ola*,' she heard Gina say outside. 'How lovely to see you both.' A male voice was almost audible in the distance. Or was that two male voices? Alice shrugged and continued to trace over the lines of her design.

Someone rapped on the door and she looked up to see Carlos smiling at her. He was swiftly joined by Ignacio.

'*Ola*! What a surprise. Have you come to look at the design?'

Ignacio looked surprised. 'Design?'

'You know. For the mural.'

He looked blank and glanced at Carlos.

'For your café. The wall. The one you asked for?'

'Oh, yes, of course. No.'

'No. No …' echoed Carlos. 'We trust you. We were passing and thought we would pop in and see Gina.'

'I was passing. I have a special aromatherapy oil I sourced recently which is excellent for encouraging creativity, so I told Gina I'd drop a bottle in. Carlos decided to join me,' said Ignacio, smiling.

'Okay. I'll get back to work then?'

'Gina is bringing us some lemonade.' Carlos turned to see where she was. Ignacio pursed his lips.

Alice stood up. 'Have you been here before, Carlos?'

'I came a few weeks ago,' he said, still looking away. 'For a meeting.' He turned back to Alice. 'That's when I came up with the idea of having the tiles.' He beamed. 'Gina's late husband used to collect old, abandoned ones and we got talking.'

Ignacio moved towards the house. 'Gina. Let me help you with that tray.'

Carlos followed. 'That must be very heavy, Gina. Are we sitting outside? I will move the books from the table over there.'

Alice sat down again and decided to get back to work as she had so much to do.

Gina appeared in the doorway, looking a little flustered. 'Alice, please do join us … please?'

'Oh, okay. Are you sure?'

'I know you're busy. But it's such a nice day.'

Alice followed her out and sat at a table under the tree with Carlos and Ignacio as Gina poured the lemonade.

'Home-made, I'm sure,' said Ignacio.

'Only the best.' Carlos smiled.

'I think this is a lovely garden,' said Ignacio. 'I told Carlos after I came the last time …'

'… I thought that when I came over that time a few weeks ago,' cut in Carlos. 'But didn't think to mention it to my brother …'

'The time before, do you remember, Gina? I said how beautifully you cultivate the flowers.'

'This lemonade is delicious,' said Carlos. 'Is it from the recipe I gave you?'

'It's lovely to see you both.' Gina smiled. 'It can get very quiet here when the classes aren't on.' She took a sip of the lemonade. 'That's why I hold the networking events here every other month.'

Carlos smiled. 'I decided I needed to meet other business owners since we are about to be business owners.'

'He was very nervous,' said Gina gently. 'So I took him under my wing.'

Carlos picked up his glass and drank slowly, hiding what Alice thought was a blush creeping up his face under his beard.

Ignacio looked at him. 'It's been a long time since he's been nervous. The life and soul of the party.'

Carlos put his glass down and smiled again. 'Gina is a most excellent host.'

'Oh, I agree completely. I really must come to the next event …'

Alice sat back and watched them continue their verbal ping-pong, Gina nodding and giggling girlishly occasionally. She thought about how she was going to move the tiles to the café when they were eventually finished.

'… so would you like us to give you a lift … Alice? … Alice?'

She looked up. 'Sorry Ignacio, I was miles away.'

'We have to go now as I have an airport pick-up and Carlos has no other way of getting home. Would you like a lift too?'

'No thanks. I've got to do as much as I can today as I'm away for a couple of days. I'll walk back. It'll be nice.'

They all stood up and said their goodbyes. Then Gina patted Carlos on the arm. 'I've just remembered. I found them – remember what we talked about. Stay there.' She hurried into the workshop and brought out a plastic bag and gave it to him. 'There. I'm so pleased I managed to unearth them.'

'Thank you.' For a moment Carlos looked like he was going to cry. Instead he shook Gina's hand.

'What's that?' Alice heard Ignacio ask.

'I told you about it before. Remember? I'll show you in the car.'

'I'll walk you to the gate,' Gina said.

Alice watched the three of them – Gina gliding elegantly in the middle flanked by the brothers, chatting as they went.

'I wonder what that was all about,' she muttered, then walked back to the workshop.

Chapter Twelve

The cat food and instructions on watering the plants were on the worktop in the kitchen, the shutters closed, and Aphrodite was asleep on the bed. 'Right.' Alice grabbed her suitcase, locked the door and took the lift downstairs. 'See you late tomorrow,' she said to the doorman.

'Bye, Alice.' He waved.

She got into the car Duarte de Silva had organised to take her to his hotel and relaxed into the plush comfort of the seat. Taking out her phone, she examined the brief text sent by Luis that morning.

All fine.

All fine, what? she thought. *All bloody fine. Where is the kiss … where is the information?*

It had arrived at 8 a.m., and she had stared at it, walked away from it and continued to pack, looked at it again, put the phone down, decided to call Luis, decided not to call Luis and eventually sent a reply.

Ok x

Now she was looking at it again, feeling she was being dragged back to the ups and downs from when they first met. All from two words. Or the lack of more words. *Actually*, she thought, *because Luis didn't want her to go on this trip*. And that was not like Luis at all.

'Working trip,' she said out loud. 'A trip for my work, for my future, while he's sorting out another issue from his past.'

She leaned back and massaged her neck, trying to keep a headache at bay. *Surely he can't think I'm interested in Saul Pires? Or that he's interested in me? That's almost funny.*

The chauffeur spoke through the intercom as they joined the motorway. 'We will be collecting Senor Pires from his friend's restaurant near to Setubal, so there will be a detour once we have crossed the bridge.'

'Okay, thanks. How long will that take?'

'About an hour depending on traffic.'

'Right. I'll listen to some music then.'

Alice found a Norah Jones album on her phone, put on her headphones and tried to empty her mind as the car sped southwards. Eventually it slowed and turned off the coast road into a car park at the top of a ridge.

'The restaurant is at the bottom of those wooden stairs,' said the chauffeur. 'I am ringing Senor Pires now. Would you like a few minutes to get some air?'

'Yes, that's a good idea.' Alice climbed outside, the midday heat welcoming her after the cool air conditioning inside the car.

At the bottom of the steps Alice took off her sandals and wiggled her toes in the warm, white sand. The sea was still and turquoise, melting into the sky towards the horizon. A ship glided silently towards the Atlantic as the gulls swooped and dived over its bows. Walking into the cool, clear water, she got lost for a moment in its different shades of blue, green and gold. Only the sudden roar of a speedboat brought her back to the present. Taking her camera out of her bag, she began to photograph it, knowing the colours, the sounds and the seascape were going to be important in the next few weeks for her bracelet designs.

'I see you're a workaholic like me.' Alice turned around as Saul waved from the restaurant.

'Oh, yes.' She laughed. 'Always something to inspire me. Are you ready to go?'

'Yes. Thank you for waiting. I'll meet you at the car in a few minutes.'

He went back inside, and Alice walked up the steps, the sun beating down on her back. She turned to look at the view again and took her camera out of her bag. *Is this being a workaholic?* she thought. *I know I used to be, and this was my escape.*

The driver got back into the car as she walked towards him, then she put her camera away and climbed in.

'I hope you don't think I'm being rude,' Saul said as he eventually sat down next to her. 'I've just got to go through some paperwork and accounts.'

'Of course not,' said Alice. 'I'll probably just have a doze as we go.'

'Ah, you'll miss the beauty if you do. And you may miss the dolphins.'

'Are we going on a boat?'

'Well, a tiny ferry, for a few minutes. But if we're lucky, they'll join us, too.'

He took his laptop out of his bag, put on some headphones and got to work. Alice stared out of the window as the car moved along the cliff-top road towards the ferry, still captivated by the bright blue of the sea peeping through the lush green trees as they passed.

Luis would love this, she thought. *He's been here already, though, but … no … can't send him a photo … he's not messaged me and I don't want to push in with him and Mario.*

You're his bloody girlfriend, muttered the voice in her head.

'Ah, no queue for once.' Saul took his headphones off and smiled. 'My family used to use the ferry when I was a child. I still get excited.'

'Have you been to Duarte's hotel yet? I know it's new, but do you know the area?'

'Not been, but I know where it is. Stunning location. Quite remote. I've got the ideas for the menu already as I grew up around here. I've just got to get the details finalised.'

The car moved onto the boat and the driver opened the windows. 'They just told me the dolphins are around today, so be alert and we may get lucky.'

As the ferry chugged into the channel, Alice leaned out of

the window as far as she could, allowing the refreshing breeze to brush her face.

'There!' shouted Saul excitedly, pointing to her right. 'Look.'

Alice saw the tip of a fin peep through the water, then disappear. 'Oh yes, yes! Look there's two. I can see them.' All at once, six dolphins surrounded the boat, jumping and disappearing into the surf. 'Oh, wow!' shouted Alice.

'I'm back to being five years old again.' Saul laughed. 'It's wonderful, isn't it?'

Their eyes met briefly, and then they both looked away quickly.

'Not far now,' he said, putting his headphones back on as the ferry began to dock. 'Need to finish this. Excuse me.'

Alice picked up her phone so she could tell Luis what she had seen. She looked at it for a moment then put it back in her bag, deciding not to send a message out into cyberspace to join the other one he hadn't answered.

How have we got to this so quickly, Luis? she thought. *How, when we are both trying so hard to be fair to Mario? And to each other?*

As the car travelled south the shadows of the pine trees dappled the road, and Alice let the low thrum of the engine calm her mind.

After a while she heard a quiet snore from Saul as he leaned, fast asleep towards her, his head almost touching her shoulder. She shifted sideways to avoid him and looked fixedly outside for the rest of the journey. The car eventually turned into a hidden driveway past a golf course and along an empty track, until it came to a halt in a cobbled courtyard in front of a beautiful yellow and white mansion.

Alice looked at Saul who was still contentedly snoring, then as the car stopped he fell against her. She gently tried to push him upright and said quietly 'We're here,' so as not to startle him. He snorted, moved, mumbled something and threw his arm across her.

116

'Saul, Saul,' she said more loudly. 'We're here.' She took her seat belt off and tried to wriggle away.

The driver opened the door, and she slowly began to climb out of the car as Saul's head rested on her shoulder and he began to nuzzle her neck.

Alice tried not to laugh. 'Saul, Saul,' she said more loudly, getting out as he fell to the seat.

His eyes opened, surprised. 'Oh, Christ,' he said. 'I was having a dream. A dream about … I thought I was with …' He sat up quickly and took off his belt as Duarte de Silva walked towards them.

'It's fine. You were asleep,' Alice said kindly.

'Could you pretend that never happened?' He looked mortified.

'It never happened.' Alice smiled and looked away quickly.

'Welcome to the Quinta de Azelejo.' Duarte grabbed her hand as she got out of the car. 'You had a good journey? Excellent. Only the chalets in the grounds are completely finished so you both have one of those.'

The chauffeur took their bags out of the boot and followed them as Duarte guided them to the foyer, still talking.

'The kitchen is ready for you, Saul, with the staff primed to be of every assistance to create the menu. They can only provide us breakfast until we open. In the meantime, a local restaurant is feeding us.'

They walked up the steps into a grand entrance hall which had walls of yellow and white and a Hollywood-style spiral staircase reaching up to a mezzanine, decorated with tiles and pots of laurel. Alice itched to get outside to find the shoreline and gather some inspiration.

Duarte waved at a waiter who brought over a bottle of champagne and three glasses.

'I need to get to work,' said Saul. 'I haven't got time.'

Duarte passed them glasses anyway. 'Let's celebrate our new partnerships first.'

Saul sighed, then finished his drink in one gulp. Putting the glass down on the tray, he walked towards one of the doors next to the reception desk. 'Where's the kitchen?' he asked, rather grumpily.

'It's to your right,' said Duarte casually. He turned to Alice and spoke quietly. 'Take no notice. He is now in "I'm a Very Important Chef" mode. He has eyes on being on TV a bit more and seems to think he should be in a bad mood when he's around his staff to get some kind of persona.'

'Really?' asked Alice.

'Yes. Well, he wants to be on TV, and he's fairly moody. So let's put them together, shall we?'

Alice sipped her wine again, beginning to feel under pressure herself. Saul's attitude had somehow rubbed off on her, and she wanted to get some ideas for her designs down on paper quickly.

'You on the other hand, serene Alice, can settle into your accommodation and have a look around without anyone pestering you.'

I don't feel very serene all of a sudden, she thought. But she smiled enigmatically and followed a doorman out towards her chalet.

'We meet at seven-thirty for dinner,' shouted Duarte after her, hurrying the other way. 'Busy, busy, busy. I have a hotel to open.' He laughed. 'I love my job!'

Alice followed the concierge along a cobbled path snaking through the trees to the chalet. It stood on the brow of a hill overlooking a long, wide beach stretching the length of the bay, with a lagoon surrounded by parasols at the far end. Remembering she was working, she made a mental note to write down her sense of the colours and light before getting the camera out to take photographs.

The concierge opened the door to a bright, wide room with glass doors leading to the decking at its front. On the wall was a beautiful photograph of an *azulejo* on a traditional white house which was surrounded by orange and crimson flowers. At the bottom was the name of the photographer. *Luis Simal*.

The sense of floating free without an anchor which had been imperceptibly creeping over her again over the past few days eased as she touched the photograph.

Well, at least you are here somehow, she thought and tried to call him. But there was no signal.

'Senor de Silva will collect you from here at seven-thirty,' said the concierge. 'I believe you will be walking to the restaurant this evening.'

'Thank you.' Alice took her camera out of her case and walked into the sunlight.

'I'm doing what I've always wanted to do,' she said to herself. 'Enjoy it. I honestly forgot to dream for a while. And when I began to believe again, look what happened.' She turned to the photograph on the wall. 'Back soon,' she said.

Dressed in a red floral, floor-length dress and wearing the bracelets and a necklace she had made just for herself, Alice sat outside the villa waiting for Duarte. Still trying to cultivate the bohemian-artist-yet-extremely-capable-businesswoman look, she had made another attempt at putting her hair up in a loose-yet-artful way but had abandoned it because she looked like a four-year-old who had stuck things in her hair without the aid of a mirror.

She looked at her phone and wondered whether to tell Luis his photos were already on display but didn't want to start another argument.

Eggshells, she thought. *When did we suddenly start walking on eggshells with each other? I should just message him.*

You are in the place he isn't happy about you being in for some reason, and you will be telling him you are in that place and that he isn't although his photographs are, so whatever the reason, even if it's a stupid reason, why bother? she thought.

'I still don't understand why he wanted me to wait,' she said to a gecko, illuminated by the light on the wall. 'When he knows this is part of my job and there's a deadline.'

On the other hand, he is your partner. You live together most of the time. And this is silly, whispered the voice in her head.

'It is actually.' She stood up and walked into the room. There was enough light, so she took a photo of his photo and decided to send it to him when there was some wi-fi.

'*Ola*, Alice.' Duarte was at the door with Saul, who was dressed in white trousers, a white polo shirt and was also wearing a frown. 'Are you ready for dinner? You can tell me what you think of the place. Saul has already had one hissy fit in the kitchen so needs to calm down.'

'Do you want me to stay?' growled Saul. 'If you do, I wouldn't use the words hissy fit. Makes me sound like a toddler.'

Duarte laughed and squeezed his arm. 'Just trying to lighten the mood, Saul. We wouldn't want Alice to have to sit and listen to us argue about the menu all night would we?'

Saul looked at her and nodded, almost smiling. 'Of course. I'll switch off for tonight and get back to shouting at the staff tomorrow.'

'Good,' said Alice, not sure what else to say.

'I was joking,' he said as she locked the door.

'Good.' She laughed and began to follow them along the path to the beach.

'We're going to a typical beachfront café,' said Duarte. 'But the food is fantastic. And Alice, I know you will love its ambience. It's very nicely done.'

'The fresh fish is excellent I've heard,' grunted Saul who seemed to be trying to be sociable.

'Well, I'm very hungry,' said Alice. 'And I'm looking forward to an evening meal with a sea view.'

As they turned along the sea path, Alice saw the distant glow of blue, yellow and pink lanterns hanging from the trees around the restaurant and heard music playing softly in the background.

'I recognise that song,' she said.

Saul stopped walking for a moment and listened. 'Norah Jones. "Don't Know Why"...'

'... love that song ...' she said.

'... one of my favourites ...' he said.

'... reminds me of ...' she continued.

'... someone I used to know ...' he finished.

'Me too,' she said.

'I don't know why she ...'

'I don't know why he didn't ...'

They glanced at each other. *From this angle*, Alice thought, *he definitely looks like Harry the Holiday Fling again, who disappeared from my life after a magical endless summer and re-appeared again briefly when it was too late.*

'What do you think so far Alice?' asked Duarte as they walked towards their table. 'The previous owner just dressed the place with odd, quirky things in a fairly random way whenever he came across them. I liked it so much that when I bought it I decided to keep it the same way.'

'You own this too?' Alice looked up at the ceiling where multi-coloured fairy lights were wrapped around the beams, trailing outside along the patio pillars.

'He owns everything, didn't you know?' said Saul.

'It's so close to the hotel it made sense. Saul's going to have a look at the menu for here too, just to update it a bit.'

They sat down and Alice looked around. One wall was covered with old paintings and photographs, with mounted ceramic windows and doors dotted between them. Outside, there was a small reproduction of Michelangelo's 'David', Rodin's 'The Thinker' and what looked like a mermaid hidden behind some pot plants.

'The light's a little dim,' muttered Saul as a waitress handed them their menus and placed a bottle of water on the table.

'Ahhh, ambience,' said Duarte. 'Your eyes will get accustomed to it.' He began to look at the menu.

Suddenly the room was plunged into darkness and, for a moment, everyone fell silent. Then someone scraped a chair back and said, 'Again? This is happening again?'

'Sorry, problems with the main power supply,' shouted the waitress. 'Our backup generator will be on in a moment. I'll just come and light more candles in the meantime.'

'Another thing on the list to do,' muttered Duarte. 'Money, money, money, money ...'

'Water anyone?' asked Alice, pouring herself a glass without really looking.

'What happened?' muttered Saul, looking up. 'It just got even darker.'

Alice picked up her water and put it down again without taking a sip. 'That smells odd,' she said. 'It smells a bit smoky.'

'You poured your water into the candle holder.' Duarte laughed. 'It looks very much like a glass. But it isn't ... you've doused the candle out.'

'Oh dear.' Alice giggled.

'I'll get you another glass, and another candle holder for the table.' Duarte waved at the waitress to get her attention.

Alice accidentally caught Saul's gaze as the new candle the waitress placed in front of them briefly illuminated their faces. 'Thank you for the text you sent me last week,' he said quietly.

'Text?'

'New adventure, you said.'

'Ahh, yes, that ... I didn't ...' Alice was thankful that the light was so bad he probably couldn't see her blush.

'Right,' said Duarte, turning back towards them. 'Indulge me. I'm going to order for us.' He laughed. 'I've tried this with my wife and she never allows me to. I saw it on a film once ...'

The plates soon arrived and Saul picked his up, holding it in front of him with one hand, appraising it as if it was a painting, then he put it down and began to eat. 'Ah,' he said, noticing Alice and Duarte's confused faces. 'I'm sorry – that's rather a bad habit. I'm very interested in presentation. More in the taste, obviously. But sometimes food looks like a work of art.' He laughed. 'And they did like it for the cameras when I did that TV thing.'

Alice examined her plate, too. 'I've never thought about it like that.'

'Food is as much a work of art as a painting … or a bracelet, for that matter.' Saul smiled. 'Its creative and uses all the senses.'

Duarte patted him on the back. 'This is why he is part of this project!' he almost shouted. 'All the senses … all the senses.' He chuckled to himself and began to eat.

Alice wasn't there any more. She was nineteen years old, sitting in a café in the south of France. Harry the holiday fling took a forkful of cassoulet, held it up to his face, took a breath and waved his arm around dramatically. 'All the senses … all the senses,' he said.

'Are you enjoying your food, Alice? … Alice?' Duarte touched her arm to get her attention.

'Oh, gosh, sorry. Just remembered I had to do something when I get back to the chalet. Yes, it's delicious.'

'You looked for a moment like you weren't here any more.' Saul smiled.

Alice shifted in her seat, a little surprised. 'I do look like that sometimes,' she said quietly.

'You creative people!' Duarte laughed. 'Your minds are always off somewhere else. But that is a good thing.'

'Well, I have to linger here for a while and talk to the manager,' sighed Duarte after their meal. 'The lights are still lit on the path to the hotel, I think. Are you two happy to find your way back to your chalets?'

Alice looked towards the sea, the low white moon casting a bright glow across the black waves, stars glittering in their thousands in the sky. 'We'll be fine.'

'So, Alice, you have a story. I know you do.' Saul fell into step beside her. 'What is a woman like you doing moving away from her home to Portugal?'

'I fell in love with it. I feel more a part of it than I did in London. I know that now.'

'Ahh, there is more to it than that,' he said quietly. 'There is something about you. You are ... guarded ... is that the word? Friendly, but there is a hesitation there. You are more reserved than the last time we met. You were relaxed then, I could tell. Something's happened?'

She glanced up at him, then looked away. *I am guarded*, she thought, *because ... because ... when I have allowed men into my life, I feel they will leave me. And now Luis ... Don't say it out loud.*

'How is the new menu going?' she asked, changing the subject.

He smiled. 'I will find out more about you,' he said, pushing back a branch that was hanging over the path. 'But if you really want to know, this is not too difficult. Locally sourced food with a little bit of a twist. A special seven-course tasting menu. The occasional special occasion. It's what I do in all my restaurants and cafés. The challenge is to make each one different.'

'You obviously enjoy a challenge,' said Alice.

He stopped for a moment and looked at her again, the silence hanging heavy between them. 'I do,' he said, then carried on walking.

Her palms began to sweat, and her heart began to beat a little bit faster. She walked more quickly, confused by the intensity of whatever it was she was feeling, wanting to push it away. She had spent years waiting and almost hiding when she was with Adam and, during that time, had not let anyone in her life. Then she met Luis and everything changed. She had let her guard down for him. She hadn't been able to stop it. What was this?

'Best get back to our chalets in case the power goes again,' she said quickly. As soon as she said it the lights along the path went out.

'Oh dear,' she said.

'Oh dear indeed,' said Saul.

'It's like the universe is having a laugh.'

'It is quite funny, after all. Your timing is impeccable.'

'Second time this evening I've made the light go.' She laughed.

Saul held out his hand. 'It's a light night,' he said. 'So, it's not too bad. But there were a few ups and downs in the path as I remember. Trip hazards …'

Alice looked at him.

'I'm simply offering to be a guiding hand. And I need you to help me too. You can be my knightess in shining armour!'

Alice took his hand. 'Come on then,' she said. 'If you need me to look after you …'

'I didn't say that,' he huffed. 'I merely wanted some equality here.'

'Fine by me,' she said. 'If we're not quick, one of those clouds is going to drift across the moon and we won't be able to see anything.'

'Point taken.'

They began to walk silently towards the lights of the hotel far in the distance.

'I'm not being rude,' said Saul eventually. 'I'm concentrating on not falling down any holes.'

'Me too,' said Alice, at which point she lost her footing slightly and fell into him. But it felt more than that – it was as if she was being gently pushed towards him. He smelt of barbecue and spices and his chest felt welcoming and warm. Alice found herself transported back to that holiday with Harry again, laying in his arms on nights just like this as they looked at the stars and talked of the adventures they would have. In that brief moment she felt the intensity of that summer, the way she had fallen quickly and helplessly in love for the first time. It rushed over her unexpectedly and then subsided almost immediately. Saul had grabbed her waist and they both stayed there for a second too long.

'Are you okay?' he whispered.

Alice almost jumped up. 'Yes, thanks. That was a close one.' She felt her heart race again. A long-forgotten memory of how she'd felt then fluttered into her mind – the Alice before she met Adam, when she'd been happy and relaxed and hopeful – then it quickly flickered out. Saul took her hand and squeezed it tightly. 'I will look after you. I promise. Honestly.'

'How far is it back?' she asked.

'A few more minutes,' he said quietly. 'You will be back safely by midnight, Cinderella.'

They walked on in silence again, accompanied by the gentle lapping of the waves on the sand and the singing of the cicadas.

'Bye Alice,' he said when they got back to her chalet. He kissed her hand. 'Thank you for a lovely evening.'

'Yes, you too,' she said. 'Best go. Lots to do tomorrow. Must ring Luis.'

He smiled. '*Adieus. Até logo.*'

She watched him disappear into the night, and opened the door, pulling out her phone as soon as she got in. The message she had sent Luis had bounced back. *Try again*, it said. So, she did. It came back again, unsent.

Alice ordered breakfast in her room the following morning. Whatever she had felt was in the air between herself and Saul the previous evening had surprised her, and she wanted to keep it at bay. Whatever it was. It was nothing. It was in her head. It was the past. She had drunk one glass of wine. *Next time I see him*, she thought, *that will have all gone. It will be daylight, and there won't be fairy lights and candles and music and food.*

126

She wanted to speak to Luis but her phone was still not connecting to the internet and seemed unable to send messages or even to call, so she looked at the sea, breathed in and out a few times, and decided to give in.

'I can do nothing. Nothing at all. I'm going with the flow!' She almost punched the air. 'Look at me, going with the flow. Now that's progress. I'm giving myself a holiday from my own brain.'

She gathered her notebook and pencils, ready for a day collecting ideas. *Whatever that is.* She smiled. Collecting ideas, who'd have thought someone would actually ask her to do that for a job? 'An actual job as an actual artist,' she said out loud.

A piece of paper was pushed under the door. *I've most unfortunately been called back to Lisbon urgently. I've been cooking since 6 a.m. The results are in the kitchen for you and Duarte. Just ask one of the staff to plate it up for you. SP.*

All for the best, she thought, relieved.

Chapter Thirteen

Alice's phone began to buzz as soon as the car turned from the tiny track leading away from the hotel onto the main road. *Ping, ping, ping*, it went. She studied it, bewildered as message after message landed. For a moment, she wondered, terrified, if something awful had happened. She tentatively opened the first one which was from her mother

Ignacio is in bits, it said. No cross words between them before. Ever ...

'Oh dear ... started another. That one was from Kathy.

And there was one from Luis. Home tomorrow evening. Will head straight to the farmhouse. Have electricity and water. Will call when I'm there. L.

Alice felt sick. *He's avoiding me*, she thought. *But why?*

She put her headphones on and closed her eyes, deciding to read all the other messages when she got back to the apartment so she could piece it all together. The silent peace of the past couple of days had disappeared in an instant.

She walked into the foyer of her building, and as she pressed the button for the lift, she knew there was no way of avoiding whatever had been going on whilst she'd been away.

Real life, she thought. *Real flipping life ...*

'Dona Alice.' The doorman hurried over to her. '*Bom dia*, Dona Alice. A gentleman has been waiting to see you for nearly an hour.' He nodded his head to a young man in a smart suit who was sitting reading a paper by the window.

'Me?'

'Yes. It's to do with the apartment. He said that Mary had contacted you about his visit.'

'Oh, right. She may have.'

Well, here we go, she thought. *I have to confront all of*

whatever has been going on in my phone in the past couple of days.

'I'll just check the rest of my messages and e-mails.'

She began to scroll through the list … Mum, Tara, Kathy, Ignacio, Carlos, Duarte, Saul Pires. Oh, oh … Mary, Luis.

She opened Mary's message. Ola lovely! Someone who's representing the person we are selling to wants to come and have a proper look around and measure. He said tomorrow at 6 p.m. Hope that's okay. Let me know if it isn't. Such a pity you can't buy it yourself, but I absolutely know you will be happy anyway.

Alice glanced back at the man. *It isn't really okay*, she thought. *But as the message was sent yesterday, I suppose I'd better see him.*

'*Ola. Bom dia,*' she said, walking over to him.

He stood up and smiled.

'*Chama-me* Alice. *Fala Inglais?*'

'Hello, yes, I do speak English,' he said, shaking her hand. 'I've been sent to do a report on the apartment for the buyers. They haven't seen it. It's been organised by another person.'

'Oh, right.'

'I just need to take some photographs and do some measuring. Is that all right? I shouldn't be much more than an hour.'

'Of course. I'm sorry, I've been away and my phone hasn't been working properly so I've only just found out about this.'

'You won't even notice I'm here.'

They travelled up together in the lift in silence. *It's real*, she thought. *This is happening.* Her stomach churned a little. 'I've got to unpack and make a few calls,' she said. 'I'll just open everything up for you and you can get on.'

'Fine, thank you.' He took out his iPad and got to work.

She checked the rooms for Aphrodite but there was no sign of the cat at all. *Kathy must have let her out when she fed her earlier*, she thought, walking to the kitchen to put the kettle on.

'Cup of tea or coffee?' she asked, glancing at this person who was appraising the apartment for someone else. The new owners. *I was only ever passing through*, she thought.

'No, thank you.'

He started to measure the windows, and she switched the kettle on, wanting to pretend it wasn't happening. There were a couple of tea leaves on the worktop and a small droplet of water by the sink. 'I thought I'd cleaned everything before I left,' she muttered, glancing at the airing cupboard door, which was ajar. 'And I know I closed that.' She looked at the message Kathy had left again. *Oh dear* it said. 'Oh dear,' muttered Alice. 'I think ... oh dear, oh dear ... I told you ... I warned you ...'

She noticed something race from the bedroom to the balcony, made herself the tea, then heard a noise from the living room.

'Can you get your cat off me?' asked the man who was cornered by the wall by tiny Aphrodite aggressively attacking his feet, her ears erect, eyes wild and bright. Jumping at the bottom of his left trouser leg she bit into the material, hanging on as he tried to brush her off.

'That's not like her,' she said, rushing over. 'She's normally very friendly. Never bites feet. Or trousers. Well, only play biting.'

Alice tried to prise her away, but the cat did not give an inch.

'I don't want to hurt her,' he said. 'She's so tiny. But very fierce.'

'I think something has disagreed with her,' muttered Alice, thinking about the stray tea leaves in the kitchen and planning what she might say to Kathy when she got hold of her. She sat down and tried to get a bitter grip on Aphrodite. 'May I?' she said, trying to pull the fabric from the cat's teeth.

'Of course.' He laughed and joined her on the floor. This confused the cat, who let go and then stood hissing at them both.

'I'm too frightened to move,' she whispered, giggling.

'Me too. I don't like to admit to being scared of something that size. But on this occasion ...'

They both stared at Aphrodite for a moment, until a bird fluttered across the balcony, luring her outside in pursuit. Alice jumped up and closed all the doors. 'I'll just let her calm down for a few minutes,' she said. 'I'm really sorry.'

'It's okay. When I tell people about this,' he said, standing up, 'the small cat may turn into a huge dog,'

'My lips are sealed.' Alice smiled. 'I've just got to make a quick phone call.' She walked back into the kitchen.

'Alice, welcome back,' whispered Stephano on the other end of the phone. 'Kathy is unexpectedly sound asleep.'

'Why are you answering her phone?' Alice whispered back.

'She was saying things about tea when she got back from feeding your cat. Then she just curled up into a ball and went to sleep on the sofa.' He sounded very tired. 'I'm having to work from home and I had to organise for someone else to cover her evening appointments at the salon.'

'She sent me a message that said "Oh dear" earlier. So that's what she meant. I thought something terrible had happened.'

'Well. It's not good, to be honest, it's not terrible, but ...' James began to cry in the background.

'I'll let you go. When she wakes up ... eventually wakes up ... can you tell her I would like a chat?'

'Have you spoken to Ignacio or Carlos?'

'No, but I've got a few messages from them. I haven't read them yet.'

'The last time this happened was fifteen years ago and it took months to ...' The baby's cry became a howl. 'I've got to go. Bye.'

Alice stared at the phone for a moment, wondering what on earth had been going on in the last two days. 'Well, I hid the tea,' she said to Aphrodite, then remembered that the cat was throwing itself around on the balcony, but carried on talking to her anyway. 'So, she went looking for it. And I did say ...'

She took a sip of her drink, wondering whether she was ready to read the other messages and, once again, be confronted by the lack of contact from Luis. Walking to the balcony, she spoke to her visitor. 'I'm going out,' she said. 'I'll close the doors behind me, so she can't attack you again. Don't worry.' Then she sat for a while, watching Aphrodite unsuccessfully attempt to catch a wasp, a nagging sense that some kind of chaos was in the air unsettling her. She tried to hold on to the relaxing void the other side of the river that had been hers for a short lovely day and night. She consciously edited out the bit that had Saul Pires in it.

Which is most of it. The voice in her head laughed.

She put her sunglasses on and closed her eyes. 'Oh, be quiet,' she said.

The tap on the balcony doors made her jump.

'I've finished,' he said 'Thank you for allowing me to do this with such short notice'

'That's fine.' Alice stood up and noticed Aphrodite sprawled, fast asleep, under the table. 'Is she snoring?'

'I should be safe now.' He laughed. 'It's a beautiful apartment,' he said as he left. 'I'm sure you'll be sad to leave.'

'Yes. But it has always belonged to someone else, so I knew it would end. Although I am quite attached to it.'

He stepped into the lift. 'I'm sure you will find somewhere just as beautiful. *Boa-tarde e obrigado.*'

'*De nada.* It's nothing.' She closed the door and thought about the little yellow house and all the other little houses she'd looked at in the past few weeks. 'You have the farmhouse when Luis has finished it,' she said out loud, 'even though it's not yours.' But somehow that was beginning to feel out of reach, and she couldn't quite work out why.

She looked at her watch. Luis would have landed by now.

Then she glanced at her phone and the unread messages from Carlos and Ignacio.

I cannot work with him any more. That was from Carlos.

He is restricting me, said the last text from Ignacio.

Are you okay Alice? Is there a problem with your phone? Carlos

Alice, is there a problem with your phone? Are you okay? Ignacio.

Has there been a full moon or something? asked the voice in her head. Then Luis rang and her stomach did the warm, familiar loop the loop.

'Hi. You're back. How did it go?'

He sighed. 'It was … more complicated than it needed to be. And stressful.'

'Shall I make us a nice meal and we can have a glass of wine and talk about it?'

He paused. 'Alice, I've missed you, but I'm going to head straight to the farmhouse. I've just collected Elvis from Carlos, and I just …'

'Shall I pop over then?'

'I'll see you tomorrow. I just need a bit of time … the enormity of this … I mean I knew it was enormous when Fran and Mario appeared but didn't have time to think. It's all been so fast, but—' she heard him open the car door '—I don't think much of myself at the moment so I … I'll speak tomorrow.'

The phone disconnected and Alice felt sick, her mind racing again. She opened the fridge and took out a bottle of wine, poured herself a glass and joined Aphrodite on the balcony, watching the afternoon sun slowly set over the horizon. A little knot of anxiety settled itself at the back of her neck.

'Remember when you were hiding in your house in London? No one could touch you. No one could hurt you. You could shut the door and be alone,' she said out loud.

Alone is the right word, she thought. *Or lonely. But no-one could hurt me. Because I'd trained myself to feel nothing.*

Massaging her neck, she rolled her shoulders, then stretched her arms.

Feeling something is better than feeling nothing, she thought. I don't want to be that person any more.

You were quite boring to be honest, whispered the voice in her head.

Alice almost laughed.

So do something.

Do something.

Aphrodite stirred and opened one eye.

Alice tried to call Luis again. This time it went to voicemail. 'I'm here if you need me,' she said. 'And I'm coming over tomorrow whether you want me to or not. Love you.'

Then she sent Carlos and Ignacio the same message. I think you should tell me what's going on.

Picking up her bag, she opened the door. 'I'm going out, Aphrodite. Where there are people. Laters.'

As soon as she stepped out of the lift, she got a message.

I've got to work on a build in Carcavelos tomorrow. I'll call you.

Then another. X.

Alice stopped at the door and took a deep breath. *You know he loves you*, she thought. *You know this is about what's just happened. Give him space. Understand. Don't make this difficult. This is not about you.*

She tried to fill her mind with ideas for the jewellery, designs for the café and working out a timescale for finishing the tiles. Then there was the website she needed to set up for the bracelets. *Can't live off the money from the sale of the house for long, don't want to fritter it away before I've bought something,* she thought. *Need to invest it in bricks and mortar and get my holiday let business going.*

Without even realising it, she found herself standing outside the little yellow house. All that had changed was the for sale sign now said sold. *Vendido*, was written in big black letters. She peered into the windows, and for a brief moment, forgot it wasn't hers. Would never be hers. Noticing another house with a for sale sign a few doors down, Alice walked towards it. A light was on upstairs and the shutters were closed in the windows on the ground floor. Making a mental note to arrange a viewing, she turned around and began to walk towards the square. And just for a split second, she felt like the little yellow house was glowing again. Shrugging it off, she carried on walking.

The square was busy with people chattering and laughing, and a busker was playing next to the statue. Alice felt her mood lift as she moved around the tables and sat down. Almost immediately Carlos appeared at the doorway with a glass of wine. 'Welcome back,' he said. But his smile was muted.

'Thank you. Have you got two minutes to sit down?'

'It's too busy, Alice.'

'Okay. Well, firstly, I have an idea for the patio. And secondly, are you and Ignacio all right?'

A shadow fell across his face. 'I don't want to talk about it.' A customer got his attention, and his smile returned as quickly as it had faded. 'Can you come tomorrow morning?' he asked.

'Is ten-thirty all right?'

'Yes. Enjoy the wine. Busy, busy, busy.'

Alice took a sip and pulled her phone out of her bag.

I'm back. Are you okay? she messaged Ignacio and watched Carlos work the tables, in control and in his element.

Ignacio replied almost immediately. I am afraid not, Alice. My brother and I last had an argument fifteen years ago. I am in pain. But I am sending him love. Even though I don't forgive him.

Alice looked at it for a few moments, trying to work out a suitable response, but before she could another text arrived.

As he was wrong to do that.

Taking another sip of wine, she decided not to fuel the flames of whatever was going on and stick to work. 'I am coming to the square tomorrow at ten-thirty to talk about my wonderful idea for the patio. Will you be there?'

If it's about the café and therefore my investment, I will do my best.

Well, at least it's not about work, then, she thought. The image of Carlos and Ignacio walking either side of Gina when they visited her popped into her head. *Oh dear*, she thought. *Oh dear*.

In for a penny, in for a pound, she decided and sent a message to Kathy.

Hello Sleeping Beauty. Once you have awoken, give me a call. I assume you accessed that tea, given the way Aphrodite behaved when I got home. She thought she was a tiny tiger and attacked someone. And … what's going on with Carlos and Ignacio…? x

She pressed send and finished her wine. Then composed another message.

And I could do with a chat xx

She waved to Carlos so she could pay.

'On the house,' he mouthed from another table, and then he waved. '*Ate amanha*. Until tomorrow.'

Alice waved back, picked up her bag and walked towards the beach, where she sat on a bench and looked at the moon reflecting on the marble sea until her feet guided her home.

The first thing she did when she woke up the following day was call Luis, but his phone was still going direct to voicemail, so Alice decided to send him a message.

Morning …

She looked at it for five minutes, her mind going around in circles.

This is not about you; it is not about you. Give him some space. Is he okay? Has he fallen back in love with Fran? Don't be ridiculous. They were never in love. He could have fallen in love with her, though. Don't be ridiculous. Two months ago he didn't have a child. Now he has a ten-year-old. Check he is okay.

… how are you this morning?

She put the phone down and took some treats from the cupboard to give to Aphrodite.

… looking forward to catching up later xx

She pressed send, put the phone in her bag, picked up her portfolio and laptop, and headed to the square.

Carlos was sitting on a table under the awning, looking out towards the other cafés. His arms were folded, and he wore his sunglasses like a shield.

'*Ola*!' Alice waved, sensing this meeting was not going to be very effective.

He stood up, pulling out a chair for her. 'Sit, sit,' he said, shouting into the café, '*Galao para* Alice.'

'Lovely, thanks.' She sat down and pulled out her laptop. 'So, we'll wait for Ignacio and then I'll get started.'

'You'll be able to sense his arrival, you won't hear. He'll appear, floating, surrounded by the smell of lavender and patchouli oil. Probably chanting.'

The drink was placed on the table and Alice began to stir it, slowly, trying to think of something sensible to say. 'I think he's just very keen on discovering his more spiritual side.'

'This counselling business is taking over everything. At the wrong time.'

Alice sighed. 'Ahhh ...'

'He says it won't interfere. But it's too much change all at once.'

'Well ... you had already both decided on the counselling business being in the café attic?'

'And he ... here he comes. I don't want to talk about it.'

Ignacio sat down, kissed Alice on the cheek and nodded at Carlos.

'No counselling workshops to go to that are more important than our business?' huffed Carlos.

'There is no point talking to you whilst your energy is like this,' said Ignacio evenly. 'I am here to see the plans that Alice has, then I have to go to take a client to a golf course near Sintra.'

'Energy,' muttered Carlos. 'Energy ...'

'My point entirely,' said Ignacio, folding his arms.

Alice opened her files to stop them arguing.

'So, I was at Duarte's hotel the other side of Troia and we went to this beachfront café for a meal one evening. It had fairy lights everywhere, plus quirky little statues and colourful plants. It was gorgeous. In fact, it was magical. Here are some photos.' She moved the screen so they could both see it. 'I went back during the day, too, and it looked just as beautiful. Look at the lanterns – they don't need light to look effective.'

The men nodded but didn't say anything.

'So,' she carried on. 'This is my idea. Something similar but on a much smaller scale.'

She clicked on the file. The sketch had clusters of fairy lights shaped like flowers hanging from the trellis and draped around the ceiling. On the back wall was a ceramic windmill and a sunflower in a pot, with a statuette of Venus partially obscured by small palm trees. The tables and chairs were ironwork and painted bright blue.

They both smiled and nodded. 'That is wonderful, Alice,' said Ignacio.

'So imaginative,' echoed Carlos. 'And simple.'

'Simple, yes.' Ignacio nodded. The brothers' eyes met, and for a moment they seemed to forget that they were in the middle of an argument. Then there was silence.

'Do you want me to tell you how much it will cost? If you're happy, I'll add it to the final bill with the rest of it.'

'Yes, yes,' said Carlos.

'You are impressively business-like, Alice.' Ignacio smiled.

She opened another file and showed them the figure. 'I think that will get us what we need, and I've factored in my time, too.'

'That is all right, in my opinion,' said Ignacio.

'Yes, that is okay,' said Carlos. 'Just a minute, though. I have something else.' He rushed inside the café and came back out carrying a plastic bag.

'That's not what I think it is, is it?' Ignacio looked uneasy.

Carlos ignored him and took out ten large lettered tiles, which he re-arranged.

'What does that say?' asked Alice, unable to work out the words from her seat.

Ignacio sighed. 'It says "Raul Coelho 1952".'

'I would like it put there in the patio somewhere.' Carlos smiled sadly.

'I already told you. It is bad luck. Why would we want that?'

'What's the problem?' Alice looked at them both, confused. 'I don't understand.'

'The past is what it is,' said Ignacio firmly.

'Our heritage.' Carlos folded his arms.

Then they both looked at their watches at exactly the same time. 'I'd better help to set up,' mumbled Carlos, gathering the tiles and putting them back into the bag.

'Got to collect my customer,' muttered Ignacio.

Alice watched them both walk off, put everything away and decided it was time to talk to her mother.

'Look, Mum.' Alice pointed the phone towards the sea, and then around to the prom towards Estoril.

'Isn't FaceTime great! It's the kind of thing they'd have had on *Star Trek* years ago and we'd say "that could never happen".'

'Thing is, when you speak to me, you don't have to put the phone by your ear. All I can see is your ear.'

'Sorry, darling. Is this better?' Her mother's left eye came into view.

'Much better. Mum, there seems to be an issue about Ignacio setting up as a counsellor. Even though Carlos already knew. Has he said anything to you?'

'No. When he talked about it to me he said Carlos seemed excited about it. Why?'

'He and Carlos are arguing about it. I don't really know

why ... and there's a woman ... I think ... possibly, and now, there is a sign ...'

Her mother moved her head so Alice could see her right eye. 'A sign? Oh Alice, at last you are connecting with your spiritual side. What kind of sign was it? A butterfly? A flash of sunlight?'

'No, Mum. It was an actual sign. Made out of tiles. And whatever it was made them both angry. One liked it and the other didn't.'

'That's a pity,' sighed her mum. 'I always thought of them like The Blues Brothers. But without the hats. Or the music.'

'Can you talk to Ignacio? I don't think he realises that his commitment to counselling is unsettling Carlos. Maybe he can slow it down a bit? And can you ask him about that sign. He said it was unlucky.'

'Of course I will, darling. They are such lovely men. I don't like to think of them arguing. You'd think Ignacio would be more understanding with all the workshops he's been going on.'

An idea began to form at the back of Alice's mind. It came out of nowhere, and she was unable to stop it. 'There is another thing I wanted to talk to you about, actually ...' Alice hesitated. *Do I really want to know this?* she thought. 'My biological father ... have you heard from him?' Alice finished the sentence quickly and regretted asking immediately. 'I mean, Joseph is my father, but ...'

'With all this going on with Luis, it was bound to stir things up,' said her mother, whose mouth was now taking up most of the screen.

'We'll put it here, shall we?' Alice heard Joseph say, as the phone was propped up on a table. 'Hello Alice.' He waved. 'Serious stuff, so I'm off.'

'Hi Joseph!' Alice felt guilt overwhelm her. How could she ask about the man who abandoned her when she had a perfectly wonderful stepfather?

'We've been waiting for you to ask for years,' her mother whispered.

'Oh.'

'Tara started asking when she was fifteen. But not you. You were old enough to remember the upset, I think, so didn't want it anymore. And when I used to try to talk to you about it you'd walk away. Every time. You kept it all inside, so we decided to wait. Taken a bloody long time, though, Alice.'

'She was fifteen? She never said.'

'Although when you were nineteen you announced you wanted to know. Just after that holiday you had in France. When you were grape picking and travelling ... remember?'

'Did I?'

'Yes. But we didn't have mobile phones or the internet then dear, so you rang me up from a university phone box ... I was about to tell you, but it ran out of money and when we next spoke you told me you didn't want to know.'

'Oh ... I don't remember any of that.'

'Do you know, I was very confused, darling.' Her mother disappeared from view.

'Mum?'

'Hang on ... sorry, had a really bad itch on my ankle.' She sat up again, so Alice could see half her face on the screen. 'I think it's because you were back at university and got caught up in all of that. Probably too much for you to take on.'

'So, what did happen to him?'

'Well, the answer wasn't very interesting to be honest.'

'What was it?'

Her mother took a deep breath. 'You know he contacted me when we had just moved back in with my parents. But I was so angry with him for abandoning us and leaving us homeless. I mean look at the effect that's had on you for goodness sake, what with your house fixation.'

'Thanks, Mum.'

'I wouldn't speak to him. Then when I met Joseph, he

tried again … some men are like that, aren't they? A sniff of another man and they're there, and I told him he could see you. But all of a sudden there was another woman around, and it never happened.'

'Oh … okay.'

'I think they moved to Canada.'

'So since then he hasn't tried to contact you at all?'

'No … Alice …'

'It's fine, Mum.' Alice smiled widely.

'I don't believe that for a minute.'

'Well …'

'How are you and Luis?'

'We're fine,' she said brightly. 'Absolutely fine. Got to go.'

Alice disconnected the phone and turned it off. The sea glistened like glass, lapping gently on the sand. It looked so welcoming. She wanted to wade in and swim across the bay and forget she had ever asked her mother anything about her past. Stepping onto the beach, she took off her sandals, enjoying the familiar sensation of the warm sand under toes. She stood for a few minutes in the shallows, allowing the water to caress her feet. *I feel*, she thought. *I feel … flat.*

Which is good, she thought, *because I can still remember how I felt when he disappeared. And now I'm terrified of losing anything: Houses, people, love.* She walked slowly up the hill to the apartment, changed into her swimming costume, and then dived into the pool to try to wash the dull ache away.

Alice coped by spending the afternoon making bracelets and researching websites so she could build her own. 'I've managed fine without knowing anything about my father except his name. This doesn't matter. At all,' she said to Aphrodite, who was sat staring at the baubles as if she was planning something.

'*Are* you planning something?' she asked and rubbed the cat's ear. 'Personally I am. If Luis doesn't call me, I'm going to get a taxi to the farmhouse anyway.'

At 6 o'clock, Alice called him, but his phone was still straight to voicemail. 'I'm just ringing to say hello,' she said. 'Call me. I'm coming over at seven-thirty.'

The tension started to creep over her neck again as she sat in the cab whilst it climbed the hill, the dark fields tumbling towards the sea.

'Can you stay for a second?' she asked the driver as she closed the door. 'I just need to check that someone's home before you go.'

Elvis barked from inside the house and bounded towards her, followed by Luis, who stood in the doorway.

Alice paid for the taxi. 'Thanks. It's fine. Obviously he's here.'

She cuddled the dog and followed him along the path to where Luis was waiting. They stood, silently, for a moment before he opened his arms and pulled her towards him.

'I'm sorry.'

'I've been worried about you.'

'So much has happened. I'm so ... I can't explain how I feel, but I just needed to hide. Not talk about it.'

'If you don't want to talk about it, we don't have to.'

'Thank you for coming. I wouldn't have blamed you if you hadn't.'

Alice stroked his hair and sank into him, enjoying the smooth, familiar curve of his neck.

'You still love me, don't you?'

'Of course I do. I love you more than anything.'

He pulled her even closer. 'I was such a selfish idiot when I was younger.'

'Easy to say. Hindsight.'

They stood back. His hair was unkempt and his face unshaven. 'I've got chairs we can sit on.' He indicated two green plastic chairs dumped in the middle of the room.

'Just like the ones we sat on when we went for that date near Cabo Da Roca.' She smiled.

'Actual chairs, yes. I can open the plastic sheeting in front of the door so we can try to recreate the view.'

Alice laughed. 'Shall we wait until we can sit outside and recreate it then?'

They sat and looked at each other again. Elvis sighed and lay down next to Luis.

'They are coming over in three weeks for the summer,' he said.

'Yes, that's a nice idea.'

'Rented a house in Quinta da Marinha.'

'Lovely.'

'My sister is insisting on coming over too for a couple of weeks,' he said irritably.

'Okay ...'

He sighed. 'Let's not talk about her. How was your visit to Duarte's hotel?'

'Useful.' Alice glanced at the floor, trying to choose her words carefully so she wouldn't mention Saul Pires. 'One of your photographs was hanging up in my room. It was beautiful. I tried to send you a photo of it in place, but the signal was really bad.'

He leaned over and took her hand. 'I'm sorry how it sounded when I asked you not to go. It's not what you think. It's so beautiful, I wanted to be with you the first time you saw it.'

She kissed him. 'I think you were stressed. And so was I really.'

'I've got to get this place finished quickly.'

'Right.'

'I'm going to have to borrow to do it.'

'Why the sudden rush?'

'I need it for Mario.'

'But they are staying somewhere else. Why push it?'

'Something my sister said ...'

'What did she say?'

144

'She ...' he hesitated then stood up. 'Nothing. She has a way of getting under my skin.'

'So, this didn't come from Fran then?

'No. She's very laidback about all of that. Doesn't even want money for maintenance. I asked her. I'm going to put some away for him for college or whatever he decides to do and have him here for holidays.'

'That's good.'

'But she didn't tell me about my son, you know? She should have done. That's ten years of his life I haven't been part of.' He picked up a beer and walked to the window. 'What would my life have been like if she had?'

'It's natural to think that but—'

'—we could have co-parented. Or maybe we would have got together, Fran and me. Who knows ... my life would have been so different. I wouldn't have felt so adrift all those years.'

Maybe we would have got together ... Alice felt like someone had hit her in the stomach.

He felt adrift. Like you Alice, just like you, the voice in her head said evenly.

But he's considering what a life with Fran would have been like and I am standing in the room, she thought.

He looked at her, his face horrified. 'I'm sorry. I didn't mean that. Everything that happened has brought me to you, and I would never want it any other way.' He walked over to her and pulled her to him again. 'Sorry, so sorry. I'm having to say that a lot at the moment. To everyone.'

'I know, I know. It's a lot ... you aren't yourself.'

'Mario likes you by the way. He really does.'

'He's great. I like him, too.'

'And Fran, too. Although, I think I should stop talking about her, shouldn't I?'

'Well ...'

He looked around the house, which was empty apart from

the chairs, an empty box and one lightbulb illuminating the room.

'Can I come back with you tonight Alice? You deserve better than to spend the night here. And I want to be with you.'

'I'm so glad you said that,' she said, trying to lighten the mood. 'I think Aphrodite will be pleased to see Elvis, too.'

'Happy families,' he said, grabbing his car keys and his overnight bag. 'I won't ask you to do my washing by the way.'

'I will, though.'

'Have you got anything to tell me? There's something, isn't there?'

Mary and Frank are selling the apartment. I can't afford to buy it. I have to find somewhere else to live soon. They think I can move in here ... but she didn't say any of that. 'Please don't borrow money to get this finished,' she said, as he closed the door behind him. 'Remember the mess you got into when we first met when you ended up with three houses and couldn't afford any of them.'

Kathy manoeuvred the pushchair into place and sat down next to Alice.

'Oh, I forgot. I've got some bread for the ducks.' She stood up and began to rummage in her baby bag. 'I know it's here somewhere. Can you hold this for a minute?' She handed Alice a bottle of milk, then a plastic book, a bag of clean nappies, a diary, a tube of Vaseline, three dummies and a clockwork dog. 'Here we go, it must have fallen to the bottom.' She took the bread out, then began to refill the bag with all of the items which Alice had placed on her lap.

'It's very therapeutic, chucking crumbs at birds,' she said as the baby chuckled. 'I'm not sure whether I do this for him or for me.'

'Can I have some?' Alice pulled out a slice and began to pull it to pieces.

'The peacocks will be along in a minute. He loves those.' Kathy looked at Alice. 'I can't apologise enough for stealing your tea and accidentally drugging your cat.'

Alice laughed. 'When you put it like that, how can I not accept?'

'I am just so very, very, very tired most of the time.'

'Bringing up a child and running a business will do that to you.'

'It's a pity you had to stop working with me at the salon to sort out the London house. My new assistant is great, though. But she's still an assistant and it's still my salon … I'm so weary …' Kathy showed James how to throw the crumbs, and he delightedly dropped them onto the floor next to the pushchair. 'My brain has enough energy to imagine not being exhausted. And can remember what it was like not to go out with splashes of Weetabix dotted on my clothes in very surprising places, to be honest.'

The ducks began to waddle to the bench and were soon joined by the peacocks, making James shriek with pleasure.

They both laughed. 'But when he does that, I don't care.' Kathy threw more bread. 'I did have a fantastic sleep after that tea, though. I felt amazing when I woke up.'

'So did I.'

'Lasted a day. I'm back to normal exhaustion now.' She turned to Alice. 'Can we do something silly, Alice? Can we? Remember when we went paddle boarding, and you were rubbish? And we danced on a bar, and you drank far too much …'

'And Luis took me home and I asked him to sleep with me, but I was a bit worse for wear and he wouldn't.'

'Happy days.'

'Aren't you starting tile painting with me later?'

'That's relaxing and edifying, not silly.'

'What did you have in mind?'

'Karaoke.' Kathy beamed. 'But in Lisbon, where no-one knows us.'

'You know I can't sing.'

'That is completely the point.' She grabbed Alice and hugged her. 'I took you paddle boarding to cheer you up. This is what I expect in exchange.'

A peacock pecked at Alice's foot which made her scream. The baby chuckled loudly and clapped his hands.

'I feel so sensible, Alice. So very, very grown up and I just want not to for an hour. Maybe two.'

Alice squeezed her hand and looked into her friend's eyes. 'Okay. For you. But as long as its where no-one, repeat, *no-one*, knows us. I wouldn't want to put anyone through listening to me sing, and I mean sing in inverted commas.'

'No-one will know,' whispered Kathy. 'We'll pretend to Stephano we're going out for a meal in Lisbon. Then he won't book a babysitter and come and laugh at our expense.'

'When will this be?'

'Let me sort out babysitting and work and I'll let you know. Spontaneous or what!'

'I'll try to look forward to it.'

The baby began to grizzle restlessly once the ducks and peacocks had eaten all the crumbs. Kathy jumped up. 'Got to keep him moving when he's like this,' she said. 'I'm off to the playground now. I suppose you have more grown up things to do than that?'

'Yes, I've got to go home and finish a training plan before I go to Gina's. I'll see you there later.'

As they both stood up, Alice leaned over to Kathy. 'Do you know what exactly happened between Ignacio and Carlos?'

'Oh, the argument?'

'Yes, the argument. When did it happen?'

'The day before you came back from Duarte's hotel.'

'Well, I hope they sort it out soon – I can't get them to concentrate on the interior design for the café!'

'Do you think Gina's got something to do with it? They

both seemed to be rather captivated by her when we had coffee.'

'Maybe. Not that they've said anything, though.' They began to walk towards the playground. 'And now there's a sign.'

'What sort of sign? A robin? A shaft of sunlight?'

Alice laughed. 'No, no ... a sign made out of tiles that said something like Coelho's and then there was the year. Carlos wants it put in their patio garden. Ignacio said it was bad luck. And, apparently, it's from their past.'

'Ahh. They're arguing about a sign, Ignacio's interest in mindfulness and such and possibly a woman. That's a lot all at once. They never argue. Well, actually ...'

'Stephano did say something. The night of the tea. You wouldn't remember. You were fast asleep.'

'Oh, that tea did make me feel lovely, though. I'm going to ask Stephano about this old argument between them. I feel like a detective!'

They reached the gate and Alice kissed her friend on the cheek. 'See you later.' She waved at the baby. 'Bye bye James. Bye bye,'

As she turned, Kathy shouted. 'I forgot to ask ... how's Luis? How did that go? And we haven't talked about your time away. You said you needed a chat and I forgot to chat ... baby brain.'

'Oh, everything is fine,' lied Alice.

Although shouting some karaoke in front of strangers may do me some good, she thought as she walked back towards the apartment.

Chapter Fourteen

The workshop was the calm sanctuary that Alice needed, the ladies around her chatting and laughing as usual whilst she dipped in and out of the conversation as her mural began to slowly take shape.

Gina moved around the room smiling, encouraging everyone, occasionally pausing behind Alice. 'It is coming along very well,' she said. 'It will be beautiful. I can't wait to see it when it's finished.'

Kathy sat next to her, painting some tiles with brightly coloured flowers. 'Placemats,' she said. 'It's all I can cope with.'

'How many have you done so far?'

'Two. But two is better than none.'

Gina rubbed her eyes and sighed. 'I think I may need glasses,' she said.

'Can you only read a menu if you hold it at least a foot away from you?' Kathy laughed.

'Sometimes. But I don't want them.' She sat down between the two of them. 'They don't suit me.'

'Maybe you just need reading glasses.' Kathy put her brush down. 'So, what's been going on with you?'

'Me?'

This is Kathy attempting to interrogate, thought Alice. *Here we go.*

'Anything been going on at all? Any exciting news. Fun? Dates ...?'

'Oh. No. No dates. I met Carlos on Sunday morning for coffee as he wanted some advice about networking.'

'Nice of you to help.'

'And on Sunday afternoon, Ignacio went with me to my regular Hot Yoga class in Carcavelos.'

Kathy picked up her brush again and dipped it in some blue paint. 'They are lovely guys, aren't they?'

'Yes.' Gina leaned forward. 'These were not dates, though. Just time spent with friends.' She started fiddling with her necklace. 'I'm not used to male company. I feel it's awakening something in me.'

'Are you seeing anyone at the moment?'

'I haven't been involved with anyone for quite a long time,' sighed Gina.

Kathy leaned back and yawned. 'Oh, God, sorry. That came out of nowhere. Exhausted and still not sleeping. I need some of Mary's tea.'

Gina giggled. 'Oh, Mary's tea. I used to have a recipe for a very relaxing one.'

'This was a really, really relaxing one.' Kathy laughed. 'She hid it behind the airing cupboard so Frank couldn't get hold of it. I found it last week and boy did it make me sleep. The following day I felt wonderful.'

'I have been a little tense myself recently,' said Gina. 'I think I'll message her and ask for the recipe.'

'Not that one, though,' said Alice quickly, remembering the texts she'd sent when she'd drunk it.

'No, not that one,' said Kathy. 'One of the gentler relaxing ones.'

'You could just go and buy some camomile tea from the supermarket,' whispered Alice.

'Mary's tea is famous,' said Gina. 'I'll send her a message now.'

'Mary's tea?' asked one of the other ladies. 'I would like the recipe, too. It helped me when I couldn't sleep last summer.'

'Mary's tea?' said another of the ladies. 'Yes, please ask her.'

'Make sure you get the right measurements,' said Alice, feeling things were about to get out of control. 'Just, you know ...'

'Of course,' said Gina, squinting at the screen.

Alice suddenly felt very, very sensible again, and she didn't like it.

Alice watched from the kitchen as Luis began to cut back the banana trees in the farmhouse garden whilst Elvis ran around, exploring and barking excitedly in the late afternoon sun. A light haze hung over the mountains like a gauzy cloud, and the sea shone a bright blue under the clear, hot sky as dragonflies danced around the grass.

It looked perfect, but it felt far from it.

Alice opened the window. 'Do you want a drink?' she shouted. 'There's water and juice in the cool bag.'

Luis turned around and nodded. 'Thirsty work,' he mouthed.

She picked up two bottles of water and walked outside. 'I've put an undercoat on a downstairs living room wall,' she said, handing one over to him. 'I've opened the window, but it still smells very badly of paint.'

'Thanks for helping.' Luis gulped down the water and put the bottle on the floor. 'I want to make it look half decent for Mario and Fran before they come.'

'I don't think they'd mind if it didn't.' Alice sat on the grass and stretched out her legs. 'They aren't staying here.'

'I don't want to look like I'm some kind of slacker,' he said irritably.

Alice began to stretch, searching for the right words that wouldn't drive him back in on himself again. 'You're not,' was all she could say.

'I'm trying to make amends.' He picked up his drink again and took another swig. 'For the years I wasn't there.'

'Getting stressed about finishing the house isn't ...' She trailed off, deciding not to pursue it.

He grabbed the scythe and began to cut the branches again. 'Let's not talk about it. It's just got to look like it could be a home instead of a building site. I've got to do it to show his mother I'm worth him knowing.'

'Can I do something to help here? I've finished what I can in the house. We've run out of paint.'

Luis paused for a moment and sighed, agitated. 'I'm never going to get this done in time. I've got all this renovation work on too.'

Alice stood up and walked over to him. 'What do you mean finish it in time? They are here next week. You aren't going to finish it. You know you aren't. It's not possible.' She put her hand on his shoulder, but he turned and carried on working.

'I just want it to look less like a ... I don't know ... I just ...'

'I'd go into town and get more paint but I haven't got a car.'

'It's fine, it's fine. I'll do it later,' he muttered.

'I've got three viewings of houses from six. Can you drop me off on the way?'

'But I said I'd view houses with you. Can you put it off to another day?'

'It's fine. I'll look at them and, if one stands out, you can come for the second viewing.'

He turned to her. 'You could just not look for a while? There's no urgency to get out of the apartment. This place will be almost liveable for us both in a few months.'

Alice wanted to say, 'Mary and Frank are selling the apartment and I have to leave. They think I can move in here now. But I can't. And I don't want you to worry about that too. And I just need something of my own. I just do. I need to put the money into something solid. And the longer it goes on, the worse I'm feeling.'

But all she said was, 'Just humour me and don't worry about it. You know what I'm like.'

He reached out and touched her cheek. 'I said I'd help. I don't want to let you down.'

'It's okay.'

'And Cassie's coming this weekend. Oh God ...'

Alice kissed him. 'Let's work for another half an hour, then you can get your paint and I can feed my craving for house viewings.'

Maybe this time I'll be lucky, thought Alice, following the agent through the bright blue door into a wide, light room. It was the first place she had viewed that actually had people living in it, and it felt warm and welcoming and, most importantly, homely. It felt good.

'The vendors are looking for a quick sale,' said the estate agent. 'I told them you are a cash buyer, and I think there may be a deal to be done if you like it.'

A wind chime tinkled in the courtyard and a clock struck seven from the kitchen. Alice could hear its gentle ticking as a soundtrack whilst she explored the rest of the house.

'My grandparents had this really old clock that rang on the hour, even during the night and ticked very, very loudly,' she said.

The agent smiled. 'I think this one is a family heirloom,' he said.

Your grandparents' house where you all hid when you were all homeless all those years ago, said the voice in her head. *Not that I think history is repeating or anything … but it is.*

'No it isn't,' she said sharply.

'Excuse me? I didn't quite understand,' said the agent.

Alice walked up the stairs. 'Thinking aloud. Take no notice.'

The main bedroom had a balcony looking over the cobbled street full of pots of red and white geraniums; the flowers tangled around the wrought-iron curled frame, and strings of fairy lights almost cascaded from the ceiling and walls. It was as if Alice already lived there.

'Who owns this at the moment?' she asked.

'I think the husband is a doctor and his wife is an artist.'

'It is beautifully designed.'

'They're expecting a baby and want more room, so they are buying a house in Birre.'

'Have you had many viewings?'

'You are the first. I have one booked in for later this week. It's a good house, at a great price, so it won't take long to sell.'

'No, I'm sure it won't.'

For the first time since she lost the little yellow house, Alice began to feel excited about somewhere again. 'I'd like to come back and do some measuring up and get a second opinion.'

You could put an offer in now.

'I absolutely love it, but I have to be sensible.'

Boring.

'As it's a big investment for me.'

What if you lose this one too?

'I must be very, very rational and not allow my heart to lead me.'

Are you directing this at me, meaning you, or the estate agent? whispered the voice in her head.

'Can I come back tomorrow?'

'Of course. My clients are away at the moment, so I'm sure we can arrange a time that suits us both.'

Alice almost skipped onto the street. *I think I may have found what I'm looking for*, she thought.

'Hopefully I will see you tomorrow,' said the agent.

'I'll call later,' she said, then took her phone out of her bag. She put it straight back in again. *I can't ask Luis*, she thought. *He's got too much on. And I can't ask Kathy as she's exhausted.*

So Alice walked straight to the square to talk to Carlos.

'I think I may have found a house.'

'That is very good news, Alice.' Carlos was clearing some plates from a nearby table. '*Galao?*'

'Yes please. The thing is, I want to look at it again tomorrow before I jump in and make an offer, but I'd like another pair of eyes.'

'*Galao para* Alice,' shouted Carlos to the kitchen.

'I mean, I know what I'm looking for. I used to help my

155

stepdad all the time in his houses and I've renovated my own. But this is the first one I'll be buying on my own, and I just want someone with me to keep me grounded.'

Carlos smiled. 'I can tell you are excited. Have you told Luis?'

'No … he's under a lot of pressure, and I don't want to bother him.'

'He won't think you're bothering him. He'll be pleased you've found somewhere, especially as you have to move out of the apartment.'

'Well, the thing is, I haven't told him that.'

Carlos looked at her sternly, then pulled out a chair. 'What do you mean?'

'He's gone into a workaholic spiral, trying to get the farmhouse into some kind of liveable shape before Mario and Fran arrive.'

'But I thought they were renting a big house somewhere?'

'They are. I think he's trying to prove something to himself.'

'But Alice, you need to tell him.'

'I will. But if this house is the one I can tell him once I know.'

The coffee arrived, and Alice began to stir it, not looking up so she couldn't see the expression on Carlos's face. 'I mean, I haven't got a date for moving out, yet. It could be months. You know how it goes, so why worry him when there's probably nothing to worry about?'

Carlos still didn't say anything.

'I am worried about Aphrodite, though. I've got to find somewhere for us both.'

'But you are moving in with Luis?'

'Of course I am.'

'You haven't changed your mind because of all of this … business?'

'No, no! I've found a house I like, that's all. I want to invest my money. And it seems silly not to do something about it just because Luis has other things on his mind. I just don't want to put any more pressure on him.'

Carlos stood up. 'Customers,' he said.

'It's just I love him and ...' she trailed off.

'What time is this viewing?'

'I haven't organised it yet.'

'Well, either me or Ignacio will do it.'

'Are you two speaking again?'

'Not really, Alice. But if I can't do it, I know he will.'

'Thank you. I wish you and him would sort whatever this is out.'

'It takes two,' he said sadly. Then he turned up his smile as he walked over to take an order from the people on the table next to her.

She finished her drink, then walked quickly up the hill, full of ideas for the house. As she got to the fort her phone rang.

'You have to tell Luis. I can't believe you haven't.' Alice could hear calming whale music in the background.

'Hi, Kathy. How did you know about this?' She already knew but asked anyway.

'Ignacio messaged me.'

'I haven't told him yet ...'

'Well, Carlos asked him to go with you for the viewing. Why didn't you ask me?'

'Because you are very busy and very exhausted. Are you phoning from work?'

'No. I decided to try to recreate that serene feeling I have there at home. I've got lavender oil burning and this really annoying music.'

'So, it's not working then?'

The baby began to cry in the background. Kathy sighed. 'No.'

'I'll let you deal with James. Speak tomorrow.'

'Wait a second, you ... before you go ... do *not* keep things like this from your partner. It will cause trouble.'

'But I don't want to worry him.'

'He tells you things and they worry you. Where's the equality here?' James began to erupt into a full-blown wail. 'Got to go.'

Alice sat on a bench for a moment, absent-mindedly watching some workmen replace loose cobbles on the pavement. She realised there was a tiny part of her that wanted to buy the house without any advice from anyone close to her. The beloved London house had belonged to her and Adam, and the farmhouse belonged to Luis. This was the very first place that would be totally hers. To rent to others, of course. But hers.

A stray cobble had rolled under the seat. *I can decorate that*, she thought, *and put it in my new house*. She dialled the estate agents.

'Hello, I'd like to arrange a second viewing of a property I looked at in Rua Melo earlier please. Could you do ten-thirty in the morning? Great, thank you.'

Alice sent a message to Ignacio, then picked up the cobble and put it in her bag. 'I'm going to make you look like a little white Portuguese cottage,' she said, 'And you are going to be living on the windowsill in the living room. With me. Wherever I am!'

She walked towards the apartment gate the following day, a spring in her step, her mind full of plans for the house, picturing herself drinking coffee on the window seat in the bedroom, the morning sun streaming in and illuminating everything, or tending her pots in the little courtyards. *My parents can stay in it for free*, she thought. *And Tara and her family. And the rest of the time I will have people on holiday in it. It's perfect. Absolutely Perfect.*

She looked up and saw the Aphrodite's tiny form far above her on the balcony. *Off to get us a house*, she thought. *We won't be living in it. But it will be ours. All ours.*

Her camera was in her bag, along with a tape measure, notebook and pencil, so she could consider everything properly back at the apartment before diving in and making the offer. And she'd tell Luis after that. And it would be fine. Completely fine.

Just as she was about to turn the corner to the sea road, her phone rang.

'Hello? When did that happen? They paid over the asking price? So there's no chance? Okay, thanks for letting me know. Bye.'

For a moment, Alice didn't feel anything. She turned around, walked back up the path towards home and glanced towards the swimming pool, which was glistening welcomingly between the trees. She paused for a moment and composed a message to Ignacio.

Ola. Change in plan. No plan ... the house is off the market. They've taken a cash offer over the asking price from someone they know. No house to view now. Thanks for offering to come with me though. A.

She continued up to the apartment and climbed into bed, covering herself with the duvet, exhausted and sad. She closed her eyes and blocked everything out for a while, eventually waking to the purring and contented padding of Aphrodite on the pillow next to her. 'That's four houses now. And Luis is getting his ready to impress someone else.' She rubbed the cat's ear and stroked her neck. 'No, I know that's not fair, but ...' The feeling of floating adrift again caught her by surprise, and she rolled over and held onto the mattress. 'God, there's a lot going on Aphrodite,' she whispered. 'All of a sudden.'

Climbing slowly out of bed, she opened the wardrobe door and found a rucksack tucked in the corner. She opened it and took out the small pink and green bowl she and Adam had bought for their house. Her house. Who was she kidding? She'd chosen it; he didn't care. It was the first thing they'd bought for their new home. The first thing *she'd* bought.

Alice carried it to the kitchen and put it on a worktop.

'Wherever I lay my … bowl … is my home,' she said. Then she found the cobble stone in her bag and put it next to it. 'Right,' she sighed. 'I am an artist and I better do art, hadn't I?' Alice took her notebook and diary, checking through her list of jobs.

1. *Jewellery designs to Duarte de Silva.*
2. *Source items for Carlos/Ignacio's café patio, including tables and chairs.*
3. *Paint mural (constantly – urgent).*
4. *Ask Luis for four photos for interior of Carlos/Ignacio's café.*
5. *Get paint samples for above.*
6. *Check in with stallholders to see if they need more bracelets.*
7. *Online training work.*
8. *Design website for bracelets (urgent).*
9. *Make bracelets, paint walls, put up décor, fix mural to wall.*

At the bottom she wrote, *Find house to buy. Or possibly rent. Just in case.*

Looking at everything that needed to be done, she suddenly felt exhausted. *Isn't this what I was like for years in London? Hiding in my work … workaholic Alice … be careful.*

Turning on her computer, she waited for it to flicker into life, and glanced around the room of white and pink. The trees outside were swaying gently in the breeze, accompanied by shouts and laughter from people enjoying the pool and garden.

'And what exactly is wrong with this list?' She smiled to herself. 'I'm an artist, and that list is the list of an artist who has work to do, plus a couple of extras. So, as work to hide in goes, this is quite all right.' 'Lists are great,' she shouted to Aphrodite, who was still sitting on the bed. 'Let's try to tick some off. Here we go.'

Picking up her phone, she messaged Gina and asked for

regular extra tile painting sessions over the next four weeks to finish the mural. She texted Kathy to ask her for guidance on improving her website and left a voicemail for Luis offering to help him paint the house that evening (to show support, even though Mario and Fran would not be staying there). She didn't mention that bit, though. Alice took her sketch pad and pencils from the drawer and laid them out in front of her, preparing to put her jewellery ideas on paper.

As she looked at the blank page, the image of Luis trying to clear the garden to impress his newly found son floated into her thoughts, and before she could stop herself, she picked up her phone and sent a message to her sister, Tara.

Have you thought about trying to track down our father recently? xx She looked at it for a moment, her finger hovering over the send button, then pressed it and regretted it immediately. She switched her phone off and put it in her bag. For the next few hours she managed to lose herself in her designs, and it was only once she had e-mailed the samples to Duarte that she felt able to re-engage with the world again and switched on her phone.

Of course, Gina had replied. Send me some times and dates x

Will do, Kathy had said. If my baby brain will allow any coherent thought. I've got time tomorrow in between spa appointments. Meet in the square at four? x

Are you sure? messaged Luis. I would love you to, you're my best building mate! I'll be there at five. Coming from Lisbon so quicker to go straight there. Can you get Ignacio to drop you if he has time? xx

The last one was from Tara. I thought you'd never ask. I need to tell you something xx

Alice looked at it and caught her breath. Was she ready to hear whatever this was?

She answered the other messages, put on her swimming costume and went downstairs to the pool to hide from the cacophony of feeling she knew was about to overwhelm her. *I'll deal with it in a minute*, she thought. *In a minute.*

Chapter Fifteen

'How are you today, Alice?' Ignacio smiled as she stepped into his car.

'Oh, you know … busy, busy, busy. Good busy, but busy.'

'Are you sure you're all right?'. He smiled sympathetically and turned on the engine.

No, I'm not. I'm not. I asked a question and now I don't want to know the answer, she thought.

'I'm fine. Why do you ask?' is what she actually said.

'You're in your bright orange and red trousers, Alice. Generally, it signifies you mean war.'

'Oh … oh, no. I just pulled them out of the wardrobe. Didn't think.'

'If you say so.'

'I do wish someone didn't keep buying the houses I want. Or the apartments I'm living in, though.'

'Ah, yes, about that. I was talking to my friend who is an estate agent over in Estoril, and he told me that someone has been buying up houses for cash in the area over the last few weeks. Often for over the asking price just to get them off the market.'

'Oh, right … why?'

'He thinks it's a large organisation that wants to add to its property portfolio. Either to renovate and sell on or to rent. It's a very popular place.'

Alice leaned back and bit her lip. *How am I supposed to compete with a faceless organisation with loads and loads of money?* she thought and gazed out of the window as the car passed the beach at Guincho, then followed the road inland, the landscape becoming more green and gentle as they went.

'I'm looking forward to seeing the progress on the farmhouse,' said Ignacio. 'Luis seems to be working on it day and night.'

'It's beginning to take shape. There's a lot to be done, but at least he's got water and electricity now.'

'This must be difficult for you,' said Ignacio eventually. 'You are a very kind and sensitive woman, Alice. But Luis finding he has a son from another woman must have stirred things up for you.'

'Well.'

'With your father abandonment issues ...'

'Not ...'

'And Luis' previous reputation ...'

'I ...'

'If you ever want to talk—'

'—Ignacio,' said Alice firmly, deciding to take charge of the conversation. 'Are you going to tell me why you and Carlos have been arguing?'

Ignacio was silent for a few moments. 'When Carlos asked me to be his partner in the café I was very excited.'

'And?'

'He is fulfilling his dream to own his own place, and I am happy to be part of it.'

'Right ...'

He sighed. 'Alice, it is not my dream. I have driven people to a lot of places for many years and many of them have confided in me. I am a good listener. And now I realise that I like listening more than driving and I want to do more ... he knows that. We agreed.'

'So why are you two arguing?'

'I am his business partner. But it is his baby, and he will be in charge. Whether I like it or not. Which I do. I am fine with it. I very much am. But I am used to being my own boss, and I need to be in charge of something ... and of course there is the past ... there is an issue.'

'So what exactly?'

'So now that's stirred up, he's being very strange about the counselling. He thinks I'm using it as an excuse to not be involved.'

'What is this thing from the past?'

'I don't want to talk about it.'

'Oh, but—'

'—no,' he said, opening the car door.

'Ignacio—'

'—no.' He smiled, helping her out. 'I can't bring myself to say it.' He closed the car door behind her and walked ahead to the house.

'Luis,' he shouted. 'We are here.' He turned to Alice, almost smiling. 'I must say it has improved since last time I saw it.'

'How long ago?' asked Alice.

'About three months.'

Luis walked towards them, a bucket of paint in one hand and a brush in the other. 'Hi. I was just about to start.'

He kissed Alice and nodded at Ignacio. 'Sorry, no hands to shake,' he said. His smile was strained, and his eyes looked tired. 'Appreciate your help, Alice. You're happy to look around yourself Ignacio? I've got to get on.'

'That's okay with me.' Ignacio looked at the garden, a combination of overgrown greenery and mounds of brown earth. 'I understand the rush, what with Mary and Frank selling the apartment as well.'

'*What*?'

'You know, Alice has to move out sooner than she thought.'

Alice sighed inwardly. *Oh dear*, she thought. *Oh dear.*

Luis stared at her. 'You haven't told me this.'

'No, well, I didn't want to worry you. And it's not urgent.' She smiled to try to show that everything was fine.

'Why didn't you tell me?'

Ignacio took a few steps backwards, then began to walk towards the car. 'Well, I should be going. It all looks very good, Luis. Carry on. Bye.'

'Like I said, I didn't want to worry you.'

'But it's important.'

'I know, but you've gone into some kind of decorating frenzy, and I didn't want to make it worse.'

He shook his head. 'I'm doing this for us, Alice.'

'But you don't need to rush.'

'I need to have something to show, to prove I'm ...' he trailed off and walked back into the house as Ignacio turned the car engine on and began to drive back towards the road. 'Please don't keep things from me again,' said Luis.

'Where do you want me to start?' Alice said to his back.

'There's more paint in the garage ... maybe you could start on our bedroom?'

Alice felt a pressure on her head and her stomach began to churn, sensing things were only going to get worse. They worked in silence for two hours, the upbeat chattering and feel-good music from the radio providing a soundtrack that belied what was really going on. By the time Elvis got so restless that he had to be taken for a walk, they were both exhausted.

'I'll drop you off at the apartment,' Luis said. 'I'll stay here tonight so I can get a couple of hours in before I collect Cassie from the airport.'

'Why don't you come back with me? You'll get a better night's sleep?' Alice touched his arm, but he wouldn't meet her gaze. 'Luis ... please, you're burning yourself out for nothing.'

'Cassie is coming tomorrow.' He sighed and rubbed his temple. 'She means well, but she drains me sometimes.'

'You aren't doing this to prove something to her too, are you?'

'No! Of course not. I've let it go on for too long. This is just a bit of a kick up the backside for me.' He picked up his car keys. 'Come on, let's get you home.'

'I'll meet you at the hotel when she arrives tomorrow.' Alice climbed into his car after Elvis had jumped into the back seat.

'You don't have to.'

'I'm going to anyway.'

Just before he closed the car door, she kissed him on the cheek as if everything was all right.

Chapter Sixteen

Alice submitted her brief to the online training company, then added two lots of bracelet orders for the stalls in town to her list. She picked up the folder with the designs of the mural in it, closed the door to the balcony, picked up her bag and keys and strode out, feeling pleased with a busy morning's work.

But as the lift took her down to the foyer, the thoughts that had been kept at bay by all her tasks gradually began to creep in again, and anxiety started to make its little stabs into her mind.

Cassie is arriving, she thought, *and Luis is not happy about it. There's a wedge between us I've never felt before and I hate it, hate it. I've got so much work to do, I'll never finish it ... I need to find a house ... I need to buy some orange juice and bread ... I need to reply to my sister's text ... I'm not ready to do that yet ... I should, though ...*

The door opened on the ground floor. Alice stood for a moment, then held the closed button. *You don't owe your father anything*, said the voice in her head. *Whatever Tara's got to tell you, it's up to you when she does.* She felt that familiar sudden surge of anger which dissipated almost immediately, then she allowed the door to open.

A man walked past holding the hand of a curly-haired little girl. Alice watched them for a moment, then stepped forwards into the sunlight.

Cassie's hotel was perched on a tiny headland in the centre of town, overlooking a little beach surrounded by sandstone cliffs. Alice sat at the café opposite while she waited for Luis and his sister to arrive and began to take photographs to calm herself down.

No experience wasted, she thought, wondering if she could

incorporate the way the golden glow of the sand eased into the clear turquoise of the shore into her designs. A car beeped its horn as she stood up to walk to the steps that led down to the beach to take more pictures, and she turned. Luis waved, unsmiling, and pointed to a lay-by further down the road.

Alice followed the car and waited until he parked.

Cassie almost jumped out towards her, waving.

'Hello, hello, hello. It's great to meet you, Alice.' She grabbed her hand and squeezed it tightly.

Alice nodded, 'Lovely to meet you, too. I've heard a lot about you.'

'Only bad stuff!' she said, pulling her into a tight hug. 'I know. It's my brother. We have a real, well, brother and sister relationship!'

Letting Alice go she shouted at Luis, who was getting her three suitcases out of his car. 'Be careful now, Luis. Don't want you to hurt your back. You're not getting any younger after all!' She turned back to Alice. 'He hates me winding him up. I personally love it.

'I'll just go and help him with the luggage, Cassie,' said Alice.

'Thanks,' she said, still loud. 'Hope I've got a sea view from that room.'

Alice took one of the cases from Luis, his face set like a stone. 'Is she not going to help?' he whispered. 'For God's sake.'

'I was hoping I'd be able to stay with you at your place, Luis. But as usual, you're painting, or selling or renovating.' Cassie laughed. 'Pity Luis didn't park outside.'

'No room outside,' said Alice, 'He's parked as close as he can.' They began to walk across the road to the hotel entrance.

'Quite a turn-up, Luis having a son,' said Cassie, watching them pull her suitcases. 'Although, not really. His flaky past was bound to catch up with him eventually. Eh, Luis?'

A doorman put the cases onto a carrier, and they followed him in.

'But I said to him, you'd better get Mario tested as soon as possible to make sure he's yours. I mean, he hasn't seen Fran for years. You do hear things. Mario could be anybody's.'

'Mario is my son,' Luis said sternly. 'Fran talked about a test virtually as soon as I met her. And you shouldn't have said that to her face.'

'Calm down, calm down.' Cassie laughed again. 'You can't be too careful, brother mine. I'm a solicitor, remember. Even if I'm on a career break. So, Alice, Luis tells me you've been helping him get his house sorted?'

'Yes, virtually from the first day.'

'Well, I'm here now, so you can get a bit of a rest.'

'No, I'm happy to—'

'—it'll do me good,' interrupted Cassie. 'It's all very well taking time off work but I'm so used to being busy I don't know what to do with myself. Plus the twins are all grown up now so they don't need me so much. But now my brother does.'

'You don't need to help. We are getting on fine. Have a rest. Enjoy Cascais. Do some sightseeing.' Luis' voice dropped. 'Please.'

Alice smiled at him reassuringly as his sister checked in.

'She's a force of nature, isn't she?' she said quietly.

'That's one way of putting it,' he sighed. 'She saves all of her sensible, thoughtful, rational behaviour for work, and lets her real personality out after 5 p.m. Only now it's all day. She'll calm down soon. She's always like this with new people.'

'You make her sound like a puppy,' Alice said.

'She sort of is.' He sighed again.

'I've asked for the suite at the front for when Bobby comes over – that's my new chap, Alice – he's meeting some friends for a golf binge in Estoril.'

'Lovely.' Alice smiled.

'Nothing but the best for me and Bobs. I was a bit lonely

when my husband left two years ago. But now I'm anything but. He rocks my world, in more ways than one!'

'Your voice does carry, Cass,' Luis said quietly. 'Not everyone wants to know—'

'—about my sex life?' she interrupted. 'Sorry.' She covered her mouth with her hand.

'It's okay. She's got friends nearby so she'll be otherwise occupied most of the time,' Luis said to Alice quietly.

Alice touched his arm reassuringly. 'I'm sure she means well.'

Luis didn't answer for a minute. 'She's bored, Alice. She was a bigwig at work, and now she isn't. She needs to be a bigwig somewhere … and I've got a bad feeling she'll be launching her bigwig takeover here, with me.'

As the concierge took her suitcases to her room, Cassie said. 'So, when am I going to look at this old farmhouse then? Looking forward to getting stuck in!'

'You don't need to,' said Luis. 'I've told you. It's fine.'

'But I want to!'

He sighed. 'I'll meet you back here in an hour and take you up there.'

'I've got to go and do some work, so I'll see you later.' Alice kissed Luis. 'Got to go.'

'Oh, yes, painting tiles and making bracelets.' Cassie laughed. 'Great work if you can get it.'

As the door closed behind Alice, she unclenched her teeth and let the afternoon sun cover her in a warm and comforting glow. The phone buzzed in her bag, and she checked the message.

We need to talk. You can't run away forever. Tara xx

'I can run away a bit, though', muttered Alice.

Alice hurried into the square after spending an hour and a half painting tiles in Gina's workshop and sat down in the shade.

A *galao* was placed on the table almost immediately.

'You look like you've had a busy day.' Carlos smiled. 'And I know you have been spending extra time on the tiles. Gina told me.'

'Well, it's not long till the refurbishment, and you haven't got much time.'

'I appreciate it.'

'I spoke to Ignacio yesterday.' Alice decided to make another attempt to get to the bottom of the argument.

'Well, I'm sure he would appreciate your work, too.' Carlos's smile had disappeared.

'Are you going to tell me what's going on, really?'

'He isn't taking this seriously.' Carlos folded his arms. 'This is my dream ... our dream ... and it takes commitment.'

'Have you spoken about it? Told him?'

'No. He knows and there's that other issue. I don't want to talk about it ... oh, here's Kathy. I'll go inside and get her another coffee.'

Alice sighed and put her laptop on the table as her friend sat down.

'Hello. I've got half an hour then back up the hill for another appointment,' she said, almost falling into the chair. 'I'm tired. As always.'

'Well, I appreciate your time.' Alice opened her laptop and switched it on.

Kathy leaned forward and touched her arm. 'Guess what? I've found exactly the right place for our karaoke adventure. You haven't forgotten, have you?'

'No, no, I haven't,' said Alice, wishing she had.

'You'll love it. God, I'm looking forward to being stupid again, and not in an absent-minded "I have a baby" way. In a totally frivolous and silly way.'

Carlos placed another *galao* on the table and went to serve a group of customers.

Alice leaned forward. 'I have almost solved the "Why have they argued" mystery,' she whispered.

'What is it?'

'Well, the straightforward wanting-different-things-from-work thing which, if they just sat down and talked to each other, would be sorted out in an instant.'

'But they *are* men.' Kathy sipped at her drink. 'Ohhh, I needed that.'

'But Stephano said they'd had another argument a long time ago. And Ignacio said there was something else from the past ... and it may be about Gina too. But maybe not.'

Kathy's eyes lit up. 'I have an idea. She must come on our karaoke night. I love a mystery.'

'She may just tell me,' said Alice.

'That's no fun. Now, let's talk about your website Mrs High Powered Businesswoman. I've got a packed evening of facials and leg waxing to look forward to.'

'And I've got a quiet evening on my balcony whilst Luis shows his sister the farmhouse.'

'What's she like?'

'She's very nice. Quite forthright. Not unpleasant.'

'Right ...' Kathy laughed. 'I'd call that damning with faint praise. But this is about you – let's sort out this website. Your homework tonight, my dear, is to get it online.'

Alice opened her e-mails before they started and saw one from Duarte de Silva marked urgent.

Alice,

A glossy magazine has a last-minute gap and wants to do something about my new hotel. They are speaking to Saul Pires, and I mentioned your exclusive jewellery line, so they would like a few words from you and two high quality photographs of your bracelets. I have seen the designs and I am very happy, so you choose.

P.S. Luis gets a mention too!

I have copied in the journalist you need to speak to, and she will be in contact.

The deadline is in two days … Soz, as they say!

D

Alice almost bounced up from her chair and squeaked.

'You sounded like one of James' toys.' Kathy laughed.

'Look …' Alice turned the screen round to show her the message.

'Oh, wow!' Kathy ran around the table and hugged Alice. 'Fabulous!' Then she ran back to her seat and sat down. 'Right your website is now urgent. You need to include the link in the article, so stop giggling and let's concentrate.'

Alice almost skipped up the sea road, excited to finish the site and make up the bracelet samples for the magazine piece, managing to forget for a while her very long list of 'to do's' and 'to worry abouts'. She put on some happy music, threw open the balcony doors and answered the questions the journalist had just sent, losing herself in her work until the sky turned black outside.

As soon as she looked up, the 'to do's' and 'to worry abouts' started to return, so she went down and sat by the pool to keep them away for a while, hoping to cling on to the positivity of the last few hours. She sat listening to the cicadas, then closed her eyes, enjoying the scent of the evening jasmine.

'Hi beautiful.' Luis sat down next to her and sighed.

Alice opened her eyes and smiled. 'Hello gorgeous. I thought you were spending the evening with Cassie.'

'I have spent enough of my evening with Cassie,' he said. 'She got bored of helping me and decided the hotel bar was a better option, so that is where she is.'

'I've got news!' said Alice.

'What? It must be good, judging by the look on your face.'

'I've just been interviewed about my bracelets for a piece in a glossy magazine about Duarte's hotel. I think you and your photographs are mentioned, too.'

'That's amazing. I'm so proud of you. I haven't checked anything today so this is news to me.'

'And I've updated my website. Hurrah!'

He leaned over and kissed her. 'I'm so proud of you, I really am.' He kissed her again. 'And I'm sorry about yesterday and all that business about the apartment. I know you weren't telling me because you didn't want to worry me. But don't please. We are in all of this together.'

A solitary bark rang from a balcony above.

Luis laughed. 'I brought Elvis over and left him upstairs. I was hoping we could stay the night with our best girls – you and Aphrodite.'

'I was hoping you would,' Alice said, stroking his face.

He kissed her again and ran his finger down her spine.

'Are you being nice to me because of all the sex?' she murmured.

'The question is,' he sighed, 'do you just want me for my body?'

'Well, if you're offering,' she murmured.

Chapter Seventeen

'So, today's the day.' Luis sat on the end of the bed holding a glass of orange juice. 'Cassie, Fran and Mario all in the same place at the same time. You are coming this evening aren't you? Please ...'

'Yes I am, and I'm sure it will be fine.'

'You weren't there the last time.' He put the glass down and pulled on a T-shirt.

'When are they arriving?'

'Fran and Mario are landing in about two hours, and I think her partner will be over in a few weeks.'

Alice stretched and sat up. 'Well it may be Saturday, but I've got loads to do – another couple of hours in Gina's workshop on the tiles. She's not there today so I've got the key, and I've got to set up social media to link to the website, according to Kathy.'

'This month is going to be busy.' Luis sat down and scratched his face. 'I need to spend time getting to know Mario. But I don't want you to feel I'm letting you down.'

Alice kissed his neck. 'It's okay. It's an adjustment ... and it's real life, isn't it?'

'God, I'm so embarrassed about the state of the farmhouse. I don't want them to think I'm useless.'

'They don't think you're useless.' Alice put her arms around him. 'You're the one putting the pressure on yourself about the house, you know. It was going to be ready—'

'—when it was going to be ready,' he interrupted. 'Yes, but things have changed and now you have to move out of here.'

'But I don't know when, so please no more stress for you.'

'Easier said than done,' he said, standing up and picking up his keys. 'I'll pick you up around six. We're eating at a restaurant on the Guincho Road. Fran's booked.' He kissed her and walked to the door. 'Is there a way we can sedate Cassie?' he said. 'Just saying ...'

'I've got two more house viewings arranged for this afternoon,' she said quietly. But he had already gone.

As soon as the door shut behind him, Alice picked up her phone and looked at the message from her sister again. It was as if Luis had been protecting her from asking the question just by being there – the question she needed to ask but still didn't know if she wanted the answer to.

Whatever it is, I'm ready to hear it now x

No you are not, said the voice in her head.

She pressed send anyway.

Fran waved at Alice as she walked towards the table, her bump significantly bigger than it had been when they'd last met. Mario was following her, concentrating on his phone.

'*Ola*!' said Alice, as they hugged. 'You are looking very, very well. And hi, Mario.'

Mario looked up briefly. 'Hi,' he said, then turned his attention to the phone again.

'I can't get him off the damn thing,' whispered Fran. 'I wouldn't have let him have it, but you know, it seems to be everyone has them at his age now.' She sat down. 'Where's Luis?' she asked.

'He's in the car park with Cassie searching for her purse. She thinks she dropped it in his car.'

'Oh, yes. I thought I heard her. Anyway, how are you? Luis mentioned you're being featured in a magazine. That's fantastic.'

'Well, just a mention,' said Alice, feeling herself glow a bit. 'But it's all good.'

'Hello!' Cassie shouted from the doorway, waving her purse in the air. 'It was in my handbag all along. Dropped right to the bottom.'

Mario looked up, frowned and looked back at the phone. Luis sat down next to him. 'Hello,' he said awkwardly.

'Hello, Dad,' said Mario casually.

Luis' face lit up, and Alice's stomach did that loop the loop again.

'What a lovely evening,' said Fran, 'It's all blue and gold and red isn't it? What with the beach and the cliffs and the sky.'

'It's gorgeous.' Alice looked out of the window as dusty pink clouds hovered above the sea.

Cassie flopped down into her seat. 'So what have you been up to, Al? Making bracelets and whatever?'

'Yes, and painting tiles and website stuff.'

'I think it's great you get to do that.' Cassie grabbed her wrist. 'Is that one of yours?'

'Yes.'

'It's so pretty. What a job! Faffing around with beads and such. Still, if you can do it, why not!'

'It's—'

'—it's so funny, you and Luis finding each other. When he was back home in Melbourne studying architecture he used to go off taking photos and doing that busking stuff. I was working hard at my first job after uni and I used to look at him and wonder what he was playing at. Teased you rotten, didn't I?' She laughed.

Luis ignored her and tried to talk to Mario. Alice and Fran caught each other's eyes.

'Mum and Dad never thought he'd amount to anything, you know? Running away to Portugal after his fiancée left him like that for that guy who owned all those restaurants. Throwing away his degree like that.'

'He renovates houses,' said Alice, who could feel herself getting angry. 'And he's a successful photographer.'

'Yes, but it's not being an architect, is it? I mean I'm a solicitor; at least I used my degree. Why would you study something and not use it? What was your degree in, Alice?'

'Art,' said Alice.

'Oh, one of those.' Cassie laughed. 'Sorry ... no offence.'

'Cassie, can you think before you speak, please?' said Luis. 'Don't be rude to Alice or Fran.'

'I wasn't ... I didn't mean to. I apologise.' Cassie took a sip of water and stared out of the window.

'She spent the afternoon round the pool drinking champagne,' whispered Luis, before turning his attention back to Mario.

Just don't overreact, thought Alice. *It's all a bit stressful for everyone, so be calm. Be calm.*

Cassie waved at the waiter. 'Can we have some bread please? I'm famished. What about you, Fran. What's your job again? I didn't ask when we met in London.'

'I'm a primary school teacher,' Fran said with a fixed smiled on her face. 'It fitted in really well with Mario, with it being just him and me, you know.'

'Well, it will be easier with the father around this time.'

'Yes it will be.' Fran began to study the menu. 'The fish looks amazing.'

'They do a sea bass baked in salt,' said Alice. 'It's gorgeous.'

The waiter put a basket of bread on the table, and Cassie grabbed a piece and began to chew it. 'It must be so hard for single mothers you know ... trying to do everything.' She dropped her voice. 'I mean, they can't be expected to do as good a job as two parents, can they? It's not possible.'

After a few moments, Fran threw the menu down on the table. 'Look, that's really not fair. I think I've done a good job with Mario.'

'Sorry, sorry,' Cassie grimaced. 'My mouth gets the better of me sometimes. I didn't mean it like that.'

'My mother was a single parent for a few years,' Alice cut in.

Cassie looked at her blankly. 'Yep, it came out wrong. I apologise.'

Luis looked up, his face strained. 'Can we just talk about the weather and what you've been watching on television. Please?'

'Mum,' said Mario. 'Can I have the chicken?'

'Of course you can.'

'And can me and Alice go for a walk on the beach with Elvis?'

'If that's all right with you, Luis?'

He smiled. 'It'll be nice for you to have a chat with Alice and get to know her.' He took the car keys out of his pocket and passed them to her. 'Elvis is asleep in the back. Did you say you wanted the sea bass?'

'Yes please,' said Alice, trying not to run out of the restaurant to get away from the tension hovering around the table. She could almost see it in a cloud and it felt like it could burst at any time. Mario slid off his seat and followed her out to the car. Elvis's ears were visible in the window, and Mario laughed. 'What's he doing?'

'Probably biting his own foot or something. He's that kind of dog.' Alice opened the door and dug around on the floor for a plastic football he liked to chase as Elvis bounded out and skipped around Mario before trotting down the steps to the beach.

Mario followed him. 'Does he like to swim?' he asked as the dog headed straight to the shore.

Alice gave him the ball. 'He seems to like chasing the sea in and out but that's as far as it gets. Loves a paddle though. Why not throw this along the beach and see what happens.'

Mario took a run up and threw the ball into the distance, chuckling as Elvis ran after it, accidentally pushed it into the sea, then splashed around it whilst barking.

Alice smiled, recognising Luis in the way his eyes lit up when he was laughing. 'What's your villa like?'

'Cool. It's got a swimming pool and a trampoline. And there are bikes there, too. And trails through the woods.'

'Plenty for you to do then.'

'Does Cassie like me?' he said, beginning to search for shells.

'I'm sure she does.'

'She says things that aren't very nice. About checking Luis is my dad, and single parents and money and stuff.'

Alice looked at him, and knelt down, smoothing the sand to help him search. 'She doesn't think before she speaks. I think she's excited to have a new nephew.'

Mario sat down and took off his trainers, wiggling his toes to make a pattern, and Alice sat down next to him. Elvis dropped the retrieved ball in front of him and he threw it again.

'Alice ...?'

'Yes.'

'I'm frightened that my mum won't want me any more when the new baby is born.'

Alice stared at the waves cascading gently onto the beach.

'Your mother loves you very much,' she said evenly. 'And I think she is looking forward to you having a brother or sister.'

'Half brother or sister.'

'Families come in all shapes and sizes, Mario,' she said. 'Have you talked to your mother about this?'

'No.'

'I think you should talk to her, and she'll tell you herself.'

'I thought if we found my dad ... my real dad ... Luis ... that it wouldn't matter so much ... but Cassie ...'

'Forget about Cassie,' said Alice. 'She doesn't think before she speaks. Your father ... Luis ... is just so excited that you've found him. Me too. Really. He isn't used to it yet, though, so you both have to be a bit patient with each other.'

'Will you be my friend?'

Elvis dropped the ball in front of her. 'Of course I will be.'

'Cool,' he said, and Alice threw the ball again.

Her phone buzzed. Come back. Please ... HELP! L x

The waves continued to break calmly, but the spell was broken. 'I think our food has arrived. Time to get back.' Alice stood up as Elvis ran towards her, dropping the ball and shaking his fur dry, the water and sand splattering over her sundress. 'Elvis,' she sighed.

Mario laughed. 'You're funny,' he said, and they walked back up towards the restaurant side by side, leaving Elvis to sit in the shade by the window.

'We're all going to help Luis at the house tomorrow.' Cassie waved at them from the table.

'Oh, you said you might play with the band at lunch time?' Alice sat down. 'So you could relax a bit.'

'I just want to get on with it.' He smiled. 'The sooner I get it done the better. You are coming, aren't you?'

Alice glanced at Mario. 'It'll be really nice to spend time with you and Mario and Fran,' she said.

'And me!' shouted Cassie. 'Bobby is arriving on Thursday, so we'll be busy doing other things … ha ha … when he's not playing golf that is.'

'Oh blessed relief,' muttered Fran under her breath.

Luis checked his phone. 'In fact I'm going to go straight off after this – something's being delivered so I've got to be there. And I need to do some paperwork for my rental property – I've got behind over the past few weeks.'

'So, you're not at the apartment tonight?' said Alice quietly.

'Got the internet connection. No kitchen, no furniture and half of one bathroom, but at least I've got wi-fi.' He squeezed her hand. 'I've just got to catch up and get an early night … you understand, don't you?'

She nodded half-heartedly, taking a sip of her drink, then turned to talk to Fran.

Chapter Eighteen

'Well this is certainly a hive of activity,' said Ignacio as they got out of his car the following day. Luis and Mario were supervising whilst a workman in a digger was moving earth, and Cassie's frame could be seen in the kitchen window. Fran sat in the shade of a magnolia tree reading a book.

'I will just go in and say hello to Cassie,' said Ignacio. 'Out of politeness.'

'Hi.' Luis waved at her and walked over.

'This is all very impressive. How's it going?' Alice asked.

'It's going well. I've brought forward laying the foundations for the swimming pool.'

'Oh, okay.' Alice felt uneasy. 'I thought you were waiting until you'd finished the interior. And the exterior ...'

'I thought it would be more fun for Mario to watch a digger than help me paint,' said Luis. 'One of the guys in the band rents them out and let me have this cheap.'

'Okay, so you'll have a pool before a kitchen?'

'No – I'll get it lined and plumbed in but not tiled yet ... it's fine, I know what I'm doing.' He smiled but she could hear the irritation in his voice. 'Cassie has decided to get on with sorting out inside. She's brought a load of bin bags and is throwing out all of the rubbish.' He turned away and walked back to the hole in the ground. 'Her boyfriend has had to cancel his visit – last minute work, apparently. She's not in a good mood, so I decided to let her get on with it.'

'Alice!' Ignacio was at the door, waving at her to come over. 'Can you come in?'

'Is everything okay?' she asked as she stepped inside.

He didn't say anything but nodded towards the pile of rubbish on the floor. On the top were two photographs Alice had given Luis for the house, and her ceramic window.

She picked them up and leaned them against the wall.

'What are you doing?' Cassie was pushing piles of paper into a bag.

'These aren't to throw away,' said Alice.

'Yes … I found them upstairs. They're from the old house, aren't they? Luis always was a bit of a hoarder to be honest.'

'They aren't from the old house.' Alice felt her voice raise. 'They were for Luis to make the place a bit more homely for a while instead of it all just looking like a building site.'

'Calm down, calm down. Can't have any old stuff in the house. Soon enough it won't be a building site – may as well get rid of them now.'

'I took the photographs and I made the window. They are a gift.'

'Oh … sorry, I didn't mean to offend.' Cassie looked embarrassed.

'My photographs sell for quite a lot of money in a local gallery, and my ceramic windows were sold in town when I used to make them.' She felt Ignacio put his hand on her shoulder. 'So …' she trailed off, unable to find the words and began to walk upstairs. 'I'm going to get on with some painting.'

'No, it's fine. I've already put a first coat on one of the bedrooms. We've run out of paint.'

'Right.' Alice walked away then paused. 'That's good news. I've got an appointment to smoke some tiles anyway. New technique for me.' She walked outside, followed by Ignacio.

'I think she is only trying to help,' he said kindly.

Then why do I feel I'm being pushed out? she thought, putting her hand on the wall to anchor herself to something, that feeling of floating adrift hovering in the back of her mind.

'I know. But …' Alice sighed. 'She just seems to know when to say the wrong thing … at the right time.'

'I think she may be very unhappy, Alice,' said Ignacio. 'She's taken a break from her job, her new partner has let her down, her children are travelling … there's more to this than just a case of foot in mouth.'

'You are very wise.' Alice smiled. 'I've got plenty of things to do myself to be honest, if I'm not needed here. Could you drop me off at Gina's? She said I could paint more tiles if I had some time spare and have a go at that smoke firing thing.'

Ignacio's eyes lit up. 'It would be my pleasure,' he said.

Alice waved at Luis. 'I'm going to get on with some other things. You've got plenty of people here,' she shouted.

He ran over to her. 'Are you sure? Can't you stay?'

'I think that Cassie is happy working on her own in the house … only make sure she doesn't throw out anything of value.'

He pulled her to him. 'She's having a bit of a strop,' he whispered. 'When we were teenagers I learned to keep out of her way.'

'Coward,' whispered Alice. He kissed her and turned back to Mario. 'Yep. Yep I am.' He laughed.

'Gina … Gina …?' Alice knocked on the kitchen door. 'Hello?'

'What a pity,' said Ignacio. 'I have an airport pick-up to go to. I was hoping I would catch her for a moment.'

'She's usually in the workshop if she leaves the garden gate open,' said Alice. 'She must be here somewhere.'

'Well, send her my best,' said Ignacio as he walked back to the car.

Alice began to take some tiles out of a drawer and placed them next to her design.

'Oh, Alice.' Gina stood at the door looking flustered.

'Hello, are you okay? I knocked, but you were nowhere to be found.'

'Oh … I … there was …' Gina patted her hair. 'I can't make head nor tail of this, Alice,' she said, placing an instruction booklet on the table. 'I'm glad you're here. You can help.'

Alice picked it up. On the front was a picture of a small

brick structure and underneath a photograph of a beautifully finished ceramic bowl. 'I've never smoke fired anything before,' she said. 'It's new to me.'

'I've had it built around the corner out of the way, and I've been trying to get the fire going, but it's very frustrating. I'll show you.'

Alice followed her to the side of the house where the brick kiln had been put on some tarmac and filled with wood and straw.

'You're so very good at everything Alice. You can help, can't you?'

Alice almost looked over her shoulder to catch a glimpse of this other Alice who was very good at everything. 'Maybe we should do it together?'

Gina smiled. 'I've got three bags of sawdust and all of these twigs,' she said, walking over to the smoke kiln. 'And some firelighters and matches … I've kept it away from everything flammable to make sure it's contained and safe.'

Alice glanced again at the instructions. 'They look like they're in Dutch … do you speak Dutch?'

'Ah, yes, I got it from a family who were moving back to The Hague.'

Alice felt her phone buzz in her bag and checked the message.

I hope I didn't offend you. Cassie xxx

You sort of did, thought Alice, striding towards the new kiln. 'Let's do it, shall we? I'm sure we can work it out. I mean you *are* a professional artist, Gina.' She looked into it. 'As, in fact, am I,' she whispered.

After they loaded it, both women stood back and examined their handiwork. Alice picked up the paper again and showed it to Gina. 'It looks like we've put enough in there. Have you got any matches?'

Gina handed Alice a packet and stood back. 'I'm quite excited.' She giggled.

'Not sure if I am.' Alice knelt down and lit the match. 'I think we have to add twigs to it to keep it going,' she said.

They both sat on the floor, watching as the fire began to catch, occasionally putting in some more tinder and prodding it with a stick. 'This is rather relaxing,' sighed Alice.

'It will open up a whole new world of effects and finishes for the pottery, once we have worked out how to do it!' Gina laughed.

'When do you put the pottery in?' asked Alice as the flames began to grow.

Gina glanced at the instructions. 'Oh, I forgot I can't read them.' She stood up. 'Let's check the internet. Do you want some lemonade?'

Alice followed her inside the house, enjoying the respite from the heat of the fire and the sun. Gina picked up her phone and began to search for information. 'Would you get the lemonade from the fridge? I made it earlier. I can see the smoke kiln from here, so don't worry.' They looked out of the window. 'It's looking very healthy,' she said. 'Hopefully I can put some test pots in soon to see how it goes.'

Alice went into the kitchen and got some glasses out of the cupboard. 'By the way – has Kathy asked you to come for a night out in Lisbon? Karaoke – do you like singing?'

'Oh, that sounds nice. I must say since my husband died I've been just hiding away, but I'm feeling a lot more sociable lately. So yes... although does it have to be karaoke?'

'I'm afraid so.' As Alice began to pour the drinks, she heard a scream and shouting coming from outside, and rushed back into the living room to see Gina staring out of the window, confused. 'What on earth is that woman doing?' she whispered.

Alice followed her gaze. Cassie was in the garden emptying the contents of a five-litre bottle of water into the kiln.

'Putting out a fire by the looks of it,' said Alice, trying not to laugh.

'That took me all morning to organise,' muttered Gina rushing outside. 'Who are you?' she shouted. 'And what have you done to my smoke kiln?'

'There was smoke,' said Cassie sternly.

'There was supposed to be!' Gina shouted.

'This is Luis' sister,' said Alice, putting her hand on Gina's arm to make sure she didn't get any closer just in case. 'Hello, Cassie. What brings you here?'

'Oh, Alice. I made Luis bring me – I think I accidentally upset you back at the farmhouse and I didn't think an apologetic text was enough.'

Alice looked around. 'Where is he?'

'He had to make a phone call from the car. Thankfully he had a big bottle of water in it so I could put that out.'

'We can start another one,' said Alice. 'It's okay.'

Cassie rolled her eyes. 'I thought your barbecue was getting out of control. Honestly, I was just trying to be helpful.'

'I'm sure she was, Gina.' Alice smiled. 'It's quite funny really.' Gina didn't look like she was going to laugh. '... when you think about it.'

'I panicked,' sighed Cassie.

The corners of Gina's mouth began to twitch. 'It was quite a sight ... watching a strange woman pelt up the path and throw water at some bricks.'

'I saw it, ran back to the car, and ran back again.' Cassie began to laugh.

Gina sank to the floor and looked at the damp mess in the kiln. 'Oh dear.' She giggled. Alice sat down next to her. 'Do we have to wait for it to dry before we try again?'

Cassie sat down next to them. 'I'm sorry,' she said quietly.

'What was that all about?' Luis appeared from the other side of the house. 'You just took that bottle and ran?'

'She channelled her inner fireman.' Alice couldn't stop herself from giggling.

He smiled at the three women sitting on the floor. 'So, you're friends now? She managed to apologise?'

'She more than apologised,' said Alice. 'She also entertained.'

He sat down next to her. 'Us artistic types,' he sighed. 'Do you need a lift?'

'I've got to do some more for the mural,' said Alice. 'It's less exciting overall than this but has to be done.'

He kissed her. 'Well, I'd better get back to the farmhouse. No rest for the wicked. Come on, Cass.'

'Can you drop me at the hotel? I think I've had too much sun.' Cassie stood up and followed him along the path.

'See you girls.' Luis waved.

'Is there a song I could sing at the karaoke about trying to get this thing going again?' Gina picked up a nearby stick and began to prod the twigs in the kiln.

'Relight My Fire!' Alice laughed, scrambling to her feet.

Cassie turned. 'Did I hear the word karaoke?' she shouted. 'Count me in! I need to cheer myself up seeing as Bobby's let me down.'

Gina looked up at Alice. 'She seems nice.'

'Of course. I'll let you know when Kathy sorts out the times and transport.' *There may be trouble ahead*, the voice in her head whispered.

'See you soon, and it was nice to meet you, Gina' said Cassie, disappearing from view. 'And like I said, Alice … sorry.'

The next few days flew by – Alice working hard on her bracelets and designs, and Luis dividing his time between work, getting to know Mario and renovating the house. Even Cassie seemed to have calmed down, arranging to see her friends nearby instead of getting involved with the building work.

So when the planned big night out in Lisbon arrived, Alice

was almost looking forward to dressing up and having some fun.

She carefully picked out a long, blue, silky sundress, applied her make-up, tousled her hair and stared at herself in the mirror for a few moments. *I have come a long way*, she thought, remembering how pale and drawn she was when she first arrived in Portugal all that time ago. 'I look almost healthy.'

Alice put on her sandals, sprayed some perfume on her neck and went down to the road to meet the transport that Kathy had organised, which she assumed was a taxi. But as the bright pink limo turned the corner and halted next to her, she wondered if the driver thought she was someone else. Because this couldn't be it. But it was, because Kathy jumped out and gave her a hug. 'Party time! I'm so excited, Alice. You've no idea how excited I am.'

'This is very pink.' Alice giggled.

'I don't get out much.' Kathy got back in the car. 'Come on.'

'He's going to put the hood back up though, isn't he?' shouted Cassie. 'I don't want Bridget Jones hair when we get to the bar.'

Kathy smiled in a gritted teeth kind of way. 'That's why I bought the scarves – like I said. I did watch the film, you know?'

Alice stepped in and was handed a drink by Gina. 'This is all very … very … new to me'

Kathy passed her a piece of silk material. 'Wrap it around your head, darling. We're driving down The Marginal topless.'

Gina looked horrified.

Alice touched her arm. 'She means we're keeping the car roof open.'

'What's The Marginal?' Cassie took a swig from her glass.

'The road along the river into Lisbon.' Alice put on her seat belt. 'On the day I first arrived, Ignacio took the route from the airport to Cascais so I could get the best view.' She sighed at the memory. 'I'll never forget it, the sea sparkled in the sun as if it was full of millions and millions of sapphires.'

'How lovely,' said Gina softly.

'Thank you for inviting me, ladies.' Cassie took another sip. 'I have to say I've been feeling pretty miserable over the past few days knowing Bobby had to cancel. So this will cheer me up.'

'You're very welcome,' said Kathy, standing up. 'Drive on ... driver!' she shouted. 'Lisbon here we come.' She pointed dramatically into the distance.

The chauffeur turned his head. 'I'm afraid you have to sit down and do up your seat belt before I can begin our journey, madam.'

'Sorry,' she muttered, sitting down with a bump. 'Just a sec.' She fiddled with the belt for a few moments. 'There we are. All done. So, drive on, driver,' she shouted again. 'Not as effective as last time though, is it?'

The car began to move, turning onto the sea road and joining the evening traffic making its way towards the city.

'So how was your day, ladies? Hard at work creating fripperies. Have you ever had a real job? You know nine to five?' asked Cassie.

'I beg your pardon?' Gina poured another glass of wine.

'Floating around making pretty things.' Cassie laughed.

Alice shook her head at Gina. 'She has a tendency to speak before thinking ...' she said quietly.

'I believe that is what is known as putting your foot in your mouth, Cassie,' said Kathy firmly. 'Shall we all enjoy the journey? Because I am having a night out for the first time in quite a while, and I fully intend to enjoy it.'

Cassie sighed loudly, rummaged around in her bag and began to scroll through the messages on her phone. 'You know, I thought when I took a career break I'd enjoy being away from all of the politics, the long, long hours, the stress, but I can't stop checking my e-mails. And when there's nothing there, I feel irrelevant.'

'You're not irrelevant.' Gina smiled kindly.

'Oh, that's nice of you to say, but you really wouldn't understand.' Cassie carried on scrolling. 'I was … sorry am … a senior partner in an international law firm. Your e-mails are all about ceramic mugs, I expect. No offence.'

Gina poured more wine in her glass and stared out of the window.

'God, I'm so sorry.' Cassie put her arm around her. 'Like I said, the words come out and then I realise what I've said. And I've been drinking.'

Gina nodded politely but didn't say anything.

Alice leaned forward. She was about to say 'You can't keep saying things like that and apologising afterwards. You can't say it then take it back. Because it's said.' But Kathy put her hand on Alice's arm, smiled and shouted 'Let's practice singing. How about "The Sound of Silence"!'

Alice began to laugh. Gina's shoulders began to shake, and she started to giggle. Cassie bit her lip, then began to sing quietly. She paused. 'I suppose if you give me lyrics to sing, at least we'll all know what's going to come out of my mouth.'

Kathy waved her arm in the air. 'I'm counting us in … one, two, three … and they started to sing as the car headed east along the river towards the city.

The car pulled into a space close to an old archway at the top of a hill. 'I can't park any nearer,' the driver said. 'When you are ready to leave, can you text me and I will be here within fifteen minutes?'

They clambered out onto the pavement. 'Where are we?' asked Gina. 'None of this looks familiar.'

Kathy checked her phone. 'We're in Biarro Alto, and the club is through here, then we turn left.'

'It's very hilly,' muttered Cassie.

'Lisbon is hilly,' said Kathy. 'Come on, ladies. Follow me.

We're two minutes away. Oh ...' She waved the phone at Alice. 'This has come up on the map. I've been meaning to mention this to you anyway ... look.'

Alice stared at the screen. 'I don't know what you're pointing at.'

'Just down the bottom of that hill and to the left, there's this place. You'll love it. Full of tiles and light. It's called ... Casa Andrade ... it's a community hub in a very old building, and anyone can pop in and see it.'

Alice smiled. 'I'll put it on my list of places to visit.' They turned the corner.

'Here we are.' Kathy pointed at a building half-way up the street.

'It doesn't look very inviting.' Alice looked at the half-hearted neon sign above the door, glowing a limp pink. '*Fechado*,' it said.

'Why's the bar called "Closed"?' Cassie asked.

'It's a joke.' Kathy stepped forward and pushed open the door, the distant beat of an unidentifiable song creeping down the corridor. 'Come on, ladies. We're here for some fun!'

'Where's Gina?' Alice turned around. 'Gina?'

'She hasn't run away, has she?' Cassie leaned against a wall and adjusted the strap on her shoe. 'Honestly, these cobbles are not good for three-inch heels.'

'You do look like you're trying to walk on a boat during a force ten gale.' Kathy laughed.

'I hear you ... or walking through a bowl of jelly.'

'Or on a trampoline!'

Cassie stood up and took some lip gloss out of her bag. 'Armour on!' she said.

'Gina?' Alice walked back down the hill. 'Gina?'

'Alice ...' A voice whispered from the darkness. 'Here.'

Alice stood for a moment, scanning the street, then noticed her friend standing on the steps of a nearby alleyway. 'Thank goodness. I thought we'd lost you.'

'I'm not sure about this, Alice. I mean, singing in public …
I can't sing.'

'Neither can I!'

'Can we just go to a nice little bar and look at the view?'

'I would love that. But I promised Kathy that I'd come, and
it's her night. We don't have to sing. We could just watch.'

'It does look a bit tatty from the outside. I'm not sure I
want to go in.'

Alice walked towards her, holding out her hand. 'It's got
great write-ups. Apparently it's the best in Lisbon, so we'll
be fine. Shall we jump out of our comfort zones? It's an
adventure. Kathy's a big one for adventures.'

Gina grabbed her hand. 'Okay. It's only a couple of hours,
I suppose.'

'That's the spirit. Come on. Let's live a bit dangerously.'

Only it's not dangerously, thought Alice. *It's just a bar,
with some music, and some noise, and some alcohol. And
Cassie, who actually at the moment does feel just a little bit
dangerous.*

'What's the problem?' Cassie waved at them from the
doorway.

'We'll be there in a sec,' shouted Alice. 'You go in.'

'Maybe we won't be able to hear her so much inside,'
muttered Gina.

'Gina! That's not like you.' Alice laughed. 'Shall we?'

They headed back up to the club, pushed open the door
and walked into the darkness, the music becoming louder
and louder as they moved up the stairs. They soon found
themselves in a room full of tables with people clustered
around them, drinking and laughing. A man on stage was
singing 'Bat Out of Hell,' with a considerable amount of
passion.

Alice could feel her mood lift immediately.

'Goodness,' shouted Gina.

'Ohhh,' shouted Alice.

Kathy waved at them from a nearby table. 'Over here!' She pointed at a book in front of her. 'I've got the list of songs, girls.'

Cassie joined them with three bottles of champagne. 'Not quite one each, but I thought we'd hang back for a while. The champers is on me!'

The song finished and two women got up and began to sing 'I Will Survive'.

'The good news is, it's early, so if we put our names down soon, we won't have long to wait for our first performances.' Kathy's eyes glowed.

'A toast,' shouted Cassie. 'Thank you for inviting me, ladies. I'm so bereft about Bobby ... I don't know what I'd have done. And I miss my babies, even though they're both twenty-one ... they're still my babies.'

Alice picked up her glass and drank the champagne in one gulp.

Cassie scanned the room. 'I'm sure hidden in the darkness here is someone that will make me happy later. If you know what I mean.'

Alice filled her glass again. *I just want to have fun*, she thought. *Looking after actual babies and teenagers is absolutely fine but babysitting an overgrown child ...*

Not like you, nice, kind, thoughtful, accepting Alice, said the voice in her head. *About bloody time.*

She stood up and walked to the organiser to write down her song, then weaved back through the tables to her seat.

'What's happened to you in the last five minutes?' shouted Kathy into her ear.

'Two glasses of champagne,' she said. 'And I'm fed up of being the adult around here. So I'm announcing that in the form of a song.'

'Excellent. I assumed we'd all go on together as you said you couldn't sing.'

'I can't sing.' Alice took another sip of champagne. 'And I don't care. I don't know anyone here.'

Gina leaned forward. 'Isn't that Saul Pires, the chef?' She nodded over to the bar, where he stood chatting with two friends. 'I tore out some of his recipes from a magazine when I was at the hairdressers last week.'

'He was on TV on some BBC cookery show a couple of weeks ago,' squeaked Cassie. 'He's very attractive, isn't he? Very sexy.'

'He's on TV?' Kathy kicked Alice under the table. 'He's on TV.'

Alice felt her heart begin to race, and pretended not to hear. 'Oh dear,' she muttered, turning to look at the stage in an effort to make herself invisible.

Cassie stood up. 'I'm going to put my name down for a song, too.'

They watched as she walked slowly past the bar towards the stage, trying unsuccessfully to catch Saul's eye on her journey there and back. 'I've chosen "You Make Me Feel Like a Natural Woman".' She laughed. 'Let's order some shots.'

As her arm went up to summon a waiter, Alice slowly lowered it. 'Maybe later,' she said.

'I think we should definitely all sing something together,' said Kathy. 'That way Gina can sing and hide at the same time.'

'Can't I just watch?'

'No, Gina, you can't,' said Kathy. 'We are all experiencing new things tonight. Except it seems for Cassie, who is behaving as if she has done this a lot before. You will regret it tomorrow if you don't try.'

Gina picked up her glass, gulped her drink, then nodded. 'All right. I will. Just once.'

Kathy got up. 'I have decided it will be "Love Shack", everyone.'

Alice felt rooted to the spot and desperate to run away at the same time. *I want to sing*, she thought, *loudly and tunelessly, as if no one is watching. But I know he will be. And I know Cassie will say something about it.*

All the more reason to do it.

Alice smiled to herself. *Yes it is.*

'Next it's Alice Matthews,' shouted the compère. She knew Saul would be looking for her when he heard her name, but she kept her gaze ahead, taking a bottle of champagne from the ice bucket, and her glass, then walking defiantly to the stage. She had no idea who she was defying, but if felt good. The spotlight glared into her eyes as she poured herself a drink, took the microphone and tried to focus on the screen with the lyrics on.

'This is for you, Kathy. My bestie ... and you Gina ... and you ... Cassie ...' she trailed off as the music started and launched into 'Don't Rain on My Parade'. As she sang, all the people in the room disappeared, and it was just her and the music and, for a few minutes, everything just fell away. Luis wasn't stressed and irritable. She didn't care that someone was buying every house she wanted in Cascais. Moving out of Mary and Frank's flat very soon was not a problem. Cassie's ability to cause friction wherever she went did not matter at all. And Saul Pires was not standing by the bar. Most of all, Alice had never been abandoned by her father. He did not exist. He. Did. Not. Exist. As the last chords played, the room came slowly back into focus and she could hear the cheering and whooping from the audience. She laughed and waved at Kathy. 'I want to do it again,' she mouthed.

'In ten minutes you will!' mouthed Kathy back.

She took another sip of her drink, took her bottle and walked down the steps back to the table. Out of the corner of her eye she noticed Saul looking at her and stared steadily ahead, pretending he wasn't there.

'Good shouting!' laughed Kathy as Cassie got up and walked to the stage via the bar. Saul didn't notice.

Alice felt the need to zone out again, or at least not be there during Cassie's performance, which was directed at an oblivious Saul, so she decided to get some air and sidled out, hoping no-one would notice. The street was empty except for a few pigeons, the cobbles lit by a stream of moonlight. Alice stood at the top of a flight of steps that tumbled towards the river enjoying the stillness as she watched a ferry chug its way across.

'That was funny.' Saul touched her arm and smiled.

'Oh, hello. What a surprise! What was funny?' Alice stepped back slightly and noticed his dark, dangerous eyes again. She felt an unwelcome tingle of electricity, so glanced away from his face and focused on a doorway behind him to try to push it away.

'Alice, I know you saw me in there.'

She smiled and nodded. 'Yes, well, I was a bit embarrassed to be honest.'

'I thought your performance was most excellent.'

'Well, I think that's a compliment.'

'I'm glad I've seen you. I have a proposition.'

Alice stepped back again.

'No.' He laughed. 'Not that kind of proposition. Duarte showed me your bracelet designs and told me you are doing the interior of a local café?'

'Yes, that's right.'

'Well, I was very impressed with those pictures of the house in London you showed me. Do you remember? And with all of that in mind, I'd like you to come up with an idea for a room in one of my restaurants. It's for parties and things like that.'

'Oh,' Alice said, the champagne fuzzing her brain. 'That's …'

'I'll text you tomorrow when you're not in party mode.'

'Party mode … that's unusual for me.'

He laughed again. 'I'd better get back.'

'Me too.' They walked together up the stairs, Alice ensuring there was distance between them so that Cassie wouldn't jump to conclusions. Her foot caught in her dress as she climbed the last step, making her stumble into Saul as they walked into the room, and he held out his hand to steady her.

'Thanks,' Alice mumbled.

Alice noticed a flash as if someone was taking a photo.

'Who's the tall girl that sang the Aretha Franklin song?' he asked, pausing by the door.

'Cassie ... Luis' sister. My partner's sister.'

'She's ... full on, isn't she?'

'Yes she is,' Alice said quietly.

'Where've you been?' Kathy grabbed her and pulled her to the stage. 'We're on.'

'I didn't know you knew Saul Pires,' whispered Cassie. 'You looked rather close.'

'It's work, nothing else,' said Alice, her heart sinking. *Here we go*, she thought. *Something ... I can feel something coming.*

'Put a good word in for me?'

'What about?'

'What goes on tour stays on tour.' Cassie winked. 'By the way, I've taken a photo of you two. Put it on Twitter already.'

'You what? Why?'

'And Instagram and Facebook. He's a big deal. Or will be. It'll be good for your business.'

Alice walked back to the table, poured herself another large glass of champagne and strode back to the stage. *Oh bloody hell*, she thought. *Bloody hell. I don't know why this isn't good. But it isn't good.*

As the music began to play, she noticed Saul engrossed in conversation with a beautiful young woman by the bar. Relieved, Alice began to enjoy herself again, and picked up a spare microphone. Gina had overcome her shyness by drinking copious amounts of alcohol and was singing loudly and happily, whilst Kathy was alternatively singing and laughing. Cassie's eyes were fixed on Saul and the young woman, and before the last notes had played out she almost rushed off the stage towards the bar, putting herself between them.

'She ordered shots,' said Kathy. 'You weren't there to stop her.'

Alice watched, horrified, as a glass on the counter was somehow knocked onto the woman's dress, who seemed to retaliate by throwing wine over Cassie. Saul tried to intervene as two bouncers rushed towards them and ushered a screaming Cassie down the stairs. It was over within minutes.

Gina put her hand over her mouth. 'Oh my goodness,' she said.

Kathy looked at Alice and started to laugh almost hysterically.

The effects of the champagne disappeared instantaneously as another bouncer grabbed Alice's arm. 'You have to leave,' he said.

'Why?'

'You were with a woman who attacked one of our managers.'

'Well, it's nothing to do with me.'

But he wasn't listening and pulled her forward, whilst a colleague guided Gina and Kathy downstairs and out of the door.

'Oh, I've never been thrown out of anywhere before,' whispered Gina. 'That was very, very exciting.'

Cassie stood in the middle of the street, wiping her dress. 'Thank God it's not red wine,' she said. Then looked at Alice. 'Does Luis know how close you and Saul are?'

'We're not.'

'Didn't look like it to me,' she said, walking off down the street. 'You know, it's all right for you, Alice, isn't it? Moving over here, making bracelets. Everything is just fun. You don't know about the real world. The corporate world. Bringing up children. Hard work.'

Alice stared at her, then looked at Kathy and Gina, who were leaning against a wall, laughing to themselves. 'Did you hear?'

What does she mean, it's all right for me? It's not all right for me. It's not just all right for anyone.

'Hear what?' said Kathy.

Cassie paused to take off her shoes.

'It's not all right for me, Cassie,' she shouted. 'You can't say that to people just because you're angry at your life. You've no idea what's going on with any of us. How dare you.'

Cassie picked up her shoes. 'Don't you hurt my brother,' she said.

Alice stared at her, trying to control her anger. She was not going to let her do this. No-one was going to do this to her again. 'Don't you dare stir things up. Don't you dare.'

God, is that you, Alice? said the voice in her head.

'Car's waiting at the end of the street,' shouted Kathy, who seemed not to have noticed the argument at all. 'Come on, girls. What a great night. I'm officially exhausted.'

They all piled into the car. Alice and Cassie looking out of their windows so they didn't have to speak to each other, whilst Gina and Kathy dozed for the duration of the journey home. Alice was the last to be dropped off and, as the limo pulled up to the apartment block, her phone rang.

'Alice. Are you okay?' Luis' voice was deep and sleepy.

'Yes, I'm fine. It's really late. Are you all right?' she asked, confused.

'I've just had Cassie on the phone a little worse for wear, crying and wailing. What's going on?'

She thought for a moment. 'There was some silly thing that happened at the bar. She drank too much and ...' Alice got out of the car and took out her purse to pay the driver.

'She was saying things about Saul Pires. Was he there?'

'Yes he was.'

He paused. 'What was he doing there?' Alice sat on a bench

in the garden and lowered her voice. 'There with friends, I think, and talking to a woman. That's when Cassie—'

'—she said you were talking to him outside for ages,' he cut in.

'I went out for some air and he came out and offered me some work.'

'Work?'

'Yes. Designing the interior for a room in one of his restaurants.'

There was another pause. 'Are you going to take it?'

'Not sure ... why has Cassie been crying and wailing?'

'She said you were flirting with him and when she walked over to talk to you, there was a bit of an accident and alcohol got spilt.'

'Thrown.'

'You threw alcohol?'

'No. He was talking to somebody, who I assume to be his girlfriend. Cassie decided to get involved, tripped and threw her drink over both of them.'

'She said ...'

'What?' Alice could feel her stomach lurch.

'That she thought he was coming on to you, so she—'

'—no. Nope. No.' Alice's voice began to rise. 'Cassie drank too much and tried to get Saul's attention. But it didn't work. She took a photo of me talking to him, then posted it on Twitter, for God's sake.'

'Christ.'

'Yes. It's so stupid.'

'But I don't trust Saul Pires,' he said.

'I'm really confused about this. What on earth is the matter with you?'

'I just—'

'—you really mean you think he's interested in me?' Alice could feel her voice get louder. 'And even if he is, which he isn't, don't you trust me?'

He sighed. 'Yes, yes, I'm sorry. Again ...'

Alice sat for a moment, listening to the silence. 'Your sister ...' she began.

'I know.'

'Why are we even having this conversation, Luis? Why are you in the farmhouse and not here with me?'

He sighed. 'I'm trying to finish it.'

'Why?'

'I just need to.' He paused. 'Look it's 2 a.m. I'm getting up early to take Mario on a boat trip. I'm tired and stressed and ... oh God, my mother's trying to ring from Australia. For Christ's sake, Cassie.'

'Well, goodnight, then,' she said. 'I'm going to bed.'

The phone went dead. She looked up at the black, star-scattered sky and wanted to scream at him, and at Cassie, and at Saul Pires. But she just walked slowly to the apartment and threw herself into bed. As she closed her eyes, her phone began to ping over and over again. She examined it, confused. The photo of her and Saul, was being tweeted and retweeted alongside another photo taken by someone else of Cassie, Saul and the woman by the bar involved in an argument. 'Oh God,' she said, then switched the phone off.

Chapter Nineteen

'Ah, you are in disguise.' Carlos was standing outside the café watching Alice march into the square for a morning meeting with him and Ignacio. She was wearing her biggest straw hat. 'Just in case the paparazzi are lying in wait.'

'Ha, ha,' said Alice, sitting down.

He pulled a chair out and laughed. 'You don't have to keep your hat on with me, though. I know you're under there.'

'I would just like to say that all of that was nothing to do with me. It was Cassie. And she took the photo. And posted it. I've only just got an account, to be honest, to publicise my jewellery.'

'It will all blow over,' he said. 'But nothing blows over with Ignacio here.' Carlos nodded at his brother who was walking towards them. 'Him and his obsession with the past.'

Ignacio sat at the table opposite. '*Bom dia*,' he said, nodding at Carlos coldly.

'Okay,' said Alice briskly. 'Let's get on, shall we? I've got delivery information here and who needs to do what and when. I've done you both a copy of the logistics.'

'Have you spoken to Luis today?' Ignacio sounded sympathetic.

'He was taking Mario out on his friend's boat early, so no.' *Well, technically I did speak to him today, if you count 2 o'clock in the morning*, she thought.

'Quite a business last night.'

Alice sighed. 'It was nothing to do with me. I've got too much work to do to care.' She looked at Carlos and Ignacio sitting on different tables and barely talking to each other. *Not long ago, when I came back from London*, she thought, *everyone was fine. We were all happy, all hopeful. Now we are all arguing. All of us.* She closed her laptop and switched it off.

'It's all there on the paper, actually. I've got to go.'

'But we need to discuss this. We have to close for the refurb very soon,' said Carlos.

'I've just got to go. Just read it through and let me know if you have any questions.'

'Where are you going?' Ignacio stood up and held her hand.

'Just somewhere,' she said. 'Just ...' She put her bag over her shoulder, turned the corner and walked across the road towards the main street, not sure where somewhere was. When she stopped she was standing next to the ticket office at the railway station. Alice looked down at her feet. *Can we run away for a while?* she thought. *Anywhere. Anywhere nice. You decide.*

The trains go to Lisbon, so ... muttered the voice in her head.

She looked at her feet again. *I'll check again when I get there, then.*

She put on her headphones and sat, staring out of the window as the train passed through the whitewashed suburbs towards the city, seeing nothing but the blur of pink, blue and yellow of the houses as it sped on.

It slowly pulled into the station and she stepped off, following the other passengers and then stood, looking at the river. She glanced down at her feet again, then across to the south banks of the Tagus and remembered the short boat ride she had taken with Saul a few weeks before across the Sado to Duarte's hotel and how tranquil it had felt on the other side, just for a while.

Oh, I want that back, she thought. *Maybe looking at this side of the river from that side of the river will make all this feel a bit less rubbish. Rubbish. That's what it is: rubbish.* So, she bought a ticket for the ferry and sat allowing the breeze to soothe her body and lift her mood. As it did, Lisbon got smaller and smaller, and with it, the arguments seemed further and further away. By the time she arrived at Cacilhas on the southern bank, she felt almost relaxed and bought a coffee and a *bifana* for lunch at a nearby café, never losing sight of the hills and multicoloured houses of the city in the distance.

Alice watched the river traffic going back and forth for a while, allowing her mind to go blank, the tooting of horns and lapping of the water on the bank an almost melodic accompaniment to the day. She ordered an orange juice and took her phone out of her bag, staring at it for a moment, then putting it back, still turned off. Eventually the sun moved further to the west so that her table sank into the shade, the heat of the day beginning to diminish, and she felt Lisbon waiting for her return.

She made her way back to the boat terminal, but by the time she eventually stepped off the ferry on the other bank her mind began to whirr anxiously again. *Cassie was like a female version of Adam*, she thought, *putting people down and trying to control them. And Luis and his problem with Saul Pires ... Saul had offered her a great opportunity*. The memory of the first night near Duarte's hotel and that momentary flash of something flew into her mind's eye.

'Stop it, Alice,' she said aloud. 'It was nothing. Absolutely nothing. I don't want it to be anything.'

A Cascais-bound train was about to leave, but as she looked at the departure board at the station, something clicked again and she turned and walked east along the river, remembering the beautiful hidden building Kathy had mentioned, and deciding that she would rather explore that than go home and deal with everyone else.

The non-descript doorway was set back between two restaurants in a busy street in the centre. She pushed it open and began to climb the steps. The top of the stairwell opened into a wide, ornate room, with tiles on the floors, the walls and the ceiling of blues, scarlets, browns and yellows, decorated with intricate shapes and designs. Its beauty took Alice's breath away, and she stood for a moment by a fountain in the middle of the room, studying it all, then stepped forward and examined the walls more closely, almost hypnotised by the lines and shades on the individual squares. Light streamed in from a skylight, and she spun slowly around so she could enjoy the full magic of it.

Heaven, this is heaven, she thought, and shivered with excitement, her heart lifting briefly, almost forgetting the sense of constantly shifting sands under her feet. She took out her camera and began to take photographs, feeling, for just a few moments, anchored to something familiar. Music began to drift down from a room above, and she turned, following it along a corridor to another staircase and up to a hallway which led into a grand chandeliered room where couples were dancing to a slow, haunting song. Time stood still as she watched and tried to commit the scene to memory, knowing that no photograph could capture or recreate the serenity and grace of what she was seeing.

Footsteps behind her brought her back from her thoughts. She knew it was him before he spoke.

'I thought you'd take yourself off somewhere like this. Kathy told me you'd probably be here,' he said quietly, touching her hand. 'Once again, Alice, I have been an idiot.'

She turned and smiled sadly. 'Luis, for once I agree with you.'

He caught her gaze and held it, and she knew he was trying to find the right words. She wanted to help him, but it had to come entirely from him. All of it.

'I have been so frightened of losing you, that it seems that I am …'

She grabbed his hands. 'No. No, you aren't. I just…'

'It's a mess isn't it? And I've been trying to make up ten

years with Fran and Mario, and I can't. And somewhere in the middle I am letting you drift away.'

'And then you pushed.'

He took a deep breath. 'I did. Your classic insecure, in-denial male.'

'Trying to prove something to everyone, including me.'

'You are the most important person in the world to me, Alice. I'm sorry. I'm so, so sorry.'

She put her fingers gently on his mouth. 'Apology accepted.'

He took her hand and kissed her palm. 'Can I be with you tonight?' he said. 'I am spending too much time away from you. I miss you when you're not there. I miss us, I miss the curves and softness of you.'

Alice pulled his lips to hers and kissed him. 'Yes, yes you can. If you put it like that.'

He smiled at her for the first time in what had felt like weeks as the singer began another song.

'This is gorgeous,' sighed Alice. 'What's it called?'

'*Chuva* ... rain' he said. 'You know I've never been here. In all the years I have lived so close. And it is stunning.'

'It's breathtaking,' said Alice, her attention drawn by the dancers again.

'Dance with me,' he whispered.

'I'd love to,' she murmured.

So he took her hand and led her onto the floor, surrounded by the other couples dressed in their finery. Alice was wearing a pair of green patterned trousers, Luis' shirt splattered with paint, but that didn't matter. They fell into each other, feeling the other's heartbeat, sensing their breathing, and barely moving.

'I love you,' he said.

'I love you.'

And as the song came to a close, they lingered whilst the other dancers moved back to their tables, not wanting to break the spell. Eventually he squeezed her hand. 'Shall we go?' he said.

'I've had twenty orders already for bracelets.' Alice was sitting on the balcony the following morning going through her e-mails as Luis scrolled through messages on his phone.

'Oh, that's brilliant. I'm going to give you a congratulatory kiss.' He stroked her arm. 'I'd congratulate you in other ways too if I didn't have to rush off and catch up with the refurb in Lisbon.'

'Maybe later, tiger.' Alice laughed.

'Said I'd take Mario on a tram – Fran's bringing him in. You can come too?'

'No – it's fine. I've booked myself into a yoga class later. I'm spending too much time hunched over making things so need a bit of a stretch.'

'Right.' He jumped up. 'Just going to grab a shower then I'll be off.'

A bird flew from the tree opposite and settled on the balcony trellis. '*Ola*,' she said. 'I'm going to miss this place when I go.' It looked at her for a moment then swept down to the gardens and began pecking at some crumbs someone had thrown under a parasol. She went inside and began to take out her jewellery-making box, putting it down on the table next to the extra sets of baubles, beads, ribbons and wire she had ordered just before the website launched.

Her phone rang. Tara's name came up. She looked at it for a moment, wondering whether to ignore it and call her later. But she'd been running away from this particular issue for years, she knew it. It was time.

'Hi,' she said, 'How's things?'

'All fine here. What about you? Your website's looking good … and that Twitter thing with the tasty chef!'

'That was just a … someone stirring things up,' sighed Alice. 'So …'

Tara paused. 'Our biological father is living in Vancouver,' she said quickly. 'I know he has two children and one grandchild.'

'When did you start looking for him?' Alice could feel her heart begin to race.

'It's the children – when I had them, I just decided I wanted to know more, and you went into lockdown because of Adam and everything, so whenever I raised the subject ...'

'... you didn't.'

'I did! Oh, I did. It was just after he left you for the first time and you were in such a state, then he came back, left you again and I didn't want to push you. So I talked to Mum, and we decided to just do it quietly ... Alice are you crying?'

'No.' But she was. Another thing she'd delayed because of Adam. Because of someone else. 'Right, so how did you find all this out?'

'Social media can be a marvellous thing. It can be a bad thing, but in this instance it helped.'

'So, he has had two daughters and a grandchild who he has managed to be with, but not us?'

'If you put it like that ...'

'It is like that.'

'Maybe he's changed.'

Alice paused. 'Maybe.'

'Do you want me to send you the link to his Facebook page? You can't see much because of privacy but there's a photograph of him and his family.'

'Okay.' Alice knew she wouldn't like it. But she had to see it.

'And I was going to try to contact him. Friend him or something. I mean he was an orphan and only child so there's no relatives who really knew us.'

'Or not even about us ...'

'Are you happy with that?'

'Happy's not the word, but if you want to, go ahead.' Alice couldn't speak any more. 'I've got to go. Bye.'

She put the phone down and looked out at the gardens without really seeing anything for a few minutes, then she looked at her messages. Tara had sent the link and Alice stared at it before deciding to open it. There was a photograph of a family group posing happily outside a house. A smiling man, next to a smiling woman, next to two smiling younger women and a smiling little boy. There was a mountain in the background and there were trees and there was sun, and it looked perfect.

Alice wondered if he had paid for the house, or if they had ever had to argue with the building society about defaulting on the mortgage as her mother had done when he left. And the second time he left. Or if he had ever abandoned those two pretty young women when they were four and seven years old. And did that woman standing next to him really stop him from contacting his first family? And if she did, what right did she have to smile like that? And if she didn't and it was all him, as Alice suspected it was, what right did he have to look so content? Did he ever think of his two other daughters, Tara and Alice? Did he ever wonder what had happened to them?

She could feel herself begin to shake with anger and closed the link before she started to scream. *I don't want this*, she thought. *I don't want that man to make me feel like this.*

She could hear Luis inside picking up his keys.

'I'm off. Are you sure you don't want to come later?' he shouted.

Alice stood up, breathing in slowly to stop the shaking. 'I can't. See you tomorrow?'

He walked onto the balcony. 'Can't tomorrow – I'm going to the farmhouse to catch up again – not there all day today. Are you okay?'

'Yes. Just thinking about what I need to do,' she lied.

He took his phone out of his pocket. 'I only went on social media because Duarte said I should promote my photos at the hotel, but my phone keeps telling me when there are new notifications,' he said, irritated. 'I'm going to have to change the settings or something.'

Alice saw a cloud pass over his face. 'Cassie's posted another photo of you with Saul Pires.'

'What? Why? I mean how many did she take?'

'He opened the link. 'She's put a link to a … oh, you're mentioned on the website of that glossy magazine … about your jewellery.'

'Oh, I thought that wasn't out till next month.'

'This bit is online I think the article is longer in the mag. He's got his arm around you, and in the next one he looks like he's virtually nibbling your ear.' Luis looked up at her. 'Please don't say you …'

Alice took his phone. 'That's just the angle – look – you can see.' She waved it in front of him, 'And the first one was him just catching me because I tripped up the last step. You can't really think …!'

'It looks—'

'—it doesn't look like anything. I think that's his girlfriend in the background.'

'He's got a—'

'—reputation. I know … but I haven't!' Alice stared at him.

'Well, it's just as well you haven't said yes to doing that room to him yet.' Luis put the phone back in his pocket and turned towards the door.

'I haven't said yes or no, Luis.'

'I thought you said—'

'—I didn't, and this is my future, you know? Thinking about it, it would be good for my career.'

'Like I said, I don't trust him. Cassie told me he was all over you. And now she's told my mother. She was on and on at me after Cassie phoned her. For Christ's sake, as if things aren't difficult enough.'

Alice could feel it coming, and she tried to stop it, but it was like a tidal wave engulfing her. 'I have to trust you, don't

I? Resolving yet another issue from your past behaviour with other women, spending time with a woman who you got pregnant, and you are asking me not to do something that may be good for me? You are asking me to wait and stand and watch? And you don't trust me!'

Luis looked like he'd been slapped.

'I'm so tired of doing the right thing all the time, Luis. Your sister is deliberately stirring things up. Like Marcella – remember her? – and your friend Antonio – remember him? But this time she gets away with it because your mother is ringing you because she's winding her up too.' She could feel her voice rising even further. 'But Luis ... what about me?'

Alice was a little girl again, watching her father walk up the road, his grubby brown suitcase in his hand, getting smaller and smaller and smaller until he disappeared completely over the brow of the distant hill.

Luis stood silently, looking at the floor for a few moments. 'You know I'm sorry. I'm doing my best. I'm being pulled in all these different directions ... getting the farmhouse ready and trying to get to know my son.'

'Getting the farmhouse ready to impress Fran and Mario and her new property developer partner, Luis.'

'And for us. I thought you understood,' he said, suddenly cold. Then he opened the door. 'It appears that you don't.'

She walked onto the balcony and heard the door slam. She watched as he hurried to the car and drove it along the driveway until the bushes hid it from view. Then she sat at the table with her beads and baubles, unable even to cry.

A message arrived on her jewellery Facebook page.

Hey Alice, I've just spotted this. Well done – no hard feelings. You may get an order or two from us soon, but Veronique is exhausted with the baby and doesn't know whether she's coming or going! Good luck – Adam.

No hard feelings, she thought. *No hard feelings*. The anger came at her again, and she stood up, pacing around the room, furious about all the years he'd pretended he wanted them to have a family but that the time wasn't right, then leaving her to pay the mortgage once he left, then fighting her for more of the house for longer than he needed to. Because he was a bully.

She wanted to scream but nothing came out, then she looked at the drawers of beads packed neatly away ready to be used. She couldn't stop herself. She threw them furiously up in the air and watched them fall, like a multi-coloured rain storm, scattering tiny little balls of blue, yellow, pink, red, orange, silver and gold across the room.

What about me? she thought, grabbing her bag and walking out of the door. As the lift opened on the ground floor, she called Saul. It went straight to voicemail, so she left a message before she could change her mind.

'Hi, its Alice Matthews here. Were you serious about me having a go at doing the interior design of that room in your restaurant? Because if you are, I'd like to do it.'

Chapter Twenty

Alice pushed the bell at the gate, hoping that Gina would be in. She had almost walked her turmoil off along the sea road towards the Boca Do Inferno, then turned back towards the little stone bridge. The café where she and Luis had sat after he had found her taking photos from the rocks two years before was derelict, its wooden frame worn and broken. She sat on a wall and listened to the sea moving to and fro, remembering that day and how he made her laugh. And how he just knew her, like no-one else ever had. Just like that.

She picked up a pebble and scratched it along the ground, feeling flat and alone. *Paradise indeed*, she thought.

A couple leaned on the wall and began to take photographs of the view. They kissed, then laughed, caught up in each other as if no-one else was there. No-one was, except for Alice. *I must do something*, she thought. *Something. Not just stare and mope. I'm not like that any more.* So, she pulled herself up, straightened her dress and made her way towards Gina's house.

Gina had a little bell at the garden gate that linked to the workshop as well as a door buzzer that called her at the house. Alice pressed them both and waited, anxious to start painting so her thoughts would go away. She pressed them again.

Please be there, please be there, she thought, then an image of all of the beads laying on the floor of the apartment waiting to be collected and made into bracelets so she could sell them to people for money to help with her future, which could now possibly be totally alone, flew into her consciousness.

'Oh, no,' she sighed and turned to leave.

'Alice ...' Gina was almost floating across the garden towards her. 'What a lovely surprise. Or – we didn't arrange another painting session today and I've forgotten?'

'No, I just … I just wanted to paint and thought I'd see if you were around. Spontaneously.'

Gina opened the gate and gave her a hug. 'Well, I am in the middle of a … meeting.' She touched her hair and smiled. 'But you can go ahead and use the workshop for as long as you want.'

'Oh, thank you – maybe an hour or so, just to get ahead with the tiles?'

'Are you all right, Alice?' Gina unlocked the workshop door. 'You look a little bit strained?'

'I'm fine.' Alice spoke too quickly and too brightly. 'Just lots on, to be honest. Hence being here.'

'I'll just get back to my … meeting.' She touched her hair again. 'Can you lock up when you finish and leave the key under that blue flowerpot over there?'

'Yes, and thanks for letting me do this.'

Alice breathed in, the mixture of paint and white spirit enticing her into her chair and, as she took out the tiles and began to paint, she felt as if she was with old and trusted friends. The kind that would just be there and not judge, or argue, or make you feel sad. Her world was, for once, silent, punctuated with occasional birdsong and passing cars and, for a while, there was just Alice and her work.

As she began to clear it away, she heard laughter – Gina's song-like giggle and a man talking quietly, his deep voice carrying through the air.

Wonder what the meeting's about, she thought, closing the door behind her. *Sounds more fun than the ones I have*. Two figures flitted past the kitchen window then moved back into view again as she placed the key under the pot. One was Gina, and the other, the man, was around the same height and build as Carlos. Or Ignacio. But all she could see was his back.

Hurrying down the path, she decided that this was either a good thing or a bad thing. Depending on whether you were Carlos or Ignacio. 'Oh. Dear.' She sighed and stepped out of the garden onto the pavement, taking out her phone. There was nothing from Luis. But there was a voicemail from Saul Pires.

'Great news, Alice. I'll get my PA to organise a meeting. Hopefully nobody will photograph that and put it all over Twitter!'

She felt a step back again, a withdrawal, her guard slowly going up.

But she couldn't face those beads on the floor yet and jumped on a bus to the centre of town. Carlos and Ignacio were sitting opposite each other at a table in the square, stern-faced, but talking to each other.

She waved and pulled up a chair. 'Good to see you two actually communicating,' she said.

'We've been having meetings with accountants and solicitors for the past two hours so we have had to.' Ignacio folded his arms. 'But we are almost finished.'

'Yes.' Carlos drummed the table. 'We were just discussing what to do on our opening night.' He wasn't smiling.

'I've been to Gina's.' She smiled. 'Did either of you pop round there at all?'

'We have had to be in each other's company all morning,' sighed Ignacio.

'Why do you ask?' Carlos sniffed. 'Do you know our solicitor had to open the window – he was being suffocated by the smell of Ignacio's massage oil.'

'I was tense and arranged a reiki session and massage first thing, but my masseuse was a trainee and was a little ...'

'.... generous with the oil.'

'No, I told you. He put it on his hands then dropped the bottle onto me as it slipped.'

They stopped talking and looked away from each other.

'So any ideas on what to do for the opening?'

'Luis ... do you think you could ask him if his band will play?' Carlos said.

'I'm sure.' Alice couldn't bring herself to call him or even message him. 'Just text him and he'll let you know.' She stood up. 'I'd better get back. Work calls.' She almost ran out of the square and rang Kathy.

'Yes?' She could hear crying and shouting in the background.

'Two things …'

'What…? Sorry, I'm at a baby and toddler group so you'll have to shout.'

'Number one – I think Gina is seeing someone and it isn't Carlos or Ignacio.'

'Oh?'

'And two – I've had a terrible argument with Luis, and I don't know what to do.'

'Where are you?'

'On my way back to the apartment.'

'I'll be there almost immediately. Thank God you rang. We have to get out of here. Well, I have to get out of here.'

Alice remembered the beads and sped up, in no mood to explain why they were on the floor instead of in their boxes.

As she opened the door, Aphrodite almost skidded past, enjoying what looked like a game of cat marbles. The floor was covered in colourful pockets of light as if a children's ball pit had exploded into tiny pieces. Alice almost smiled.

Was that little show of frustration really worth it? sighed the voice in her head

'At that particular moment in time, yes. Now, no. No it wasn't.'

Well I would call that a spectacular act of self-sabotage.

'I can't argue with that,' she sighed.

Alice took two careful steps and felt some of her precious baubles disintegrate under her feet, so decided to travel to the utility cupboard on all fours, pushing the beads away from her with her hands as if she was the prow of a ship.

'Oh, look … Auntie Alice has been drinking again!' Alice

turned. Kathy stood in hallway behind James' pushchair, holding her phone.

'Don't take a picture!'

'Too late!' She laughed. 'Follow the yellow brick road, Alice Dorothy Matthews. Your *Wizard of Oz* namesake would be proud.

'What?'

'You've made a little clear road in the middle of verges of baubles.'

'Please don't come in until I've managed to clear them up – I need them for quite a lot of bracelets!'

'I'd take you more seriously if you were actually standing up.'

Alice laughed and pulled herself to her feet using the kitchen door handle.

'I'll take James to the pool and come back in ten minutes, so he doesn't dive out of the pushchair and try to eat them,' said Kathy. 'And good luck.'

Alice took out the dustpan and brush and began to clear the mess that she had made, finding escapees as far as the bedroom and kitchen thanks to Aphrodite, who had come to rest laying on top of a pile under the sofa. She emptied them into a box where they sat amongst the bits of fluff and dust she'd swept them up with. Then she knelt to check there were none left hiding under any cupboards. One tiny, shiny blue bauble sat by the wall under a chest of drawers, and she prodded at it with the broom, knocking the bottom of the furniture as she did. A photograph fell from the back and landed on the floor.

She pulled it out and smiled. Grinning back were Mary, Kathy and Alice, sitting outside the hotel on her first day in Portugal, just after she had somehow been persuaded to cat sit. They were all laughing, holding up celebratory glasses of champagne; it was the first day of her new life, but Alice hadn't known it then. She'd thought she was just stepping out for a while. But it turned out to be forever.

On the other side Mary had written 'Me, Kathy and Alice on the first day of Alice's fabulous new adventure'.

Alice looked at the box of beads, waiting to be sorted back into their different colours before she could even start working and burst into tears, sinking back onto the floor.

'Oh, Alice, what's the matter?' Kathy ran over and sat down with her. 'I can help you sort these out, and whatever's going on with Carlos and Ignacio will be all right in the end.'

Alice passed her the photo. 'My adventure isn't an adventure, it's a mess.'

'Oh, look at us.' Kathy smiled. 'We've had a few ups and downs since then. So what else has happened?'

'I've had a terrible argument with Luis. He's being funny about some work that Saul Pires has offered me. He doesn't trust me. And he's off looking after an ex-lover who he's had a child with. And I'm encouraging him to do it!'

Kathy put her arms around her.

'And Tara has found our father – a photo of our father – and he has a new wife, and daughters and a grandchild, as if we never existed.'

Kathy stroked her hand. 'Oh, Alice.'

'And I have to move out of here. Don't know when, but I do.'

Kathy stood up and began to rummage in her bag. 'Carry on.'

'So I have to buy a house soon, because I don't know about me and Luis if he doesn't trust me ... and his *face* when I shouted, Kathy ... oh ... so this is the reason I need somewhere for myself, so I don't get thrown out, or stuck ... you should have seen the house my father was standing in front of ... and we got thrown out of ours because of him ... and he's got a really big house now.'

Kathy sat down next to her and handed her a hankie.

'And Cassie is manipulative and confusing and winding Luis up for some reason ... and I haven't got a child and I'm not pregnant and I spent years waiting for Adam to be ready because he said he wanted them … and now …'

Kathy put a clockwork bee on the floor.

'And I've got all those beads to sort out because I threw them on the floor.' Alice began to sob more loudly, and the bee began to move. Then Kathy put a clockwork clown on the floor, plus a clockwork lion and began to squeak a soft Cheshire Cat toy.

James began to chuckle and Alice watched them as they all ground around in tiny circles, her tears slowly subsiding.

Kathy put her arms around her again. 'Always works for James, so I thought I'd give it a go.'

Alice sniffed and laughed. 'Was I having a tantrum?'

'Well, in adults we call it venting.'

'I thought all the difficult bits were over, Kathy, but I just want to run and hide in my house in London. Which isn't my house any more.' Her voice began to rise again. 'And someone is stealing all the houses here … *all* the houses.'

Kathy took James out of his pushchair and sat him on her lap next to Alice. 'I know you're overwhelmed, but it will all be fine. You and Luis, you know you love each other. It's quite lovely and sometimes irritating to watch … and me and Stephano have space if you are stuck anyway, and look at all the projects my lovely clever artist bestest friend has on.'

'I can't not take work because Luis is insecure,' said Alice. 'For a moment it was like talking to Adam.'

'Have you spoken to him since?

'I can't. I'm too angry. And ashamed. I just can't …'

Kathy gave the baby to Alice. 'Now give Auntie Alice a big, wet kiss.'

James grabbed Alice's ear and put his other arm round her neck then blew a raspberry on her cheek. Alice laughed again.

'He needs a bit of help on that – not quite worked out the difference yet.'

Alice blew a raspberry on his cheek and he chuckled. 'I rather like it,' she said.

'Now.' Kathy stood up. 'You need to get away from this apartment for an hour or so.'

'I've already done that.'

'Let's have another hour away, then. Shall we walk along the prom to Estoril and I can take James to the paddling pool and we can eat cake or ice cream?'

'I haven't got the time.'

Kathy looked down at her. 'It's an order. And, forget all this big stuff like love, where you're going to live, your career and general wellbeing. We need to find out what's going on with Ignacio and Carlos and if it's got anything at all to do with Gina. It could be a love triangle!'

'I don't think it's a triangle,' said Alice, handing James back to his mother. 'It may be a square.'

On the way back to the apartment from Estoril, Alice meandered through the back streets, passing by the houses and trying to imagine herself living in one of them and wondering whether they would be suitable for a cat, too. She bit her lip. *And I need space for my work*, she thought. *Luis was going to put a building in the garden for us both, but now …*

You haven't split up, you know? You've just had an argument. The voice in her head was sounding unusually kind.

Yes, voice in head, but … what if it goes wrong? It did with Adam. And look what happened with my … I mean our … house. I don't want to be that person again.

You want to be empowered, then.

Exactly.

That's why you're wearing those trousers and all of that jewellery.

Alice looked down and almost smiled. She was wearing

her bright yellow, multi-patterned, flowing, loud and happy trousers – plus three of her own bracelets on each wrist, a necklace, earrings and her hair wrapped up in a green and orange band. She'd put it on after her argument with Luis that morning and hadn't even noticed.

It's like a very bright suit of armour.

Alice laughed out loud. She checked her phone. There was nothing from Luis.

Her finger hovered over the call button, but she put it back into her bag and went into a nearby estate agent to arrange more viewings. When she came out, she checked her phone. But there were still no messages.

Alice filled the next two days with work – painting tiles, designing bracelets, sorting out details for the patio decoration in the café, telling herself she would call Luis in a minute, in an hour, later. But she didn't. She couldn't. Still angry and upset, she was determined to go for her business meeting with Saul without feeling she was doing something wrong.

Chapter Twenty-One

Alice pushed open the door of the empty restaurant, clutching her laptop bag. She was dressed smartly but not too brightly, keen to look business-like and efficient.

A waiter was laying a table near the window. 'Can I help you?' he asked.

'I'm here for a meeting with Saul Pires. My name is Alice Matthews?'

Why am I saying my name as if it's a question? She sighed.

Nerves, nerves, nerves, said the voice in her head.

'One moment,' said the waiter. 'I'll go and get him.'

'This isn't good enough. I've told you before you need to keep them in the pan for twenty-four seconds more. Twenty-four seconds more – that's all they need for perfection.'

Alice could hear Saul bark instructions from the kitchen and wondered why she ever thought he reminded her of gentle, sweet Harry the Holiday Fling. She watched the waiting staff set the tables ready for opening, enjoying the sense of movement; calm yet urgent at the same time.

'Tea all right, Alice?' he yelled from the other side of the room.

'Yes, thank you.'

'Sit down and I'll be with you very soon.' It felt like an order, so she found a corner table and waited.

'Here we go.' Saul placed a tea tray down in front of her. 'Shall I be mother?'

'Go ahead,' said Alice.

'I made the assumption you'd like the English Breakfast tea. Well, I decided I want it so hoped you would too.' He smiled. 'I can get you something else if you want?'

'No, this is fine. A bit of a treat. I don't really drink tea any more.'

He poured the milk into the cups and then the tea. 'Milk first for me,' he said. 'I think it should be done properly.'

'This is a lovely place,' said Alice, 'and the view is fantastic.' She nodded at the window which stretched the length of the room, looking out over the rooftops of Lisbon and the river beyond.

'The food's pretty good, too,' he said, handing her a cup. 'Sugar?'

'No, not for me.'

'Good, because I forgot to bring it. So ...' He looked at her for a moment. 'Alice. Thank you for agreeing to do this.'

'It's a great opportunity for me.'

'Excellent. I felt that you'd get what I was looking for. We have a great connection.'

Alice wiggled in her seat uncomfortably.

'Don't panic; I didn't mean that. I meant I think you understand my aesthetic.'

'Of course, yes. I know what you meant.'

He held out a plate of biscuits. 'All made in-house. They are very, very delicious.'

Alice took a shortbread.

'Do you dunk?' he asked, catching her eye.

'Not a shortbread, no.' Alice took a sip of tea and turned to look at the view again. 'Do you have a rooftop bar at all? It would be lovely to sit there at night and stare.'

He smiled. 'Not at the moment, but I am in preliminary discussions about a café-bar in Lapa with a large terrace. Don't put that on Twitter!' He laughed, looking directly at her.

'That wasn't me!' Alice knocked the tea pot which nearly fell onto the floor. 'It was my ... it was Cassie. She had a bit to drink.'

'That doesn't explain the post the following day, though.'

'No, it doesn't. Again it was nothing to do with me. I'm sorry. It's just stupid.'

'I agree. I just want to get on with cooking. My agent wants me to get on TV more, but I'm not that keen. Whatever they say about me.' He looked around the room. 'This is important. They are important.' He nodded to the kitchen. 'My staff, in all my restaurants.'

'I'm sure they appreciate all the shouting,' said Alice.

'It's all done in their best interests!' He laughed. 'Anyway, here's the space.' He stood up with his cup of tea and walked to a room next to the one they were in. 'This is a private dining room, but that sounds stuffy. I want a more bohemian vibe, a more … like those trousers you wore one day when we were at Duarte's hotel.'

'You want a room like my patterned trousers?' Alice laughed.

'I am absolutely serious,' he said. 'They said fun, vibrant, relaxed, different.' He caught her eye again and she looked away, feeling a blush creeping up from her neck.

'Well, it's a first,' she said, trying to sound efficient. 'I can give it a go. When do you need it and what's the budget?'

'This is the thing,' he said. 'I need it very quickly. I have to confess I had someone else on board but they let me down at the last minute. Can you do the initial plan by Friday? I'll get my PA to send you the budget and measurements.'

'Oh, that is quite tight. I've got a lot on.' Alice thought about the tiles, the bracelets, Duarte's jewellery, finishing the interior and patio for Ignacio and Carlos, and looking for a house.

'Alice. It's a great opportunity. I have quite a brand, and you'd be a part of that.'

'I—'

'—good. That's fixed, then. Can you bring it in with you? You have time to come in on Friday, right? Or maybe we will meet in Cascais?'

'Here's fine,' said Alice, quickly, then realised she had agreed to even more work.

'Great. Got to go. Short and sweet. But effective.' He shook her hand and walked back into the kitchen. '*Adieus, ate a proxima.*'

'Until next time,' she said as she watched him leave. *Is this good, or is this complicated?* she thought. Either way, I'm in it now.

She took a tram back down to Praca do Comercio, staring out of the window as it weaved its way up and down the narrow city streets. *Every building has a story to tell*, she thought, *I wonder what it is*, then she remembered that evening in the streets of Cascais with Luis only a few weeks ago when he'd said a similar thing. She took out her phone. There were still no messages. The tram stopped next to a craft shop, and there, in the window, was one of his photographs – of the gardens near Sintra when they went for their first picnic amongst a carpet of wild flowers.

She decided it was time to call. 'Hello, it's me,' she said. 'I hope all is good and Mario is fine. I'm in Lisbon and I saw one of your photographs in a shop window. Sintra. Wild flowers. Remember? Got a lot of work on. I know you have too. Just ...'

She left the voicemail but couldn't say 'just call me.' Or 'I've just been to price up a job that will be so good for my future. Our future.' Or 'I miss you.' Or 'I'm sorry.' *Damned if I do and damned if I don't*, she thought as she stepped off the tram and walked along the river back to the station.

You want to tell him that someone wants you to design a room based on your trousers, don't you? said the voice in her head. *Because it's funny.*

It is funny, she thought. *But he'd want to know who for and I don't understand why. And I'm not that Alice any more.*

If you're not that Alice anymore you'd just tell him, and he'd have to deal with it.

So she sent a text to Kathy instead, who responded immediately.

I knew those trousers would come in useful one day! So, when are you next tile painting? I've got a busy couple of weeks at the spa coming up soon to cover for staff leave, so am making the most of my leisure time (ha ha!) Let's go to Gina's to paint tiles and find out what's going on with her and our two favourite brothers! Xx

Alice messaged back. Actually I'm off there after lunch, so ask if she's got space at the workshop and you can pick me up and bring me back. Win Win!

Gina almost danced around the workshop that afternoon, laughing and smiling and giggling girlishly.

'You're in an exceptionally good mood,' said Kathy. 'You're always in a good mood, but this is exceptional. Isn't it, Alice?'

Gina sat down between them. 'I have discovered the joys of internet dating,' she whispered. 'And I'm finding it very enjoyable.'

'Oh, lovely. Have you met anyone nice?' Kathy was in quiet interrogation mode again.

'Well ... not just one person ... don't judge me, please, but I've been on my own for a long time and I've just been getting on with my work, so I've not had any male attention for what feels like forever.'

Sounds familiar, thought Alice.

'... and well, when I met Carlos, and then Ignacio, they reminded me of how nice it is to have male company.'

'But?' Kathy leaned closer.

Gina fiddled with her hair. 'They are just friends. And I have decided I need more.'

'Oh.'

'My friend suggested I go on this dating app, and for the past two weeks I have been having an absolutely lovely time!'

'Oh, what's his name? Do tell?' Kathy said.

'Filipe ...'

'What's he ...?'

'David ...'

'Oh ...'

226

'Joaquim … very intense … and Jorge.'

'My word. In two weeks?' Kathy laughed.

Gina clapped her hands. 'Yes! I'm so busy with dating and such.'

'Sounds fun,' Kathy said. 'Go Gina!'

'It's not like me at all,' breathed Gina. 'But I'm finding that it is actually. Anyway, Alice, how are you doing with the tiles?'

'Nearly there,' said Alice. 'Should be done by the middle of next week, thankfully. It's going to be a bit tight, but they'll be ready in time for the café opening.'

'I'm going to make us some of Mary's tea at our regular craft session next week. I've just got to get the last few ingredients.'

'Wonderful.' Kathy laughed.

Alice sighed as Gina began to help another of the painters. 'Be careful. Please remember when we got the measurements wrong. And Gina's glasses are not necessarily fit for purpose.'

'Forget that,' said Kathy. 'We thought this was a common or garden love triangle.'

'Square,' corrected Alice.

'But now it appears it is a … septa … septa … there's seven of them. Or five, or six. I got confused. And how are we going to tell Carlos and Ignacio?'

'I'm not sure their argument really has anything to do with Gina, to be honest.'

'No, but it might.'

'And it might not.'

'Ssshhh! I'm enjoying a bit of intrigue.' Kathy began painting. 'I am so looking forward to that tea. Stephano won't let me make any of it at home since the last incident.'

'Ha, ha,' said Alice, taking a tile and her tracing paper. 'Ha, ha, ha.'

Kathy dropped Alice off in town so she could track down Carlos and Ignacio who were proving elusive in the run-up to their takeover of the café. A group of drummers were entertaining passersby at Fisherman's Beach, and she paused for a few moments, enjoying the reactions of the audience as much as the drumming itself. A woman standing opposite waved at someone next to her and on her wrist was one of Alice's bracelets. Alice beamed, forgetting briefly that she was not very happy at all.

'Alice.' Someone was tugging at her hand. 'Alice.' Mario was standing next to her. 'She's here, Mum,' he said, gesturing to Fran who was sat on a bench in the shade. 'Mum's getting tired because she's pregnant,' he said. 'Where have you been?'

'Around and about.' Alice smiled. 'Working hard. I've got a lot of projects on. Why?'

'Mum said we haven't seen you for a while.'

'Oh, well, I've just been busy, that's all.'

Fran walked slowly over, fanning her face. 'Oh dear. I'd forgotten how hot the summers here can be.' She kissed Alice and messed Mario's hair.

'Mum!'

'Not too old for that, Mario.' She laughed. 'Alice, I'm glad we've seen you. Is everything all right?' Mario moved to get a better look of the group and Fran lowered her voice. 'Luis is in a strange mood. Not that I know whether it's strange or not as I barely know him, but ... he seems to have gone quiet. And when I've asked where you are he's been quite short with me.'

'I'm just busy with work, that's all,' said Alice, her voice upbeat, trying not to give anything away. 'Is Cassie still here?'

Fran rolled her eyes. 'Honestly, it's like being around a forty-two-year-old who is really a thirteen-year-old girl. Like one of those body-swap films.'

Mario turned around. 'I told her she was rude, didn't I, Mum?'

'Yes, he did. He shouldn't have really.'

'She was talking about single parents again and how single

mums can't cope and needed men and stuff and my mum has worked really hard. Haven't you, Mum?'

'Yes, Mario.'

'So I told her she was being rude about my mum and she should stop.'

'Well done you,' said Alice.

'And she did stop.'

'And then she said "no offence", as usual, and went and poured herself a glass of wine.' Fran fanned her face again. 'She bought a bottle in a cool bag to the farmhouse.'

'Still working on it?'

'Yes … Luis spends a lot of time there, doesn't he? It's like he's got something to prove.'

Alice glanced at the floor, not wanting to meet her eyes. 'You may be right.'

'My partner Pete and Luis got on very well, but Pete was showing him a lot of his multi-million-pound developments.'

'Ahhhh …'

'Men!'

Another piece of the jigsaw puzzle falls into place, thought Alice.

'We're going home soon,' said Mario.

'Oh, that's a pity,' said Alice. 'You will be back though, won't you?'

'Of course he will. Luis is proving to be the opposite of the man I knew all those years ago. Thanks in part to you, Alice.'

'Oh, I …'

'Like I said the first time we met – but I think you were too shocked to take it in – when I saw you together at that gig I could see it – what's that quote about "you make me want to be a better man"? It's from a film.'

'My mum would know,' said Alice quietly. She thought for a second. 'What was Luis like when you first new him?'

Fran smiled. 'Ahhh. Do you really want to know?'

'I think it may help me.'

Fran flopped onto a bench under a nearby tree and patted the space next to her.

'He was gorgeous, of course.' Fran smiled. 'He is now, and he was then. Talented, funny, charming. Looking back, I think he was also a bit lost. But that's the benefit of hindsight for you.'

'You said when I first met you he wasn't the kind of man you wanted in Mario's life.'

'No, he wasn't. It wasn't that he was a player, but there were always other women around and it made me feel insecure. It would, wouldn't it? And there were people that knew him who I wanted to keep a distance from—'

'—Antonio,' cut in Alice. 'His cousin Antonio.'

'Oh, yes. He was not a nice man. Obsessed by the band. Used people, I think.'

'No, I know,' said Alice, remembering how dismissive he was of her when she had first come to Portugal and how he tried to control Luis.

'He used to taunt Luis about his ex-fiancée a lot. Laughed at him about moving to Portugal with a broken heart. Said it was banter. It wasn't. I mean why would you keep going on about that?'

'Antonio moved to Brazil last year. Needed to start afresh. Thankfully.'

Fran stretched her legs. 'I wasn't all that reliable either then,' she said. 'It wasn't all his fault. When I got back to London and realised I was pregnant after what was supposed to be a summer fling, I panicked. I did not want to be in a long-term relationship with anyone, and in my young and foolish head, telling Luis about Mario meant having some kind of life-time commitment with him. And that's not what it had been about at all.'

'Have you told Luis this?'

Fran frowned. 'I suppose I should, shouldn't I?'

'He feels very bad about himself at the moment.'

'So much going on.' Fran sighed. 'I don't want his money you know. I was lucky – my parents are quite well off, so that was never an issue and they are very … well … accepting, so Mario was part of a big extended family.' She looked at Alice. 'I should have told him sooner. I know that. It's just time went on …'

'Maybe tell him that. Before you go. I think it would help.'

'He's certainly thrown himself into being a father.'

'Yes. I'm glad.'

'Are you?'

'Yes,' said Alice. 'I mean it.'

Fran put her arm around her. 'I'm so pleased we found you, too, Alice. Mario's lucky to have you in his life.'

'Well, I'd better go,' said Alice quickly. 'Work has taken off, and I've got to ride the crest of that wave.'

'We will see you before we go, won't we?'

Alice smiled and looked at Mario, his wavy, dark hair curling around his face, and wondered if that was what Luis had looked like as a boy. She felt a sob catch in her throat.

'Of course.' She stood up, but she wasn't sure if they would.

Chapter Twenty-Two

'Thank you for doing this so quickly.' Saul closed the door behind him and sat on the sofa next to Alice. 'I'm heading back to New York next week and I'm something of a control freak about everything to do with my restaurants, including the décor.'

Alice opened her laptop and clicked on a folder. 'Well, it's your business so I think that's admirable.'

He laughed. 'I've been called many things before, but never admirable.'

'So, given that you wanted a design …'

'… based on your trousers, yes!'

'I've gone for vibrant and quirky here.'

He leaned closer to look at the screen, his arm brushing hers.

'I see you've gone for a different look today,' he said, still looking at the screen.

'Sorry, I thought I'd got the brief pretty well.'

'No,' he said, catching her eye. 'You've gone for a bohemian businesswoman look. Understated nicely cut dress in a soft fabric, with lots of jewellery.'

'Oh.' Alice didn't know what to say and looked back at the computer, trying to pretend she wasn't attracted to him. Because she didn't want to be.

'Although. May I?' he took a napkin and used it to gently brush something off her shoulder. Alice could feel her heart picking up speed. 'Avocado, I think?'

'Ahh. I wish I could say that was part of the bohemian businesswoman look, but I think I just left home in a hurry this morning.'

'Well, it's very endearing,' he said, studying the screen again. 'Now, I like the colours in this.'

'Good. I've kept a neutral palette for the walls and used a lot of bits and bobs to bring the room to life as you can see – paintings, wall hangings, bric-a-brac and such – and I found a way of painting the floor as if it was wallpaper without using tiles.'

'Ah, that's ingenious.'

'Thank you. I've given it a bit of a Moroccan theme, and I've got fairy lights too, and they look like multi-coloured stars.'

He glanced at her. 'Like the fairy lights in the restaurant on the beach near Troia?'

'Yes. That's right.' Alice focused on the designs and tried not to remember the moment she'd been transported back to her nineteen-year-old self with Saul accidentally playing the part of Harry.

'I have to say, Alice, that when I got that text from you I was rather intrigued.'

'Oh, I'm sorry, that text was … it was sent—'

'—by mistake. I know.' He laughed. 'I worked that out very quickly. Disappointing for me, but that's life.'

'I'm very flattered, though,' said Alice, avoiding his eyes and clicking on another page. 'That's flattering but I'm—'

'—how long will this take to get done?' he said, business-like again. 'I want the best quality materials, and properly sourced – this room is for exclusive parties for people who have money to spend.'

'I've done some internet searches and there are one or two bespoke items but they will take a couple of months at the most. The floor is the most complicated part because I've only found one company in the area that does this, so they'd need to be booked.'

'May I?' He touched the computer to make the image bigger, brushing her arm again as he did it. It felt like a very pleasurable electric shock.

'This is very imaginative, Alice. Different. I'm very impressed. How long have you been doing this for?'

'Interior design? Well, I'm just completing my first project.'

'You are very, very talented. Has anyone told you that?'

She blushed. 'No, no, they haven't.' She giggled, embarrassed.

He looked at her again. 'As far as I'm concerned, you're booked, but I need my business team to look at the costings before we confirm. There may be a few adjustments, but hopefully not.'

'Oh, thank you.' Alice felt suddenly flustered by his closeness. She could feel herself floating again, loose and anchorless, and put her hand on the arm of the sofa. As she glanced up, their eyes locked, and they moved towards each other, lost in something she couldn't understand and couldn't stop. She didn't want to stop. It felt like she was being pushed towards him by something outside herself, and when he kissed her, she fell into it, everything else falling away. She had no sense of where she was; all she could feel was the beating of his heart, his hand touching her face, and there was nothing else there. Just them, and the kiss, and an echo of a lavender field in France, with Harry next to her looking at the stars.

She accidentally knocked a cup over and the sound of it clattering onto the floor brought her back to reality. She pulled away awkwardly. 'I'm sorry, I'm sorry. I shouldn't have done that. I'm in a relationship. I shouldn't have.'

Saul took her hand. 'I shouldn't have either. I apologise. Something came over me. It was very inappropriate of me.'

She switched off her laptop and stood up. 'I'd better be going. Busy, busy.'

'Let me see you out,' he said, sounding calm, despite the embarrassed look on his face. 'Like I said, my team will confirm the details very soon.'

He put his hand on the door and turned towards her. 'You really don't know, Alice, do you?'

'Know what?'

'How ... how ... bewitching you are.'

'Me? I thought I was just …'

'You are not "just", Alice. Always remember that, you are very much not … just.' He looked at the floor. Harry the Holiday Fling floated into her mind again. 'For what it's worth, I think you are astonishing.'

And there she was. Alice before Adam. Before the put-downs, the dismissiveness, the control.

Ahh, Prince Charming has kissed Sleeping Beauty back into life again, sighed the voice in her head.

'Right person, wrong time.' Saul opened the door and guided her onto the street, the heat and noise of the midday traffic suddenly piercing. 'I have to get back to the kitchen.'

'Okay, well, I'll wait for that e-mail,' said Alice. She tried to shake his hand, but he held it for a moment, then kissed it softly.

'Please don't think that this had anything to do with me asking you to do some work for me. I'm not trying to manipulate you. This was not planned.'

Alice nodded. 'No, I know.'

He held her gaze. '*Adieus.*'

'*Adieus.* I have an appointment to view a house in Cascais in an hour. So I'd better go. And I've got to drop the bracelet samples off at Duarte's office, too.' She smiled, then turned and walked down the hill, confused, ashamed, but also feeling very alive. It had been wrong. But for some reason it felt right, too. Why would she kiss Saul Pires when she loved Luis? It was Luis she wanted. But at that fleeting intense moment, she'd wanted Saul. Alice knew it meant something, but she couldn't work out what. As she got to the square at the bottom, her phone rang. It was the estate agent cancelling the viewing as the house had just been taken off the market.

Duarte sat with his legs on the desk, leaning back into his chair, the light flooding through the blinds behind him, his face just a shadow, his features hidden.

'I love doing this,' he said. 'It makes me look like I'm in a Hollywood film, doesn't it?'

'I suppose it does.' Alice leaned forward. 'You look like a cut out shape, to be honest.'

'Excellent! If I was into mind games I could get my employees in here and really have fun.'

'You're not, are you?'

He put his legs on the floor. 'No, I haven't got the energy for that. And I value my employees and everyone I work with. Which brings me to you, Alice.'

'Oh?'

Duarte stood up and moved around to lean on the desk in front of her.

'Last week I sent you an e-mail, a text message and left a voicemail about more jewellery for a hotel shop I am opening in Porto, but you haven't got back to me.'

Alice felt like she was in her headmaster's office at school and said nothing.

'Lucky I was here when you were dropping off your samples.' He looked at her. 'It's your turn to speak, Alice. I'm offering you a fantastic opportunity.'

'It's a great opportunity and I'd love to do it, thank you,' she took a deep breath. 'But last week, well, and this week, I've been a bit distracted because of issues about housing.'

'But you live in Mary and Frank's apartment?'

'Yes, but they're selling it, and I have to move out.'

'But aren't you moving in with Luis?'

'Yes, but … but … I can't at the moment, and I'm not sure if …'

'You can rent then?'

'I could, but I have a cat. Mary and Frank's cat. And you know what cats are like. They need security, and their own space.'

'I think you may be talking about yourself there, Alice.'

'And not everywhere takes pets.'

He sat down behind the desk again, then seemingly realised she couldn't see him and moved to the chair opposite.

'And someone is buying all the houses and apartments. Well the ones I like, and the one I'm living in.' Her voice began to rise. 'Some investment company has suddenly decided to steal all the property.' Alice realised she was sounding a little hysterical and looked at her hands.

'Ahh.'

She looked up. 'Ahhh, what?'

'I think that may be me.'

Alice stared at him. 'You're stealing ... sorry ... buying all these houses?'

'I'm not. I decided to expand into property, you know, just because it makes sense and ... I can.'

'You must have a lot of money,' she said, 'to buy all of those places all at once.'

'Actually, I have got a lot of money.'

'Including buying the place I'm currently living in.'

'Well, I'm not actually doing it.'

'And the little yellow house I had my heart set on. I was about to make an offer on that.'

'I've employed agents to do it for me. Experts who know the area.'

'Have they been following me around? It feels like they have.'

Duarte laughed. 'No, Alice. No ... but I'm sorry.'

'I'm a bit overtired. I know I'm sounding a bit ...'

'... creative?'

'Nice way of putting it.'

He leaned forward. 'So what do you mean about Luis? Is everything okay?'

Alice bit her lip. 'It's ... well ... no ... I don't know ... I can't really ...'

'But you two are so good together.'

'I know.' Alice could feel tears gathering in her eyes and sniffed to keep them from falling down her face.

Duarte jumped up and rummaged in his desk drawer. 'I have some … wait here.' He thrust a handkerchief in her hand. 'Please don't.'

'I'm not going to cry.' Alice almost shouted, dabbing her eyes. 'But thank you.'

'Have the yellow house,' he said, suddenly. 'Have it. I mean don't have it. Buy it. From me. I am a businessman after all. A very successful one. But I don't need it. It will either be sold once its redeveloped or rented.'

'I can't.' Alice said, confused. 'You can't do that. I'm not crying about the house. I'm angry about the houses. Not upset.'

'Yes I can do it. It's my company. And if it means you can carry on designing for me instead of worrying about where you're going to live, then that is a good investment in itself.'

There was a knock on the door. 'Your next appointment is here,' Duarte's assistant called in.

Alice jumped up. 'It's so kind of you, really. But I can't. It's not … I can't. But thank you. And I will happily design more bracelets for Porto.'

'If you change your mind, let me know,' he said gently. 'You don't have to be quite so British about it.'

Alice opened the door. 'You've been very kind,' she said. 'My mind is all over the place at the moment. I'm on my way to finish painting the last tiles for the café mural, so I've got to rush.'

Chapter Twenty-Three

Alice sat alone in the workshop, the radio on in the background, checking the paintwork on the tile. It was the last one, and it was perfect. She held it up and put a number on the underside so she would know where it should be on the mural when it was ready to be mounted, then studied the piece of paper with the sketch of the design on it to make sure everything matched.

'It's a pity Ignacio and Carlos are so busy arguing that they haven't even checked what I planned,' she said to the wall. 'I hope they like it. Too late now.'

Gina swept through the door carrying a box of tiles. 'These are all fired, Alice,' she said. 'Have you checked the ones I did last week to make sure they're okay?'

'Yes, all good. I'll have a look through these before I go.'

Gina put the box down. 'I'll get these last ones done later on. If you're taking them to the café tomorrow you won't have time to check them, I'm afraid.'

Alice stood up and stretched. 'It's okay. They're for the top and bottom, and I've done extra just in case.'

'I'm very much looking forward to seeing it complete. You've done so well, Alice. I'm very impressed.'

'Thank you.' She glanced at her watch, then took the tiles out of the box. 'I'll give these a look over and head home.'

'I'll see you tomorrow around lunchtime? This last lot will be finished then. I'll put all the boxes under the tree over there and label them up, so you can find them if I'm not here.'

'I can't believe it's nearly done.' Alice smiled. 'Can I just come and paint tiles for the sake of it now?'

'Of course you can. It's a pity you're so busy tomorrow. Kathy's coming over, and I've got the ingredients for Mary's tea, so a few of us are going to have a very relaxing paint.'

Oh dear, whispered the voice in Alice's head.

Gina picked up the rest of Alice's tiles and began to load them into a box. 'I'll get these dried and in the kiln. Have a good evening.'

'Bye, Gina.' Alice checked her first tile and made a conscious effort not to worry, as it was only tea after all.

Closing the gate behind her, she began to walk towards the town. The tile painting was finished, and she wanted to tell Luis. She wanted to tell him how she'd felt when the last one was taken away for firing, how she hoped the design would make a difference. That Duarte de Silva had offered her more work, and even told her she could buy the little yellow house because his company was the one that was snapping up property along the coast. She'd also kissed Saul Pires. But she didn't want to tell him that. So, Luis had been right all along. But she didn't feel guilty, and she was beginning to understand why.

He took you back, sighed the voice in her head. *He took you back to when you were full of hopes and dreams and anything was possible.*

Alice turned onto the sea road. 'I miss Luis,' she said to the waves. 'I miss him, and I might have ruined everything.'

The square was full, the hot summer night drawing everyone outside, filling the air with the familiar sound of music and laughter. Ignacio sat at a table going through paperwork whilst Carlos flitted around, dealing with customers.

Alice sat down. 'Ignacio,' she said. 'I've finished painting the tiles. They'll be ready tomorrow – I need you to help me get them here.'

He looked up, pen in hand, and smiled. 'Well done, Alice. Of course I will.'

'I've finished the tiles, for the back wall,' she said to Carlos as he walked past.

'That is very good news, Alice,' he said, looking away as Ignacio glanced towards him.

'The café is now ours.' Ignacio put the pen down. 'Everything was transferred this morning. Very smooth. We will close for two days from tomorrow to re-decorate and rebrand.'

'So, you two are talking again then?' Alice smiled as Carlos placed a cool glass of Vinho Verde in front of her.

Ignacio began to shuffle the pieces of paper. 'Only for work, Alice. Carlos will not listen to reason about the sign and it makes me uneasy.'

'What is the problem with it?'

'This is not the first time we have worked together, Alice. And the sign is a reminder of our unhappy past. I thought I was beyond it, but it has stirred everything up.'

'With all of this meditation and mindfulness you'd think he'd be beyond that kind of good luck, bad luck rubbish,' huffed Carlos, hurrying past with a tray of food.

Ignacio sat back and folded his arms. 'It's not luck. It just reminded me,' he said.

'Can I help at all?' Alice asked softly.

'No.' Ignacio looked at the floor, then he looked up. 'I haven't seen you and Luis together for a few days. Is there something you need to tell me?'

Alice looked at the floor. 'No … no …'

Ignacio raised his eyebrows.

'Um …' Alice looked at Carlos with his back to his brother at another café. *Perhaps if I mention Gina*, she thought, *that's one less thing for them to argue about.* 'About Gina …'

'Yes? About Gina?' Ignacio took a sip of beer.

'Well.' *There's no easy way to say this*, she thought. 'She's been on a dating app and has been seeing another … other men.' Alice paused. 'I hope that hasn't upset you.'

Ignacio leaned forward. 'Oh, I know that,' he said. 'You didn't think we were interested in Gina? We were both at school with her. A long time ago. Knew her husband …'

Carlos swept past. 'The dating app she is using is very good. I've just signed up.'

'Me too.'

'We used to both have a crush on her at school.' Carlos laughed.

'And when I first saw her in the square with you I couldn't place her at first.' Ignacio shook his head, smiling.

'It's been lovely to reconnect,' they both said at once.

Then they looked at each other and seemed to realise they weren't speaking. Carlos walked off.

'Of course, if he hadn't bumped into Gina at that networking session we wouldn't have all of that trouble about the sign,' huffed Ignacio.

'Right.' Alice took a sip of her wine. 'You're still arguing about a sign?'

He folded his arms again. 'I don't want to talk about it.'

Carlos picked up an empty cup from the next table. 'He wants to talk about everything. He wants … what does he say? … meaningful dialogue about every single issue, except for this.' He walked back into the café.

Alice felt tired all of a sudden. 'I'd better be off.' she stood up. 'Can you meet me at around two to get the tiles from Gina? I stored all the things to decorate the patio garden in your utility room, so I can work on that afterwards.'

'Of course.' He stood up and limped around the table.

'What's the matter?'

'Oh, I overdid a low lunge in my yoga class this morning and hurt my leg. I'll just stretch it later. It's fine.' He gave her a hug. 'See you tomorrow, Alice. I will be driving in my Rolls – I'm picking it up from the garage in the morning. It's had some work done, and I'll come straight after that.'

'Ah, that will be a treat.' She took out her phone to call Luis. Everywhere reminded her of him – the square, the apartment, the stone bridge next to the lighthouse. But she'd built a wall to protect herself again, and she felt unable to pull it down.

Alice woke up as the first pinpricks of sunlight shone through the grills in the shutters. She stretched herself in the warm comfort of the bed

Aphrodite sat staring at her from the bottom of the bed, purring contentedly. Just for that moment, Alice felt happy and positive for what the new day would bring. Then her mind began to work again, and she remembered today was the day she was collecting the tiles for the mural from Gina's to drop off at the café. It was the most challenging project she had ever done, and it was nearly finished. But she wasn't excited. She wasn't even nervous. She just wanted to share it with Luis, but she still couldn't allow herself to pick up the phone and call him. To risk him not calling back.

The cat padded over to her and nuzzled her face, then jumped onto the floor and walked towards the kitchen, so Alice slid out of bed and followed her. She spooned out the food into one of the vibrant pink food bowls, feeling flat and sad. She didn't turn on the radio, didn't open the shutters, she just quietly got ready, spent the morning doing some admin and went to the road to wait for Ignacio to pick her up.

Alice heard the music drifting from the workshop as she stepped out of the car. It was louder than usual and not accompanied by the regular happy chattering she expected.

'Is everything okay?' asked Ignacio, shutting the car door.

Nope, said the voice in her head. *Nope, nope, no, not at all.*

'Yes, fine,' she said, walking up the pathway, Ignacio limping behind her, the late afternoon cicadas screeching in unison. 'You're not okay, though, are you?'

'I have to admit, Alice, that this foot is very painful now. I fell doing the Firefly Pose in my yoga class earlier on. I thought I had recovered from yesterday's injury, but it appears that it's made it worse.'

'You can wait in the car.'

'I said I would pop in and say hello to Gina.' He groaned and tried to lean against a bush, then fell into it, twigs snapping as he went, scattering flowers and dragonflies in his wake.

'Oh God. Are you all right?' Alice held out her hand and tried to pull him up.

'Yes, yes, I'm fine.' He rubbed his leg. 'I may have twisted my ankle now, too.'

'Don't try and get up right now,' said Alice. 'I'll get Gina and Kathy to come and help.'

She hurried along the path, a growing sense of dread in the pit of her stomach, instinctively knowing somehow that they weren't going to be much help at all. The door to the workroom was flung open wide, with Etta James blasting out 'At Last' from the radio. Three of the ladies were limply attempting to paint bowls, four were dozing on bean bags in the corner and Kathy was curled up asleep on the floor. Alice picked up an empty teacup and smelt it.

'Tea. Bloody tea,' she muttered, trying not to laugh. 'I warned them!'

Two empty bottles of wine were placed haphazardly in the middle of the table. 'Oh dear,' she said.

She heard a door slam outside and went to see what it was. Gina was standing next to the kiln staring blankly into the distance, playing with her hair. 'Alice,' she sang. 'Oh Alice. It so lovely, lovely, lovely to see you …' She almost glided towards her, then stopped and looked over Alice's shoulder. 'Dear me. What is the matter with Ignacio?'

Alice turned. Ignacio was on all fours, trying to pull himself upright with the help of a tree trunk.

Gina gazed at Alice blankly. 'Tiles. I've come to collect the tiles,' said Alice. The sense of dread returned but this time with hundreds of little butterflies flying about her stomach. 'The tiles for the café wall. They were being fired last night. You told me earlier to pop back once you had sorted them out.'

Gina began to play with her necklace and looked confused. 'Tiles. I …'

'Ignacio and I are taking them to the café tonight so we can put them on the wall.'

Gina smiled serenely. 'Of course. Silly of me. Over here.' She indicated some boxes next to the tree.

Alice sighed with relief, but the butterflies continued to race around as she opened one of the boxes up. She felt sick.

'These aren't my tiles, Gina. They must be in another box.' Alice opened another one, and another one. 'These look like broken tiles, or misfires, or mistakes.'

'Oh ... oh ...' Gina's eyes began to widen as her smile faded. 'Oh ... dear ... I put your boxes last night over there and ... oh dear.'

Alice's heart began to pump faster, sending the butterflies into a frenzy. 'It's just, we're in a bit of a hurry ... you know, because of the delay in getting them finished. We only have tonight and tomorrow to put them on the wall and dry them.'

Ignacio had managed to pull himself upright and was hobbling in a slow panic across the grass towards the boxes.

'I'm sure there's some mistake. They can't be anywhere else.'

'The man took them,' breathed Gina dramatically. 'He took them ...'

'What man? Have you got his number?'

'The shredder ... the incinerator!'

Ignacio stopped moving. Alice stared at Gina as the music from the workroom changed to 'Don't Worry, Be Happy'.

'He must have taken your boxes by mistake.'

'That's okay, Gina. We can phone him and get them back.'

'He's the other side of Sintra,' she breathed, pulling on her necklace harder. 'Somewhere near Ericeira.'

'We can phone him.' Alice nodded. 'It's fine.'

'His phone isn't working. He told me.'

'We can phone the factory,' said Ignacio.

'It's a public holiday. They are closed . He did this as a favour.'

Alice felt a rush of blood to her head. 'Oh, my tiles. All that work ...'

The workroom door clattered as Kathy stumbled out. 'Let's find him,' she almost shouted, obviously having overheard. 'Follow him. In the car.'

'I don't think I can drive,' said Ignacio. 'With my leg. And my foot.'

'I'll phone Carlos,' said Alice.

'Him! No. He's looking after the café today. He won't be able to.'

'You can call Luis,' shouted Kathy.

'Kathy … no!' said Alice, angrily. 'No. I'll do it myself.'

'Okay.' Then Kathy leaned against the wall outside the workroom, her hands pressed hard against the stone as if to stop herself sliding down towards the floor.

'I told you not to give them that tea,' sighed Alice. 'And as for drinking wine with it … you should know better.'

'It's fine. We can have a car chase!'

'You know you're shouting?' said Alice.

'Am I?' shouted Kathy.

Alice stood up straight, a thousand thoughts shooting around her head, but panic overrode all of them.

Get in the bloody car and get after him, yelled the voice in her head.

'Where exactly is this factory, Gina?'

'I have the address on my phone.'

'Right, we have to go,' said Alice.

'I'm coming.' Kathy almost skipped towards her.

'I'm not sure you'll be any use.'

'I will be when this has worked its way out of my system,' she said brightly. 'Let's get Ignacio to the car.'

Alice, Gina and Kathy grabbed Ignacio and almost dragged him back towards the gate.

'It's my yellow Rolls-Royce,' he muttered. As they propped him against the door, he sighed. 'Alice. This is my pride and joy. The love of my life. But you must drive it. The others are too full of that concoction.'

'But I haven't driven a car in years. I live … I lived … in London!'

'You'll be fine,' yelled Kathy.

'And I've never driven on the right side of the road.' Alice thought she heard Ignacio whimper.

Kathy shoved him into the passenger seat, guided a bewildered Gina into the back and dragged Alice around to the driver's door.

'In you go,' she said, pushing her in. Then she jumped into the back seat, slammed the door and said, 'Come on then. Let's go and save your tiles.'

Alice and Ignacio exchanged looks. 'Are you sure you won't let Luis …?' he began.

'No,' said Alice. 'Can I have the key? And can you call Carlos and tell him what's going on. And call Stephano and tell him that Kathy is … well … you know.'

Ignacio handed her the key, did up his seat belt, took a deep breath and said, 'I trust you. Now drive.'

No you don't, thought Alice, turning on the ignition. *And I certainly don't.*

'We're having an adventure,' said Kathy loudly whilst Gina giggled.

'I can drive. I can drive. I *can* drive,' she muttered.

Ignacio looked at her. 'You said that out loud Alice. You can drive, can't you?'

She thought of all the hard work she'd put into the tiles. All of the love and thought and hours and hours of painting. And how she hoped that the mural would somehow heal the rift between Carlos and Ignacio. Then she pictured her tiles being ground into tiny sand-like pieces in a terrible grey, noisy grinding machine.

She adjusted her sunglasses, checked the rear-view mirror and pulled out. 'Of course I can,' she said with a confidence she didn't feel.

The car seemed to hop then spluttered to a halt in the middle of the road.

She glanced in the rear-view mirror and, instead of Kathy's face, she saw Adam's. '*Why don't you let me drive, Ali? Every time I get in the car with you I feel nervous. We all have our areas of expertise, and this isn't one of yours. You'll find whatever it is eventually.*'

Alice bit her lip, adjusted herself in her seat and shouted, 'I can do this. I can. And I will.'

'She can do this,' echoed Kathy. 'She can, she can, she can.'

'I will call Luis,' said Ignacio.

'No,' said Alice, pulling off again. 'No! Let's go.'

In her mind she saw the car growing a pair of wings, flying above the trees and gliding across the mountains, the *ET* soundtrack playing in the background. *Or maybe 'Chitty Chitty Bang Bang' would sound better*, she thought. *Oh, no. I'm turning into my mother and mixing films as well ...*

'Can't you go faster?' asked Ignacio, sounding pained.

'At some point,' said Alice. 'And I think at some point I may be able to talk again but currently I'm just trying to breathe. And see where I'm going. And ... guide me to the main road, then talk to me.'

The car fell silent.

That was very assertive, said the voice in her head. *Or aggressive. Not sure which.*

The car spluttered again as Alice changed gears, and it felt like all of its occupants took a sharp intake of breath as the Rolls somehow managed to keep going and pick up a small amount of speed.

They all sighed.

'And she's off,' said Kathy. 'Woooo hoooo.'

As the car began to crawl along in the public holiday traffic, Alice finally calmed down. Kathy and Gina were dozing in the back, and Ignacio was talking to Carlos on his phone.

'Yes, yes ... just ring the office and keep ringing. Someone must be there. Alice doesn't want you to call Luis ... you need to call the office. Okay, if you insist.'

He looked at Alice. 'He is going to ring Luis.'

'I don't ... Ignacio, I can't.'

'I don't want to speak to Carlos, but I did because it is in everyone's best interests,' he said sulkily.

'What help is Luis going to be anyway?' Alice looked out of the window. Luis was the only person she wanted to see now. She wanted him to put his arms around her, tell her it would be all right, and they'd get her tiles back. She wanted to close her eyes and sink into him and feel peaceful. But she felt the wall grow again and pushed it all away.

The car edged forward.

'Yes, well. He's probably too busy anyway.'

Ignacio sighed. 'If you want me to mediate, to counsel or send you good thoughts. Or maybe just some simple stretching exercises to release all the tension. You are looking very stressed. You know, very wound up. It's in your eyes, in your smile, the way you walk. You've been like this for days.'

His phone buzzed before Alice could say anything.

'Ah, from your mother. I messaged her earlier to tell her what was happening,' he said, then laughed. 'She said it was like in one of those car chase movies.'

'Only much, much slower,' sighed Alice.

He laughed again as his phone rang. 'It's Luis,' he said, answering it. '*Ola, diga*, speak ... yes, I will get the address from Gina and send it to you ... you are sure? Why?' his voice got quieter and he turned away. 'She's fine, the car's fine ... yes I will.'

Alice didn't say anything. *What's the point?* she thought. *I can't deal with Luis now.*

'We are going to have to wake those two up,' said Ignacio. 'We're about to turn off, and this is where it will get interesting. Or stressful.'

'Well, I suppose you're right,' said Alice. The cars ahead

were beginning to move more quickly, and there was no turning back. Quite literally.

'This should wake them up.' Ignacio pressed the play button on his cassette player. 'Old school for an old car.' He smiled.

The introduction to 'Born To Be Wild' filled the car. Ignacio looked in the rear-view mirror and turned up the volume. 'Desperate times,' he sighed.

'I need a drink of water,' said Kathy woozily.

Gina leaned forward and whispered to Alice. 'Me too.'

Ignacio found two small bottles in the glove compartment and flung them into the back of the car.

'Now,' he said gently to Gina. 'Can you tell me the address of the … how shall we call it? … tile recycling plant.'

'Where tiles go to die,' said Kathy.

'Don't say that,' he hissed. 'You will upset Alice.'

'It's here,' said Gina, passing him her phone, and he entered the details into his sat-nav, then messaged Luis.

'And we are on our way,' he said and, for a while, the car passengers were silent.

Eventually, Alice turned off onto a side road. 'Are you sure this is right?' she asked.

'If the sat-nav says it is,' said Kathy. 'It's right. Do you want me to take a turn driving? You must be tired.'

'Oh no,' said Alice. 'You drunk that tea and wine on top of it. Well, you two should have seen yourselves … so no.'

'Don't bite,' muttered Kathy. 'I was only trying to be helpful.'

They continued along for a mile or so. The road got narrower, and Alice's neck and shoulders began to ache.

'I keep trying to ring the office, but no-one is answering,' said Gina quietly. 'I'm so sorry, Alice.'

'It's fine, Gina. ' Alice didn't mean it, but she said it anyway. They pulled up to a crossroads. Alice put her head on the steering wheel. 'We've been going around in circles. Just bloody circles!'

'Stop, stop!' shouted Kathy. She jumped out of the car and began to hold her phone up in the air, waving it around frantically. 'That sat-nav's obviously shot to pieces. I need to get a signal for Google Maps.' She paused for a moment, one arm stretched upwards, her face serious and concentrated. She looked like a Greek statue. 'I've got a signal ... no, I haven't ... yes, I have.'

Ignacio found a small bottle of orange juice in the glove compartment and passed it to Alice.

'Sugar,' he said.

'How big is that glove compartment, Ignacio?' said Alice, taking a long, refreshing gulp.

He leaned over. 'It's a secret.'

They got out to join Kathy, who was still running around with her phone aloft, as Gina kept manically dialling and re-dialling the office. Ignacio leaned against the car and massaged his leg. 'My poor foot,' he muttered. 'Yoga ... man my age ...'

Alice looked at her phone. There were five missed calls from Luis. 'I think Luis is trying to contact us, Ignacio. Can you call him back?'

He sighed as Alice walked along the road for a few minutes, accompanied by the shrilling of the cicadas and the faraway low rumble of traffic. It looked the same as all the other bits of road they had driven on for the past half an hour.

Ignacio waved at her. 'We have to turn left, then it is the second right and on to the main road after that. Luis said we should be there soon. And he will be too.'

She trudged back, weary, dreading seeing him, but longing to at the same time.

Stubborn, whispered the voice in her head.

Yep, she thought. *Yep. I'm allowed to be*.

'You've become an expert Rolls-Royce driver,' said Ignacio as they got to the second turning.

Gina leaned forward. 'I need the bathroom,' she said quietly.

Kathy's phone buzzed with a new message. 'Stephano says he's on his way. And that we should have turned right and why are we going this way?'

'Why's Stephano on his way?' asked Alice.

'Because me and Gina are taking up tile space in the car … and he thinks he knows best.'

'Gonna Get Along Without You Now', burst out of Alice's phone. 'It's my new ring tone,' she muttered, feeling three pairs of eyes looking at her in judgement. 'And it looks like Mario's calling. Can you answer it, Ignacio? As it's Mario. What's that look for?'

'Give the man a break,' Kathy shouted from the rear seat.

'Mario says he has an app which says we should turn right, then left, then right at the big olive tree next to the old chicken coops,' Ignacio said. 'It's the most up to date on the market apparently.'

A peal of hysterical laughter rang from the back of the car as Gina sank into her seat.

'I think we've lost Gina,' trilled Kathy.

'Right then, everyone. Which way shall we go? Who are we going to listen to?' Alice said, sounding more calm than she felt.

'I can see the glint of the sea in the distance,' said Gina. 'I know it's close to the sea. He told me—'

'—I must go down to the seas again,' said Kathy. 'To the lonely sea and sky …'

'And all I ask is a tall ship and a star to steer her by …' echoed Ignacio. 'John Masefield.'

'… and the white sails … sails … um … shaking …' whispered Gina.

Ignacio turned round and smiled. 'Oh you know it, Gina. You are so poetic.'

'I know it too,' said Kathy. 'In fact, I knew it first.'

Alice slammed on the brake. 'Where. Should. We. Go?' she said loudly and slowly.

No-one responded. Alice put her foot on the accelerator, enjoying the sound of the tyres ploughing into the dust, and pulled off as quickly as the classy old car would allow. 'I'm following the sea. If you get lost in Lisbon or the coast, look for the water.'

'This is the west coast,' said Ignacio quietly.

'Well we've got to go somewhere,' said Alice, her teeth almost clenched. She somehow wanted to laugh but couldn't. *My tiles*, she thought. *My tiles*.

Suddenly all of the phones rang at the same time, creating a weird cacophony of rhythm and noise and, for a while, Alice enjoyed her three passengers arguing with each other and their callers. She just followed the call of the sea until she got to the brow of a hill overlooking the ocean, blue and blustery below. The road had narrowed again, and there was nowhere else to go but forward.

'A sign, a sign!' shouted Kathy. 'Over there!'

'It's … to … somewhere anyway,' said Ignacio, trying to sound confident. 'It will get us somewhere, which is better than here.'

'Which is nowhere,' breathed Gina dramatically. 'And there is no mobile signal … again.'

Alice looked out of the window to her right and felt her stomach lurch. The land fell away sharply to the cliffs just a few feet away and a late afternoon sea mist was rolling like gossamer across the road in front of her.

'I don't want to drive any more,' she said firmly.

'You have to,' said Ignacio

'I don't want to,' said Alice, grabbing hold of her own knee and sinking her nails into it. 'I can't see over the ridge in front. What if it's a sheer drop? And I can't reverse in this. I can't reverse anyway. I never could.' She could feel her voice rising but had no control over it.

'Alice!' shouted Ignacio. 'Calm down!'

'Easy for you to say,' she shouted back. 'I just want my tiles. I don't want them to die.'

'Now you're being irrational,' he said more calmly.

'I bloody know!'

The wind whistled around the car. No-one spoke.

Alice took some deep breaths, put the car back into gear and moved off.

'At this speed you may as well be going backwards,' muttered Ignacio under his breath.

'I heard that,' said Alice. 'I'm trying not to break your car.' As they crawled along the narrow track, Alice saw a shadowy figure appear in the mist a little way in the distance. 'Am I imagining that?' she whispered.

As they got closer, the figure became more distinct and began waving at them. He was wearing blue overalls and had a cigarette hanging from his mouth, his face brown and leathery, his hair a bright silver-grey. To Alice he looked like an ageing, off-duty superhero. But without a cape.

'It's him,' squealed Gina. 'The man. The tile man. It's him, it's him.'

Alice almost burst into tears of relief as she wound down the window.

'*Ola*!' she said.

'*Ola*! English?'

'*Sim*. Yes.'

'I couldn't stand it any more.' He laughed. 'You were driving so slowly it was like watching someone land a helicopter.'

Alice looked at him and burst out laughing. 'That bad?' she said.

He nodded. 'I shall never forget it. Now, your tiles. Someone called Mario sent me a message on Facebook.'

'You're on Facebook. Why didn't any of us think of that?' Alice turned to look at Ignacio, Gina and Kathy. They were all avoiding eye contact with her.

'He said there'd been a mistake,' said the man. 'Follow me into the yard over the ridge to the left.'

Alice did as she was told. As she parked, she realised Luis was waiting in his car with Mario and Elvis, and Stephano was in his with James.

'How did they get here before us?' Ignacio opened the door and hopped over to them, limping badly, whilst Gina almost fell out onto the floor and sat on the ground. Kathy just got into the back seat of Stephano's car silently and lay down.

Alice clambered stiffly out of the Rolls. 'Thank you for your help,' she said, wanting to move towards Luis, but her feet wouldn't take her.

'You're welcome,' he said, looking at a point beyond her. 'I know how much work you put into this, so ...'

'That was fun!' Mario laughed. 'Dropping Cassie off at the airport was boring. She was in a very bad mood. This was better.'

'Oh? I thought she was staying another few days.'

Luis looked at the floor. 'We had a very big argument. She went too far, and I finally told her to stop.'

They stood and looked at each other but neither moved.

Say something, she thought. *Say something Alice. It's not hard. I love you, I miss you, I'm sorry I shouted at you. It wasn't all you ... you don't trust me, though ... and you were right.*

That kiss happened for a reason, whispered the voice in her head.

'Are you playing at the café opening?' she asked instead.

'Not sure. The band is. I've got behind with the refurbishment.' He looked away. 'Will you be there?'

'I don't know yet.' Alice sighed. 'I've got lots of work all of a sudden, and—'

'—well. I'd better get going. Dropping Mario back to his mum and then work, public holiday or not.'

'Okay,' she said as he and Mario got back into the car.

'Bye, Alice.' Mario waved.

She watched the car move away, Elvis barking from the window as it slowly disappeared over the ridge of the hill. *Work. Concentrate on work*, she thought. 'Shall we drop these off at the café then, Ignacio, ready for the tiler, and I'll start on the patio garden?'

'Oh, for a moment I forgot you would have to drive us back,' he muttered.

'I heard that,' she said, almost smiling.

Carlos helped carry the boxes into the café as Ignacio sat outside, massaging his leg. 'You need a doctor to look at that,' said Alice, once the tiles had all been safely stored. 'Shall I drive you?'

'No. No, thank you. Very kind of you. But the surgery is just over the road. I'll just hobble over there.'

'He will be no use tomorrow,' muttered Carlos. 'With all of this with the sign and the counselling, it's as if he doesn't want our café to open.'

'Ridiculous,' huffed Ignacio. 'Why would I invest my savings in it?'

'The closer we get to it the worse you are.' Carlos picked up the car keys. 'I suppose you want me to drive the Rolls to your garage?'

'Yes.'

Carlos stalked irritably to the road. 'Not enough time. *Not* enough time.'

'Can I help you over to the surgery?' asked Alice.

'No my dear.' Ignacio smiled. 'You get on with the garden. I'm much bigger than you and I could hurt your back. We don't want both of us hobbling around, do we?'

'All right, if you're sure. I've e-mailed the mural design to the tiler, so when he gets here first thing tomorrow he'll know where to start.'

Collecting a broom from the kitchen she began to sweep the

debris from the patio, the steady to-and-fro of the brushing almost hypnotic, her mind repeating like a mantra to its rhythm. *I love Luis, but I can't speak to him ... I love Luis ... why can't I speak to him? ... I love Luis ... but he turned into Adam ... I love Luis ... but I kissed someone else ... it was only a kiss ... it was only a kiss ...*

I keep telling you the kiss happened for a reason, said the voice in her head firmly. *Think.*

As she began to decorate the space, hanging fairy lights and moving the plants around, Alice wondered what her old self would have done; the Alice that kissed Harry the Holiday Fling in the south of France, determined and hopeful and free. That Alice was almost back, hovering somewhere just out of reach, but she couldn't quite get to her. Not yet anyway.

'Are you nearly finished, Alice?' shouted Carlos from the door. 'I've just got back from parking Ignacio's car, and I wanted to close up so I could get an early start tomorrow.'

'Just a sec,' she shouted, adjusting one of the light fittings. Standing back, she quickly checked that everything had been done and, as she turned, she noticed a white plastic bag tucked away at the back of the café. She picked it up and found the tiles inside. She took them out and spread them on the floor. They spelled out 'Coelho 1952'.

I need to find out what the problem is with that sign, she thought, putting them back in the bag.

'All done, Carlos,' she said.

He locked the door behind them. 'A new era, Alice,' he said. 'A new era.'

Alice walked to the wall overlooking Fisherman's Beach and sat on it for a while, pockets of moonlight illuminating the evening sea gently washing up onto the shore. She closed her eyes, enjoying the mix of sand and salt, then made her way back to the apartment, empty apart from her cat.

Chapter Twenty-Four

'It's all gone wrong, Mum.' Alice leaned the phone against a vase on the table, then looked more closely. 'What are you wearing?'

'Off to a fancy-dress party in half an hour. I'm Marilyn Monroe in *Some Like it Hot*. Do you like the wig?'

'Very effective.'

'Joseph is going as Clint Eastwood, but he's not getting into it very much. Just got an old throw I'd hidden in a cupboard and that hat he got from Australia.'

'I'm sure you'll have a lovely time.'

'Oh, Alice, you look so very fed up. I just want to come over there and give you a hug.'

'I had this terrible argument with Luis, and I know now I was shouting at him as if he was Adam and my ...' she lowered her voice so Joseph couldn't hear. '... biological father. But it went too far, and I was angry because, for a minute, it was like he was trying to control me in the same way Adam did, and I don't think he was, and I was insecure, and everyone else has babies and I haven't, and I haven't even got a house, and I have to move so all I've got is my work, just like it used to be, and that's not good, Mum—'

'—Alice!' shouted her mother. 'Listen, please.'

'Sorry.' Alice sighed.

'Luis has a child from a previous relationship, and that was bound to cause problems, no matter how adult and sensible everyone is being about it.'

'Yes.'

'And you've had problems with the way he used to live his life already. Remember that awful silly girl Marcella and that daft-brush aunt of hers?'

'Yes.'

258

'So, you need to speak to him, don't you?'

'He's avoiding me.'

'And you are avoiding him.'

Alice looked at the floor. 'But the house, Mum, the house ...'

'Alice, its not that difficult – you can rent, you don't have to own.'

'But the cat ...'

'Will follow you to the ends of the earth.'

'This counselling course you've been doing is quite helpful, Mum. You're much more ... how can I say it? ... understanding.'

'I know. Now, because I can't give you a hug in person, I'm going to read you a story.'

'A what?'

'When you were little, your favourite story was *Alice's Adventures in Wonderland* because you thought it was about you.'

Alice smiled. 'Did I?'

'Yes ... and well, as it transpires ... just a second.'

Her mother got up, and Alice saw a swoosh of a wide-skirted dress as she walked towards the bookcase.

'We've got to go in a minute. I mean a minute. *One* minute,' shouted Joseph from another room.

'Okay, oh well.' Her mother turned back towards her. 'Right – let me think if I can remember some of it then. You used to play with your dolls and were constantly quoting a line from the book, it was something like ... "she knelt down and looked along the passage into the loveliest garden you ever saw".'

'We're going to be late.' Alice saw Joseph walking in behind her mother, wearing a very large hat. 'Oh hello, Alice. Lovely to see you.'

'Nice outfit, Joseph.'

'Thank you. Is your mother quoting *Alice's Adventures in Wonderland* again?'

'It's Alice's favourite book.'

'Yours I think ...' he smiled down at her mother.

'Think about it Alice – you're in Wonderland, you live in that beautiful garden – you've made it happen, it's all you. So, what do you need to do now? What was that quote from the book? Oh, yes it's something like, "You know very few things are really impossible ..."' Her mother blew her a kiss, Marilyn Monroe style. 'Oh, I love doing that,' she squealed. 'By darling.' The phone went dead.

Alice sat back, finally realising she'd always longed for colour and life around her when she was a little girl, even when they briefly lived in that dingy bedsit. And how trying to create that was somehow the thing that drove her, even if she didn't know it.

Logging onto the internet, she typed in *Alice's Adventures in Wonderland* and scrolled through some quotes until she found it.

How she longed to get out of that dark hall and wander about among those beds of bright flowers and those cool fountains, but she could not even get her head through the doorway; 'and even if my head would go through,' thought poor Alice, 'It would be of very little use without my shoulders. Oh, how I wish I could shut up like a telescope! I think I could, if only I knew how to begin.' For you see, so many out of the way things had happened lately, that Alice had begun to think that very few things were really impossible.

She stood up and walked onto the balcony, gazing at the garden; the delicate petals of pink and purple bougainvillea clinging onto the gates, the blue pool at its centre.

Alice closed her eyes. She was sitting next to Harry in the lavender field in the south of France. 'One day, I'm going to have a little house with a beautiful garden in another country,' she was saying. 'It will have all the colours you can think of, and I will sit in it every morning and think how lucky I am. I will make bracelets and paint and be a successful artist.'

'That sounds perfect,' he'd said.

Alice had laughed. 'There's more ... I will have a cat and a dog, and maybe it will be a bed and breakfast and people will stay. And ...'

'... you will be living your best life, Alice,' he'd said. 'Alice in Wonderland.'

'If only I knew how to begin,' she'd said.

'Everything is possible. You can make it possible.' And then he'd kissed her. But then it wasn't him. It was Saul Pires. She opened her eyes. *Thank you, Saul*, she thought. *For reminding me of who I can be.*

'Time to sort all of this out,' she said to herself. 'And the easiest thing to do is ...'

She picked up the phone and called Duarte de Silva. 'Hi,' she said. 'You know the little yellow house ...?'

Aphrodite nuzzled around her ankles and purred. Alice looked at her and laughed. *For you see, so many out of the way things had happened lately, that Alice had begun to think that very few things were really impossible.*

The following morning Alice walked out onto her rooftop terrace, the terracotta tiles warming her bare feet. In the distance the sea glowed blue in the morning sun, and a fishing boat chugged its way back to the harbour with its catch ready for the morning fish auction. The rooftops tumbled to the bay as birds swooped and soared in the perfect, clear sky, and in a nearby street a dog barked.

It's mine, thought Alice. *Mine. One phone call to Duarte yesterday and it's mine. Well, almost mine.*

The sensation of being adrift had almost gone, but there was still something unsettling; an unidentifiable lingering unease that she had woken up with. She breathed in and tried to breath whatever it was out.

'This is the first house I have bought on my own,' she said. 'I have done it. I will own it. Well, when Duarte gets the paperwork through.' Alice walked back inside and scooped up the cat who she'd carried down there with her from the apartment. 'This is my bedroom.' She laughed, then went downstairs, 'This is my living room, and this is my very bright and airy kitchen.' Some music drifted in from the radio of a house nearby, and Alice began to dance. Aphrodite wriggled away and jumped onto the floor, settling disdainfully on the bottom step.

'I'm dancing around my soon-to-be own house,' said Alice. 'And no-one will try to take it away from me. Adam has now left the building, my mind and my life. Bugger off Adam and goodbye!' She threw herself around, spinning and swaying as the music swept to a crescendo and, as it stopped, she picked up her bottle of water.

A celebratory drink, she thought, sitting on the floor and staring out to the courtyard through the kitchen window.

This is nice, said the voice in her head. *But where is everybody?*

Alice sipped her drink and pretended not to hear.

You have your lovely house. You have what you wanted. But where are your friends? Where is Luis?

She carried on drinking, trying to focus on a bird flitting around on the whitewashed wall outside.

Haven't you been here before, Alice? Didn't you spend years in your house, hiding from it all? Aren't you doing it again?

Groundhog day, she thought.

Groundhog Day, indeed. This is all very well but …

'This is all very well,' echoed Alice. She picked up her phone. The message from Tara was still there, unread, but today it seemed to shine. Alice looked at it for a moment. 'Today is the day I stop hiding,' she said out loud. 'Today is the day.'

She opened the message.

He accepted my friend request, Tara had written. So I sent him a message and introduced myself – we had nothing to lose, did we? And this is what he sent … keep a handkerchief ready.

'My dearest Tara. How wonderful it is to hear from you. I have wanted to make contact for many years, but always found a reason not to. Please forgive me. It is the act of a man who has carried his shame around for a long time. I can see from your profile now we are friends that you are married and have children, and that Alice is living in Portugal? I couldn't see more than her photo as we are not connected. Perhaps she will want to speak to me one day?

I hope we can meet, and perhaps put the past right in some small way, but before we even try I need to say this –

Please forgive me. When I left you both and your mother, I was not in a good place. My life was chaotic as was I and, despite the support and kindness of your mother, I was in the habit of making bad decisions and taking advice from the wrong people. I know now that I was not well as I have had many years of therapy, but that does not undo the past, does it? When we emigrated to Canada, I thought I could leave my bad behaviour in the UK and start anew. But it tortured me for years. I could have tried to get in touch, but I didn't – it seemed the easiest way for me, but not the right way.

I was lucky enough to meet Barb, my wife, who scooped me up, loved me unconditionally and gave me the strength to get help. I now have a secure job, two lovely children and a grandchild. I talk to them about you all the time. You have never left my thoughts, or my heart.

I want to say I'm sorry – I'm sorry for abandoning you all, for running away, for allowing my past to affect your lives, for being absent in every way. A part of me thought I was doing it for the best, but that was me making excuses.

Please try to forgive me, and please, can we all get to know each other? I never stopped loving you.

Yours, Paul (your father)

xxx

She felt a sob leap into her throat quite suddenly and allowed the tears to trickle down her face.

I have to speak to Luis. I want Luis. I want to find Luis.

'But I've got a lot to do,' she said out loud. 'I've got a deadline for another training plan, and then I've got to shop, and then …'

Luis … said the voice in her head again.

'I don't know how, I don't know how.' Alice stood up and walked back upstairs, fighting the overwhelming urge to hide in the house forever.

No. I won't let you. They are all out there. Your friends. Your love.

'I don't want to do it on my own,' she said. 'Any of it.'

So?

She put Aphrodite in the cat carrier, stepped out into the silent street and began to walk towards the square. As she got closer, the sounds of life going on around her lightened her mood slightly, and she began to move more quickly, almost being carried along by the chatter, the scraping of cutlery, the barking of dogs, the engine of a car, the constant movement of the sea in the background.

Alice stood at the top of the steps opposite Carlos and Ignacio's café and tried to spot the familiar figure of Carlos moving around busily between the tables. But there was no-one there. She walked to the door, puzzled to see a 'Closed' sign on it. Peering through the glass, she saw a figure inside and pushed the door open. 'Hello,' she said into the gloom.

'Alice!' Carlos waved from the patio area. 'I'm just clearing everything to make sure all is okay. Thank you for all your hard work with this patio – it is beautiful.'

'I'm glad you like it.' She looked at the mural – it was covered with a sheet. 'Did the tiler finish putting this up?'

'Just late last night. He says he needs to clean it, but he's coming in later to get it ready for the grand opening.'

'I assumed you'd be open anyway this morning?'

'No. No. We got too busy so had to delay it a little.' He

walked towards her and took her hand. 'Where were you yesterday, Alice? We've been trying to contact you.'

'I've just had a lot on,' she said. 'Where's Ignacio?'

'He is out buying party paraphernalia. I had to get him to do something other than chanting and breathing and trying to get me to do relaxation exercises before we started work. It was very stressful for me.'

'Are you two friends now? I mean I know you're brothers ...'

'Would you like a *galao*?'

Alice touched his arm. 'Oh no you don't. You have to talk to each other.'

Carlos looked at the floor.

Alice sighed. 'Honestly, you two.'

'And what about Luis?' said Carlos. 'Have you spoken to him?'

'No.'

He laughed. 'Honestly, you two.'

'Is the band playing at the opening?'

'Yes. He'll be here at around five.' He looked at his watch. 'I'd better get on with this, Alice. The kitchen staff arrive in an hour.'

'Okay – I'll see you later.'

Mentally ticking half of one thing off a list she had just compiled – *try to sort out Ignacio and Carlos ... failed ... try again ... check on mural and patio ... buy fruit and bread ... ring Kathy. Find Luis* – she knew there was something missing, and as she ambled aimlessly up through the bustling streets, still carrying Aphrodite, her mind jumped around, trying to search for it. *What was it?*

She stopped outside the *pasteleria* and saw her reflection – healthy and confident, and completely different to the Alice who had gazed at the *pastel de natas*, *tortas de azeitao* and *rissois* stacked high on the shelves two years ago. There was something on her mind, then: a weight, a fear. And then she remembered what she'd left off the list ... *buy a house*. A cashier appeared at the window, picked out some cakes from the display and took them to the till, and Alice carried on up towards the prom to Estoril.

She looked across the bay to the west; the boats were dancing on the waves as they always did, people were playing on Fisherman's Beach, traffic was snaking up the hill. This was the place she had chosen. Or perhaps it had chosen her.

Cutting in through the old town, the streets emptied and all she could hear was the echoing of her own footsteps on the cobbles. A small wooded park provided a welcome shelter from the heat, and she turned to walk through it. But as she opened the gate, at the other side she saw a familiar figure sitting on a bench and staring at a building in front of him.

'Ignacio?' she called. 'What are you doing here?'

He looked up, surprised, as if he'd been woken from a dream. 'Alice,' he said. 'Where were you yesterday? We hoped you would pop in to say hello.'

'Things to do,' she muttered, sitting down next to him.

'This,' he gestured towards the building. 'This was our maternal grandparents' café. We used to gather here every Sunday for a family meal, help out during our holidays. It was always busy. Successful.'

'How long ago was that?'

'They only gave up just over sixteen years ago. Can you imagine? They were in their early eighties. They persuaded Carlos and me to take it over.'

'Oh, so the café in the square is not the first time?'

'No. Carlos had years of experience already – he'd worked in Lisbon, then London, then New York'.

'What happened?'

Ignacio stood up. 'They were so old, they had almost run it into the ground. It needed so much work. And we tried ... but after a year, we had to call it a day. It was very painful. They both died six months later.'

'Is that why you've been feeling nervous about the café?'

'Carlos and I argued then, too. We felt so bad we took it out on each other. And look at us now.' He scratched his head. 'I had to take a customer to the airport from a house over there, and when I saw the café – not a café now, a house – it brought it all back. It was about three months ago.'

'Have you told Carlos?'

He looked at the floor. 'No. I didn't want to remind him too. Our childhood went with that café, you know? I don't want to feel that pain again.'

'You won't. This is different.'

'And when I saw the sign ...'

'Ahhh, the sign!'

'Gina's husband used to collect ceramics. That's why she had it and gave it to Ignacio. It set me off again.' He shrugged and turned towards her. 'Carlos has always been the optimistic one. Jumps in. I've always been more sensitive, reticent. He wouldn't understand.'

'He may.'

'The past, Alice ... you think it's gone ... but sometimes it rears its head.'

The past, she thought, *the past*. Something suddenly clicked. *Why did Luis' fiancée leave him all those years ago? Did Cassie mention something about restaurants?*

She hugged Ignacio. 'I've got something I need to do,' she said, picking up the cat carrier.

'I have, too,' he said. And they both walked off in different directions.

Alice hurried back to the apartment, ringing Luis as she went, but his phone went straight to voicemail. 'I need to talk to you,' she said. 'Can you call me back?'

I'm not going to stand and wait. I'm not going to run away. I'm going to run towards, she thought, pulling out a box full of clothes from a storage cupboard that Mary and Frank had kept for her. She rifled through impatiently, throwing pale, beige, dark, plain, safe dresses, tops and trousers onto the floor. Clothes of Alice's past. Then she found it. The bright pink dress Adam had hated. The bright pink dress she loved. The bright, silky, vibrant, noisy dress she was wearing when Luis had noticed Alice and Kathy singing tunelessly in the car park on the night they had first met. The bright, lovely, symbolic, soft, sexy, sensuous dress that she was wearing when she had accidentally dropped her mobile phone onto his head from the hotel terrace. She had looked down; he had looked up. And she was in love. Immediately, hopelessly, forever.

Aphrodite watched for a while as Alice put the dress on, applied some make-up and tousled her hair, but then wandered off to the balcony just before Alice ran out of the door. She watched as the lift lights stayed illuminated on the top floor, pressing the button over and over again to make it hurry, then ran down the stairs instead, out into the garden and onto the street, around the corner onto the sea road. She was running towards something this time. Not anxiously walking through arrivals at Lisbon airport, afraid of the future, escaping, running away. And that Alice was cheering her on.

Turning into the square, she almost ran over to the café as the band were setting up. 'Where's Luis?' She smiled. 'I've got something I need to tell him.'

The drummer looked at her. 'No idea, Alice. He said he wasn't sure he could do it, so he told us to carry on anyway, and if he could, he would.'

'Oh.' Alice looked around, deflated, then checked her phone again. There were no messages.

'Alice! Alice!' Ignacio shouted from inside the café. 'The tiler is just cleaning up the mural – would you like to check?'

'Um … no … I've got to do something. I hope you like it. I'll catch you later.'

Carlos appeared and put his arm around his brother's shoulder. 'Look. We are talking. It's the sign.'

'Where's the sign?' Ignacio smiled at him.

'Where it should be. Above the entrance to the patio garden.'

'It took a few pieces of ceramics to make us talk after all that.'

'With all of that counselling and meditation, it still took our grandparents to knock our heads together.' Carlos laughed.

'But not actually knock our heads together as they are no longer with us,' Ignacio said seriously.

'And they weren't ghosts. We didn't have a visitation or anything.' Carlos grabbed his brother and gave him a hug.

Alice laughed. 'That's wonderful. I'm so glad ... and relieved ... given what's on the mural. But, where's Luis?'

'He's parked his car at the pink hotel,' said Stephano, pushing James in his buggy towards them.

'Oh, right, thank you.' Alice turned around.

'He's not very happy,' Stephano muttered as she rushed past. 'Duarte told him you were buying the yellow house from his company, and he thinks you are moving in there and not with him. He's taking some photographs for his portfolio and may or may not make an appearance tonight.'

'Oh no ... I didn't think of that ... it never occurred to me ... Okay.'

When she got to the road her heart was racing, and she was beginning to pant as she paused at the zebra crossing. *Oh bloody hell*, she thought. *I'm starting to sweat.*

Not quite the Hollywood entrance you were hoping for. The voice in her head giggled.

'Oh leave me alone!' she shouted, startling an elderly man who was standing next to her.

A Range Rover screeched to a halt opposite. The driver rolled down the window.

'Can I help?' shouted Kathy.

'I'm trying to find Luis. Near the pink hotel.' Alice was almost hopping from one foot to the other impatiently.

'Get in!' shouted Kathy. 'I shall take you to your Prince Charming, Cinderella. Not sure it's the right fairy tale, but it'll have to do.'

Alice tried to climb in. 'This is very high,' she muttered as Kathy leaned over and grabbed her hands, pulling her up into the passenger seat.

'This is the second car chase you've done in three days.' Kathy laughed, putting the car into gear and pulling out into the traffic.

Alice leaned back and tried to slow down her breathing. 'Why's everything so difficult? Why does nobody answer their phones in this place?' she said. 'Why do I have to keep running around after tiles and men and—'

'—because they're worth it,' cut in Kathy, turning left at the mini roundabout towards the stone bridge.

'What if he's not there?' Alice looked at Kathy anxiously.

'We'll find him. Cascais isn't that big, don't worry ... but I think that's him posing enigmatically on the rocks with a camera, don't you?'

Alice's heart went loop the loop as she saw him standing opposite the lighthouse, the sea in front of him blue and green where it reflected the trees in the park. His shoulders were hunched, focused on his task. *What if it was too late? What if he didn't want her?* She put her hand on the car seat and held onto it.

'I think you need to get out,' said Kathy softly. 'I mean that kindly, obviously.'

'I seem to have run out of momentum,' whispered Alice. 'Suddenly.'

Kathy prised her hand off the seat, leaned over and opened the door, undid her seat belt, then gently pushed her out of the car. 'Cruel to be kind,' she shouted as Alice steadied herself on the path. Then she slammed the door shut and drove off.

Alice felt a bead of sweat trickle down her back then picked her way over the stones towards Luis. 'Luis,' she said, but he didn't move. 'Luis …' Alice began to panic. Perhaps this was it – perhaps he never wanted to see her again. And there was nothing to be done.

No it's bloody not, shouted the voice in her head. *He's got headphones on. For. Goodness. Sake.*

'Ok, okay.' She moved next to him and put her hand on his arm. 'Luis,' she said, her heart racing again.

He turned his head and looked down at her, his face serious.

Oh no, she thought. *Oh no …*

Then he smiled.

And so did she.

'Alice,' he said.

'Luis,' she said.

'I'm sorry.'

'I'm sorry.'

'Shall we?' He pointed at the rocks. 'Its not very comfortable, but …'

'It's very romantic.'

They sat down next to each other and he put his hand on hers.

'My fiancée in Australia. She left me as you know … it was a long time ago … and I was very young, but it was for a guy who inherited three restaurants from his father.'

'Cassie did mention restaurants, but I didn't really understand.' She squeezed his hand.

'I thought I was over it. But, you know, Saul Pires is a chef.'

'He is.'

'The past … you think it's gone but …'

Alice looked into his eyes. *I need to tell him about the kiss*, she thought.

Oh no you don't, whispered the voice in her head. *That is your secret. Harry and Saul. They found the key. They unlocked your heart. That was your past. Luis is your future.*

Alice smiled. 'Yes, the past. There's a lot of the past around at the moment.' She watched a school of silver fish dart backwards and forwards as the water lapped on the rocks. 'Is it a good thing or a bad thing, do you think?'

'I was so scared of losing you when Fran appeared with Mario. So I tried very hard to prove to you I wanted to make amends. Be a good father. And then I wanted to prove to myself and everyone else I was more than what I'd been before. But I was trying so hard, I was pushing you away. And then, there was the chef ...' He almost laughed.

'It stirred up a lot.' Alice leaned on his shoulder. 'My dad ... Adam. That day we had the huge argument, Tara had found my father, and Adam had sent me a message. And it felt like you were trying to hold me back. But it was them. Not them ... the memory of them. So you all became one person.'

'Fran appearing, Cassie winding me up. Do you think it was meant to happen?'

'Yes. I think it was all meant to happen. I feel free of it all now.' She sat up again. 'And I have a house.'

'I heard. Congratulations.' She could sense him move away, ever so slightly.

'It's for holiday lets,' she said quickly. 'And I'm proud of myself. It's the first place I have ever bought on my own. I'm going to paint a sign to go above the door – it's going to be "A Casa de Alice". And so many good things are happening, Luis, but they wouldn't be good without you.'

He pulled her close. 'You should be proud of yourself. And...' he looked steadily into her eyes. '... I really enjoy being Mario's father. That is okay, isn't it?'

'It's wonderful,' she said.

He cupped her face in his hands and kissed her, and she heard fireworks as if they were surrounded by hundreds of shooting stars, skidding across the sky, trailing bright white clouds of light.

'Did you hear that?' he asked. 'The fireworks?'

'Wow, you too?'

He looked up as a solitary white spark exploded above the bay. 'I think someone's practicing for tonight's display,' he said. 'For a minute there ...'

'Me too.' Alice laughed as he pulled her to him, wrapping his arms around her for what felt like forever.

'I think it's time to go back to the square,' he said eventually. 'After all of that chasing around the other day, I think we should see your mural.'

'Ah, yes ... I'd forgotten. I hope everyone likes it. It's a bit different.'

Elvis barked in the distance. 'And I've left Elvis in the car with the window open, and I think he's feeling a bit restless.'

'Hurrah!' Kathy shouted as Alice and Luis sat down. 'I win.'

'Win what?' Alice waved at baby James.

'How long it would take you both to sort things out. I said ten minutes with a twenty-minute journey.'

Luis glanced at his watch. 'Very accurate. I'm impressed.'

'I said it would take fifteen minutes,' said Stephano. 'Carlos said five and Ignacio said nine.'

'I said two minutes,' said Gina, 'as I'm a hopeless romantic.'

'Alice!' Carlos darted out of the café and grabbed her hand. 'Alice ... oh Alice.'

Ignacio stood in the doorway. 'Come on in everyone and see what she has done. It is just the most wonderful thing.'

Carlos pulled her to her feet. 'Come, come ...'

They all crowded into the café, but Alice edged to the back, nervous. The mural was the most personal thing she had ever created.

What if, what if ...?

Then, almost as one person, the whole crowd turned around to look at her. Luis pulled her to him. 'That is wonderful,' he whispered.

'Look!' Carlos was almost dancing with excitement next

to the wall. 'Here I am holding a tray of drinks and shaking Ignacio's hand. There's his yellow Rolls-Royce by his side … and there are all the tables and chairs and parasols in the square, and the lighthouse and Fisherman's Beach, and all the bougainvillaea framing it …'

'And look closer.' Ignacio pointed at two squares – one on the top right and one on the top left. 'See. There is Luis and Alice and Elvis and Aphrodite standing in front of the house on the hill. Mario, you are there too … and Fran … and on the other one, there is Kathy and Stephano and James … Gina in her workshop …'

Carlos threw his arms around her. 'It is us! Thank you!'

Alice almost began to cry with relief, but what felt like a sob was actually a laugh, and an almost joyful scream of happiness.

The drummer poked his head around the door. 'Are we ready for the ceremony? The square is full of people. Are you going to join us Luis?'

He nodded. 'Can't think of anything better.'

They all went outside and stood as Carlos and Ignacio shook two bottles of champagne, opened them and sprayed the contents over their friends. 'Bem-Vindo is now officially open!' they shouted.

Epilogue

Alice adjusted the flowers in her hair and checked herself in the mirror, smoothing the dress so it fell softly over her body.

'Alice, are you ready yet?' Kathy shouted from the next room. 'It's time to go.'

Aphrodite sat on the windowsill watching as Alice picked up the posy of flowers. 'I reckon that you're smiling, Aph, although you are just looking inscrutable as usual.' The cat jumped onto the floor and stretched herself out on the cooling tiles. 'Yes, it's a hot one.'

A postcard was leaning against the mirror on the dressing table. Alice picked it up and smiled. On the front was a photograph of a train racing through the Rocky Mountains and on the back was a message. *My dearest Alice. I am so very happy that you have got in touch. We are all excited to meet you in Portugal soon. The whole family will be descending on you. I hope you're ready! Love, Dad x*

'Alice.' Kathy opened the door. 'What do you think?'

Kathy stood, her long cream dress cascading into a gentle trail behind her. She stroked her belly. 'Does it hide baby number two, or announce its presence?'

'Depends which way you look at it, I think.' Alice smiled. 'Whichever way, you look beautiful.'

'Wedding number two to the same man.' Kathy laughed nervously. 'Am I mad?'

'No, you're happy.'

Kathy held out her hand. 'So, my bridesmaid for the second time to my second wedding to the same man, shall we go?'

'I want to hug you, but I'll crease your dress. And mine.'

'I think our respective bumps will mean we can't get too close anyway.'

Alice put her hand on her belly and felt a kick. 'She's

moving. We'd better get going before she decides to come to the wedding herself.'

They linked arms and walked slowly into the sunlight, under a bright blue cloudless sky, to the sound of birdsong and the sea, as dragonflies danced around the garden amongst the crimson roses and rich pink bougainvillea.

Stephano stood under a floral arch next to Luis, whilst Elvis sat obediently next to him. Carlos, Ignacio and Gina turned from their seats and nodded at them proudly. Alice's mother and stepfather sat next to them and waved, and Fran sat at the back with her baby in its pram next to her, Mario and her partner, Pete, in the seats in front. Kathy's father led her down the aisle to Luis' Latin band playing 'Better Together' and, as Kathy took her place next to Stephano, Luis grabbed Alice's hand and stroked her stomach.

'Still haven't thought of a name,' he whispered.

'I think we should call her Chuva,' said Alice, softly. 'To mark the night she was made.'

'I'm not calling our daughter Rain,' he said.

'We'll know what her name is when we meet her.' Alice squeezed his hand, and they turned to watch Kathy and Stephano as they all stood in the garden of the old farmhouse, the hills tumbling to the sea in the distance. It looked like it was glowing. And it was.

Thank You

Dear Reader,

Thank you for reading about Alice and her new adventure in Portugal.

If you have enjoyed reading this story it would mean a lot to me if you had a few minutes to share a review on the platform you purchased the book or on Goodreads, as this is a great way for people to find out about my books.

If you have any thoughts, comments or questions you can contact me via the contact details at the end of my author bio on the next page.

Hopefully I'll see you again soon with a new story.

Chris x

About the Author

Chris Penhall is an author, freelance writer and radio producer.

Born in South Wales, she has also lived near London and in Portugal, which is where *The House That Alice Built* and *New Beginnings at the Little House in the Sun* are set. It was whilst living in Cascais near Lisbon that she began to dabble in writing fiction, but it was many years later that she was confident enough to start writing her first novel, and many years after that she finally finished it! She is now enjoying her new career as a novelist.

A lover of books, music and cats, she is also an enthusiastic salsa dancer, a keen cook and loves to travel. She is never happier than when she is gazing at the sea.

Chris has two grown-up daughters and lives in the Essex countryside.

Chris is a member of the Romantic Novelists Association.

Follow Chris:
Website: www.chrispenhall.co.uk
Twitter: https://twitter.com/ChrisPenhall
Facebook: https://www.facebook.com/ChrisPenhall
BroadcasterWriter/

More Ruby Fiction

From Chris Penhall

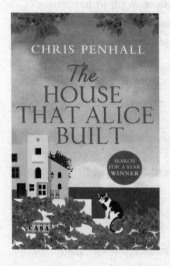

The House That Alice Built

Book 1 – Portuguese Paradise series

Home is where the heart is …

Alice Dorothy Matthews is sensible. Whilst her best friend Kathy is living it up in Portugal and her insufferable ex Adam is travelling the world, Alice is working hard to pay for the beloved London house she has put her heart and soul into renovating.

But then a postcard from Buenos Aires turns Alice's life upside down. One very unsensible decision later and she is in Cascais, Portugal, and so begins her lesson in 'going with the flow'; a lesson that sees her cat-sitting, paddle boarding, dancing on top of bars and rediscovering her artistic talents.

But perhaps the most important part of the lesson for Alice is that you don't always need a house to be at home.

Visit www.rubyfiction.com for details.

Finding Summer Happiness

**You won't find happiness
without breaking
a few eggs …**

Miriam Ryan was the MD of a
successful events and catering
company, but these days even
the thought of chopping an
onion sends her stress levels
sky rocketing. A retreat to the
Welsh village of her childhood
holidays seems to offer the
escape she's craving – just peace, quiet, no people, a generous
supply of ready meals … did she mention no people?

Enter a cheery pub landlord, a lovesick letting agent, a
grumpy astronomer with a fridge raiding habit – not to
mention a surprise supper club that requires the chopping
of many onions – and Miriam realises her escape has turned
into exactly what she was trying to get away from, but
could that be just the thing she needs to allow a little bit of
summer happiness into her life?

Visit www.rubyfiction.com for details.

More from Ruby Fiction

If you loved Chris's story, you'll enjoy the
rest of our selection. Here's a sample:

Visit www.rubyfiction.com for more details

Introducing Ruby Fiction

Ruby Fiction is an imprint of Choc Lit Publishing.
We're an award-winning independent publisher,
creating a delicious selection of fiction.

See our selection here:
www.rubyfiction.com

Ruby Fiction brings you stories that inspire emotions.

We'd love to hear how you enjoyed
New Beginnings at the Little House in the Sun. Please
visit www.rubyfiction.com and give your feedback or
leave a review where you purchased this novel.

Ruby novels are selected by genuine readers like yourself.
We only publish stories our Tasting Panel want to see in
print. Our reviews and awards speak for themselves.

Could you be a Star Selector and join our Tasting Panel?
Would you like to play a role in choosing which novels
we decide to publish? Do you enjoy reading women's
fiction? Then you could be perfect for our Tasting Panel.

Visit here for more details …
www.choc-lit.com/join-the-choc-lit-tasting-panel

Keep in touch:
Sign up for our monthly newsletter Spread for all the latest
news and offers: www.spread.choc-lit.com. Follow us on
Twitter: @RubyFiction and Facebook: RubyFiction.

Stories that inspire emotions!